Noravale

Tosca

Cymber
Mountains

Lake
Galion

Serency

Ivory Sands

ke Sire

sen

Opal Ocean

A
DIAMOND
BRIGHT
BR&KEN

A
DIAMOND
BRIGHT
BR&KEN

HOLLY DAVIS

INIMITABLE
BOOKS
UNFORGETTABLE STORIES

Published by Inimitable Books, LLC
www.inimitablebooksllc.com

Library of Congress Cataloguing-in-Publication Data is available.

First edition, 2024
Cover design by Keylin Rivers

ISBN 978-1-958607-26-8 (hardcover)
10 9 8 7 6 5 4 3 2

To Heather, my twin, thank you for always believing in me, even when I didn't. No one would be reading these words if not for you.

TRIGGER WARNING

Social inequality, classism, ableism, gaslighting, referenced (but not shown) physical abuse, on-page depiction of emotional and verbal abuse, confinement, death, murder, homophobia, stealing, and imprisonment.

ONE

If my tears hadn't paid for this mansion, maybe I wouldn't feel so bitter about living in it. But they did, and so I hate it.

My parents decorated the hallway with everything they wanted in a home. It's all a bit...*excessive*.

When there are hungry and homeless people in Serency, or those who can't pay for medical care, having anything extravagant feels selfish...wasteful. We—really any of the upper class here in Noravale—could be making a difference and helping those in need instead of hoarding it all. But I get no say, because my diamond tears belong to Mother and Father.

A lush carpet lines the floor. Custom pottery sit on pillars as tall as myself. Silk curtains adorn tall windows so pristinely clean I swear I could reach right through them. Wrought iron sconces burning cinder rose-scented candles light my way. As I walk down the hall of the grand foyer to my parents' room, a sense of dread settles like a stone in my stomach.

Unlike most people, I don't shed regular tears. Instead, the hard, tiny gems fall from my eyes. Diamond tears, my blessing and my curse.

The colorful drapes hanging from the ceiling are the most recent addition to this absurd collection of unnecessary belongings. Don't get me wrong. I don't mind luxury, but not at anyone else's expense. It jolts me back to the time I was five years old and Mother wanted a new jewelry set.

"Cry for me, Cadence. Do it for mommy."

My diamond tears have always caused me sharp, intense eye pain and occasionally cut my cheeks as they spill over. Until that day, I hadn't reached a breaking point. But that time, when I begged Mother to stop, she refused and said I mustn't love her enough to give her what she wanted. And so, I cried until my eyes turned bloodshot and I couldn't open them for days.

My gut wrenches at the memory, yet I continue my trek and pass every painting on the wall, knowing full well where they came from—who bought them. I was ten when Father wanted to replace the collection he'd only gotten the year prior.

"We have to impress our guests. Don't worry. It will all be over soon."

Except I'm sixteen now, and it's not over. It will never be over. Not as long as I need to help my sister, Al.

I approach the laughter that echoes from the door of my parents' room, open just a crack. A pattern of silver swirls coats the door frame and that pit in my stomach is now an anvil. All our doors were plain before Mother complained that Lady Amatsu was showing us up with the most gorgeously decorated doors in her house.

I scratch my back where a similar pattern of scars hides. It makes me want to rip all the silken folds off my dress and leave my wrists and fingers bare of their bangles and rings for how much pain they've cost me. I inhale deeply and push past the door.

"Cadence! Thank the gods you're finally here. We have to pay Dr. Hyu in a few hours," Mother says. She's sitting by her vanity, dabbing blush on her cheeks and admiring herself in the mirror. Her long brown hair matches my own, except hers is smoother. Mine is mixed hair, a combination of straight, wavy, and frizzy locks. I like to thank Father for giving me the variety.

I tuck a strand behind my ear and close the door as if sealing my fate. Their room looks smaller than I remember. There is so much glittering gold in the décor, from small statues and trinkets sitting on all available flat surfaces to multicolored tapestries of castles and landscapes. Globe lights hang from the ceiling, equally spread out around a two-tiered chandelier.

I have to squint at first to adjust to the brightness. When I do, my gaze sweeps the room and I stifle a scoff. Since when did they have busts of themselves made? Father stands by his statue with his arms folded, and I remember when Al and I were younger, we used to hang and swing on each arm, giggling and smiling. Now, we're on our own, struggling to hold on to something that's not even there—and maybe never was.

I've never believed my parents were on my side. After all their greed, how can I trust them? But I still hope they'll change some-day—for their daughters' sake. But I'm not sure we'll ever be the family I want us to be.

"Do you need any help, Cadence?" Father asks as he walks over to Mother, their dark brown and white skin in stark contrast to each other. My sister's and my shared skin tone is somewhere in the mid-dle—white like our mom's, with an olive undertone.

I return to Father's question. Do I need any help? Help? *If you need to help me cry, all you have to do is tell me about all the promises you two have broken.* But nothing can break my sealed lips because right now, my parents aren't worth my breath. I shake my head.

It's not the first time I've cried on command, but the billionth time isn't any easier. I usually picture something sad—like a future where I'm never allowed to leave the house for the rest of my life—and the tears flow. Other times, I'm so detached from my body—like some incorporeal spirit—that nothing comes out. That's when Mother and Father beat me—only mentally, but still awful—what-ever it takes to make me start bawling. The worry in my stomach crushes my insides. I should know better than to put up with it. But I'll do anything to help Al.

Whatever it takes.

This time, I envision if my sister was gone—if her neuromuscu-lar disease progressed so rapidly that she died, leaving me alone.

Oh, gods. What would I do?

Al is worth more than the world to me. Even though she's two years older than me, I still try to protect her from Mother and Father. But she's usually the one holding me together.

I can't help believing that if she died, I'll have failed her. All the weight rests on my shoulders, and I know whom our parents would blame for her passing.

The morbid thoughts are working. A coolness settles in the corners of my eyes, and soon diamonds are landing in my cupped hands with tiny clinks. My tear ducts scream for relief as each finely cut gem slices past my sclerae like a butcher knife.

I've gotten used to some of the pain over time, but I'll never be completely numb. I finish lamenting over my sister's imagined death, ending the torturous flow of riches. My eyes burn and my cheeks ache as if I'd been crying normal tears—the way Al looks when she cries.

The diamonds in my palms reflect the light of the other jewels and trinkets overtaking the room, mocking me. I release them into Mother's hands—her delicate fingers with long painted nails closing over them like claws. Her eyes glint even brighter than the diamonds do.

Father flashes his pearly whites and pockets some of my tears for himself. "Thank the gods again for your gift," he says, a familiar refrain so cold and lifeless it only makes me shiver.

Gift? This so-called *gift* has brought me more than physical pain. Has forced me to cry in private. Live in complete privacy. No one can know about it because then they'd want to use me. Take advantage of me. At least, that's what Mother and Father say. Isn't it funny how they're doing the very thing they're protecting me from?

But I don't voice any of my thoughts. I just nod and exit the room, wondering if they even realize I hadn't spoken a word.

4

TWO

After I compose myself, as I always do, I head to Al's room to make the most of the morning. It's the best way to get out of my sullen, post-crying mood quickly. Although we have separate bedrooms, which are annoyingly just as elaborate as Mother and Father's, I spend most of my time in hers. It's become a ritual now, a way for us both to escape reality.

Her door is open, and I close it after I enter before meeting her on the velvet-cushioned windowsill. If our parents hadn't built us a library, this spot would be the perfect reading nook. Instead, we use this space to create our own stories.

My sister moves her crutches out of the way so there's room for me to sit beside her. Because muscles and nerves breakdown in her neuromuscular disease, she has weak legs and tires quickly. Sometimes, Al uses crutches or a wheelchair to get around. The condition can worsen over time…and be fatal. The best we can do is slow it down with a physiohealer, who gives her strengthening exercises.

After I settle in my spot, she wastes no time before jumping into our game, rubbing her hands together and laughing. "All right… let's see what sort of fun people we'll encounter today! There has to be someone interesting to make up a story about—it's too nice for people not to be outside."

I grin. "Not sure anyone can beat that burly man last week who you said was King Pontifex in disguise."

We peer out the second-floor window, squinting to make out any passersby from a distance. While our home is surrounded by lush plants, flowers, and trees, bits and pieces of the city of Noravale are visible beyond. Mansions line the row across from us, each with a perfectly manicured lawn and pearl-white windowpanes. A few horse-drawn carriages make their way down the paved street, the open windows letting in the gentle summer breeze. The hustle and bustle of the city is our tiny slice of normalcy, but all we can do is look at it from inside our pretty prison.

"I doubt the king would appreciate being described as 'burly,'" Al says.

"That's what makes it so funny! And you're the one who said it!"

We chuckle the exact same way, then burst out laughing because we did. We've picked up so many similar mannerisms from all our time together, one would think we were twins.

"Okay, well, I'm going to pick that boy over there. He's cute!" She points to a long-haired redhead who's walking an old hound at a leisurely pace. He pauses when his dog sniffs a tree before continuing on.

"He does look pretty cute. The boy's not too shabby either," I joke. I crack the window open, savoring the fresh air as I watch him.

"So." Al curls her short brown hair behind her ears. "This boy has been lonely for a long time. His parents have made him study hard so he can get into Hosef Academy, but that means he hasn't had time to make any friends…or have any girlfriends."

Usually, we create stories different from our own to escape our reality. I don't know why she's deciding to stick closer to what we know, but I keep quiet and let her continue her tale about this future student at Soridente's top school.

"This boy does everything that his parents ask. He's passed his exams and is going to graduate next week, so they finally let him explore the city streets on his own. He moves slowly to make the moment last as long as possible." She inhales deeply through her nose. "On his walk, he locks eyes with the most beautiful girl he's ever encountered across the street. And in an instant, he sees flashes of not the past, but of the future—one with her. He realizes he can never go back to his old life because he's found what he wants his new life to be—his destiny."

I swallow hard. Will we ever get a chance at a new life? "Please, don't make me cry. I've done enough of that today."

She shakes her head, snapping out of her daze. "Oh, gods, I'm sorry, Cade. I didn't mean to…"

"Don't worry, I get it." I fiddle with the ends of the curtains. Al's eighteen to my sixteen. We've never found love. Never known romance. We have each other, but still feel so alone. Even though we should be able to experience life away from home—from our parents—we can't.

She clears her throat. "I'm sorry you're stuck here because of me."

"Al, come on…"

"No, I'm serious."

When we peer out the window again, the boy is gone. But I know neither of us will forget that story. Some stick with us long after the words leave our lips and the sun has set.

My lips purse. I don't know if I'll ever be allowed to find happiness outside these walls—adventure, excitement…and love. It feels selfish to want those things, especially because I know Al wishes for the very same things for herself. I take her hand and scoot closer to her on the cushion. "Don't feel bad about being you. You didn't choose to have this disease. Uncle Vinio had it, too. And I'd never trade any of our time together, even if it has to happen inside."

Now *Al* looks like she's going to cry. She closes her eyes and nods with a grin. "Thanks. I know all that, but it never hurts to hear it. I just don't think love's in the cards for me. How am I going to find someone stuck in here? But maybe we can get out. You're gorgeous and smart and deserve to find a guy who'll love and take care of you."

I lean back and laugh. "First off, you can find love, too. Second of all, I can take care of myself."

"Too true."

"And lastly, who says the someone I find has to be a guy?"

"Or girl," she instantly amends.

My cheeks warm. I can be exactly who I want to be in front of at least one person in my life. "There you go."

My sister picks at the cushion. "You know, I feel guilty that Mother and Father use you to pay for my treatments. You…you should stop crying diamonds for me."

"Al…" I sigh, tipping her head up to meet mine. "We both know they're the ones who should feel bad. They refuse to spend a single coin or gem that they honestly earn on us. It's always spent on their next new outfit or night out on the town. And then they spend mine, too. But as much as crying hurts, I don't want you to suffer. I'll make as many diamonds as it takes to help you—*you*, not them."

Al smiles. "Thank you for that."

"You know I love you."

"Love you, too, sis." She takes a deep breath, then smiles brightly. "Okay, enough sappiness. Your turn," she says, switching her attention back to the window.

I hate how bad my sister feels, but it's comforting to know she's got my back. I follow her request to move on and rub my palms together, peering through the glass again.

A couple walks down the street, arms linked like they're a hop, skip, and jump away from busting out in a dance right then and there. There's a woman carrying sacks of potatoes and other vegetables on either side of her, struggling to make it to her carriage. Why she didn't bring her vehicle to the market is a mystery.

I turn my head as a blur of black crosses to my left.

Someone is wearing a dark cloak, walking close to the bushes spilling onto the sidewalk. The person's head is down, so I can't see much as they slink in the shadows. Definitely not an everyday sight.

"I'm picking that person." I point to the mysterious figure, un-sure of whether they are male or female. Their boots are slim, but it could still be a young boy, rather than confirmation the stranger is a girl. "They're cloaked because they committed a crime and they're hiding from the authorities."

"Oooh," Al says, leaning closer to the window.

The stranger stops at an alleyway, turning their head left and right to investigate the space.

I catch a glimpse of the person—the girl—underneath. My jaw drops and I can't tear my gaze away from her. I can't put my finger on what's so mesmerizing about her, but she's unlike anyone I've seen before. She has light brown skin and striking dark eyes. A lock of light pink curls slips out of the hood.

"Cade? Caaaade?"

"Huh?"

"What happens next?"

"Oops, sorry." I bite my lip in embarrassment.

"I don't blame you. She's cute."

I laugh and settle my racing heart for the moment to return to my storytelling. "Okay, so this girl isn't just hiding from the police. She's hiding who she really is. She doesn't let anyone know her true self. But she's waiting for the…right person…to let her know it's okay to open up." I smile, staring at her before she steps back into the alley and disappears.

A blotch of darkness remains where she stood. Almost like her shadow pulled away from her and now existed on its own. I blink and the next thing I know, it's gone. It must have been a trick of the light, or an errant diamond tear from earlier blocking my vision.

Still, I find what's holding my attention isn't the shadow, but the girl. She didn't look like she belonged in Noravale. Then again, neither do I. I stare at the spot, wondering if—*hoping*—she'll show her face again.

THREE

After our people-watching session, I wheel Al down the ramp to the first floor to see Dr. Hyu.

Mother and Father used to take her to the hospital on the other side of town for rehab therapy, but then Mother got paranoid about her worsening condition and didn't want Al exposed to the outside elements. So, what did they do? They made me cry enough diamond tears to build a personal rehabilitation gym and hired a physiohealer to make home visits.

Although I appreciate Dr. Imogen Hyu for all she's done for Al, her presence only represents more pain for me since my tears pay for each session.

I sit on one of the low mat tables as my sister begins her appointment. Exercise equipment fills my vision from left to right. Bands, weights, balance pads, stretch straps, a stationary cycle, parallel bars, and more. I cried so many diamonds to deck the place out, to give her the best chance at managing this disease.

But my sister is the one person I don't mind using my gift for. I'll fill buckets if it means helping her. Plus, she's helped me more than I've helped her. She's made me want to live despite my parents giving me every reason to hate the life they've forced us into. Al and I? We're in this together.

But sometimes I find myself at a crossroads—I want freedom while still being able to help my sister. *Can I have both?*

Realizing I've been digging crescent moon shapes into the soft mat table, I snap from my thoughts and relax my hands, focusing on Al.

She's lying on her back on the low mat table beside me while Dr. Hyu stretches her hamstring, trying to straighten her leg.

I've been assisting Al with her home exercise program, but it's hard when a disease does what it wants…and when there is no cure.

I struggle seeing how much tighter her leg appears—how bent her knee stays despite the physiohealer's pushing.

I don't attend all of Al's therapy sessions, but Dr. Hyu asked the family to sit in on this one this time. I don't know where Mother and Father are, but they arrive when the session's almost over.

Mother *tsks*, working out the wrinkles in her dress, not even acknowledging we're here. Father approaches the mat table with a passive expression. Gods, they're acting like they're not even late. If I had been a second late, there'd be hell to pay.

He tilts his head as he studies the scene. "How are things progressing, Dr. Hyu?"

The woman pushes the bridge of her glasses up her nose and releases Al's leg, shifting to stretch the other one. "Her muscles have been stubborn today. They're shortening, adapting to her sitting in the wheelchair more."

"They're angry," Al says, pausing once to cough. "But I'm working on making them happier."

My spirit lifts at her optimism, something I always try to emulate, especially right after a crying session. From inspirational words and medication to the good ole sucking it up, I've tried everything. But nothing cheers me up as much as being with Al.

Mother grabs the wheelchair by the handles and pushes it off into the corner. It's a brand new one they bought for her a few months ago—gold all over, with satin cushions and floral embellishments along the armrests and wheels. "Well, we just have to get her off this thing, then."

Dr. Hyu finishes stretching Al and pats her shoulder, signaling for her to sit up.

I catch the flash of slight annoyance in the physiohealer's expression. But if she's offended by Mother's remark, she doesn't say anything. "She's been using a wheelchair for the past six years, Lady Esmerene. It's normal for her neuromuscular disease to progress this way and make things harder for Al to move. Honestly, she's doing great. Our goal in therapy is to slow the disease, but we can't predict the tissue damage that will occur. Based on her last strength and gait tests, she'll always require the wheelchair for longer distances and when she's fatigued, but she should keep walking either without assistive devices — or with the loft strand crutches, if necessary, for short distances — as much as possible."

I'm glad Dr. Hyu has Al using the crutches. They're like plain ones, except they allow her to hold objects like food or bags while walking, since she bears weight on her wrists while leaving her hands free.

My sister frowns. "I'd rather talk about what I can do than about my physical challenges. But it won't be a problem using the wheelchair less. I never get to go anywhere."

I have to force myself not to say, *Same here, sis.*

"*Allegra!* Watch your mouth." Mother glares daggers at her.

"What? You're only trying to cure me because you're embarrassed when I can't walk."

"That's not true and you know it," Father says. "We built a gym for you so you can live a better life and filled the greenhouse in the center of our home so you can experience the outside world in a safe space. You could be a little more grateful for everything we've done for you." His voice wavers, struggling to remain light and airy in front of Dr. Hyu.

But I sense the poison lacing his words.

"Sorry." Al wheezes twice and her hand shoots to her chest. "And...sorry for this..."

Dr. Hyu finally speaks again, clearly not wanting the family drama to derail the conversation. "Don't apologize for coughing, Allegra. It's something I wanted to bring up with you. Lately, you've been short of breath in our sessions. Especially during your standing exercises. The skin under your fingernails turns a little blue, which indicates you're not getting enough oxygen. We want to address it sooner rather than later, so I had your parents send for Dr. Sammer to check your respiratory function and discuss further treatment strategies."

Father runs his fingers through the coils of his short hair. "He should be here tomorrow to perform his exam."

"Well, I appreciate your promptness with the matter. It could be a simple fix or something very serious," Dr. Hyu explains.

I fixate on that last part. Any change in Al's function sets me on edge. It's a possibility I want to ignore, but it's always in the back of my mind. Al has been looking a little thinner and frailer lately. But I bite my tongue to prevent myself from asking Dr. Hyu my billion questions.

Al knows how to put on a brave face, too. But her eyes glisten, like she's going to cry. She swallows hard and smiles. "I, uh, thanks for your help."

Dr. Hyu nods and rests a hand on Al's shoulder. "Anytime. Keep up the good work, and I'll see you on Thursday?"

"Yes. I'm going to do twenty reps of the bridges without stopping next time!"

"I love that!" Dr. Hyu cheers.

My heart warms in gratitude as the woman gathers her things. She's been working for us long enough that I consider her a friend, especially since Al and I don't have any of our own.

We're not allowed to have anyone over. The townsfolk know us as the sick girls who never leave their house and, frustratingly, view Mother and Father as doting parents protecting their dear children.

Before she leaves, Dr. Hyu collects her pay, and Mother hands her a tiny pouch of diamonds—my tears.

My parents are lucky that diamonds are expensive in Soridente. It makes what we offer that much more valuable. But it also isn't too out of the ordinary in our country's currency of gems, jewels, and coins. Anything that glitters and clinks is fair game.

Father paces the floor, past bins of weights and equipment that Al uses in therapy. "I'm eager to hear Dr. Sammer's opinion tomorrow. He spoke to us earlier this month about some different experimental treatments he wants to try."

"I'm his guinea pig," Al says with indifference before coughing and clearing her throat. She motions for the wheelchair and I wheel it back to her. She transfers herself from the mat table back into her wheelchair on her own.

Mother adjusts the rings on her own fingers, gems too large to stay on straight. "We only want what's best for you. If there's a way we can get you better, don't you want that?"

I don't hear Al's reply, only my thoughts. If she gets better, I wouldn't have to cry diamond tears to pay for her treatments. But is there another way to relieve her symptoms?

And would Mother and Father still torture me to fit their agenda to get richer and rise in the royal ranks? Without a single doubt. They can't do that without me. But I'm getting tired of it. There has to be another way for me and Al to both find happiness—for Al to receive the care she needs to achieve the freedom we deserve without our parents abusing me.

Al wheels herself past the double doors into the hallway.

I follow suit. I've got to get away from Mother and Father before I find it harder to breathe, too. I've been crying on command for sixteen years. Can I endure anymore?

Mother and Father better be careful. Sooner or later, I'm going to break. After all, with enough force, even diamonds can shatter.

FOUR

Therapy sessions often tire Al out, so she returns to her room for a quick nap. But since we're planning on planting some new flowers in the greenhouse later this afternoon, I stay with her. I pull up a chair and open our sketchbook onto the easel before me, sketching out the best arrangement for the new section. From begonias to peonies, I pencil in every petal and leaf before coloring them in with my paintbrushes to create a gorgeous pattern. One bunch will be red, white, and pink. *Pink…*

The pink-haired girl I saw earlier…I haven't forgotten about her, but now that Dr. Hyu is gone, she comes back to the forefront of my mind. I bite my lip, wondering if I will ever see her again. Unlikely. Maybe I'm going stir-crazy from being inside too long and fixating on whatever my mind feels like.

A knock at the door rattles me from my musings. Al pushes herself up in bed and yawns.

One of the newly hired maids walks in, wearing an apron over a buttoned shirt and a pair of slacks.

Why did Mother and Father need to add more strangers into the mix? Why can't we be left alone to do everything ourselves? As we've always done?

"Excuse me, girls," she says in a bright voice, "but your parents are requesting your presence. They have some exciting news to share with you!"

Exciting news? Since when do we ever get that?

Al and I turn to each other.

Her eyes light up, but mine narrow in suspicion. I spring from my chair, Al rushes into her wheelchair, and we're off, wasting no time as we hurry after the maid, impatient to discover what our parents have to tell us.

They are waiting for us in the family room, sitting on one of the plush couches.

Globe lights hang above us, with a yellow hue, not stark white like Al's therapy gym. In the center of the room sits a low circular table with photo albums on top, along with a glass bowl of colorfully wrapped candies. The space is wide with tall ceilings, yet it feels small and cozy with the thoughtful way it's been decorated. So unlike the rest of the house, which looks more like a museum than a home.

The carpet underneath the table is thin enough that it's easy to wheel Al across the room. As we pass the table, Al grabs a blue candy for each of us. I park her on the other side of the table and sit on a nearby loveseat.

Mother's holding a letter with gold foil along the edges.

My heart skips a beat. The golden pattern is a signature look for King Pontifex Goldin, a play on words of his last name. What sort of news does the king send?

Curiosity. Officially. *Piqued.*

I unwrap the fruity hard candy and pop it into my mouth, the sugary sweetness coating my tongue.

Al must notice the letter, too, because her head tilts inquisitively. She fiddles with her candy, wrapping and unwrapping one end. "Well, what did you have to tell us?"

Father's grin spreads from ear to ear, but Mother jumps in excitement and speaks first. "We've been invited to the Summer Solstice Ball this weekend!" she announces, clutching her hands to her chest without crinkling the prized paper.

My eyes widen. "W-what? Oh, my gods, Al! We get to go to our very first ball!"

"*Yes!*" Al exclaims before her hand shoots to her chest and pauses to catch her breath.

Mother's forehead creases. "No, no, you misunderstand. I meant *we...*" She points between her and Father, "are going to the Summer Solstice Ball."

"What?" My elation quickly deflates as I sink into my seat.

Al's crinkling candy wrapper grates like nails on a chalkboard.

"Your father and I have been invited to the ball because we became a baron and baroness this year. We're going to be among only the best of the best. *Royalty.*"

Father grins, appearing just as clueless to the fact that Mother has crushed his daughter's hopes and dreams. "I'm going to try to speak to King Pontifex directly. You see, his royal advisor is also the captain of the guard. I want to convince him they should be two separate people, and that, of course, I should take the former role. I can picture it now..." He spreads his hands in an arc as if he were watching the scene play out right in front of him. "All welcome Lord Monticello Alcro, royal advisor, and King Pontifex's right-hand man."

I fight to keep from rolling my eyes, but my parents make it obnoxiously difficult. They have more than enough wealth thanks to my tears, but it's still not enough for them. They need to look and be the best in everything. Hells, I wouldn't put it against them angling to become the next king and queen themselves.

"That new housekeeper you hired said you had exciting news for us..." Al says with downcast eyes.

Mother scratches the back of her head. "That...that is the news."

"Yes, for *you*," Al retorts.

Mother rushes over and kneels beside her. "Well, it would probably be too much for you. There's going to be many people, a lot of dancing..."

Al scoffs. "And? You wouldn't even know what I'm capable of because I can't *try* anything."

The sweetness of the candy has now soured in my mouth, but I refrain from spitting it out at my parents' feet. They won't *let* her try.

Mother looks like she's searching for a retort, which she clearly doesn't have, so instead she says, "Well, even if we let you go, Cadence couldn't go with you. We can't risk people finding out about her gift."

I grab the letter in Mother's hand and start reading it furiously. "It says it's going to be a masquerade. So…no one's going to see me. I can hide behind a mask, right?" Not like I don't already, but I keep that remark to myself.

Father rubs his clean-shaven chin while remaining on the couch. "Hm, she does have a point there."

"Monticello!"

"Come now, Esmerene. Weren't you ready to play matchmaker?"

"What do you mean?" I scan the letter for clues.

Mother rises and grabs the paper from me, reading word for word. "This invitation extends to any eligible ladies of sixteen or older, as our son, Prince Wendell Goldin, is now in search of a bride. Please dress to impress."

My lips part in stunned horror, but nothing comes out.

Al hoots, slapping her knee. "Ooh, eligible…" She shakes her shoulders in a sultry manner, "ladies."

"You…want me to go…for the prince?" I finally eek out.

"Yes, I was thinking of having you attend, Cadence. But is it worth the risk of exposing your gift?"

I fixate on the word, worth. Is it worth it for my parents if I accidentally reveal my diamond tears to the world? If that means they would no longer belong to them?

I want to interject, but decide it's not worth it and let her continue. "Your diamond tears must stay secret until the time is right," she explains. "If we allow you to go, that is."

"But just think…" Father goes on, still hung up on his aspirations. "If Cadence marries Wendell, we'll have another way into the royal family. It'll be even easier for me to replace Rioza as Pontifex's advisor!"

"That is true," Mother muses. "A very important reason we should all attend."

My stomach churns, and it's not from the candy. I'm already controlled by enough people. Now I have to get married off to some guy I don't even know? I've seen paintings of him and sure, he's kind of cute, but I have no idea what his personality is like. And having "prince" for a title doesn't impress me at all. It's a matter of birth. And even if it wasn't, the bar is low for titles if my parents got into the nobility solely on money.

I'm about to object to them turning my one chance at a night of normalcy into a matchmaking scheme, but then I catch the look in Al's eyes. They're glistening, on the verge of tears, and full of hope. And I know, right then and there, that I have to go.

And hey, maybe it could work out in my favor. It's unlikely that the prince would actually notice me out of all the other girls who will be there, and it wouldn't be so bad to let Al have the time of her life. Worst-case scenario, I'll become the Princess of Soridente, get away from my parents, and never have to cry again. They have enough money after sixteen years, don't they?

I spring from my seat and rush to Mom. "Can we go? Please? I'll meet Wendell. Dress to impress, right? I'll do whatever you ask, as long as Al can go, too."

Mother and Father exchange looks, doing that typical parent mind-reading thing.

Al and I force ourselves to sit still while they silently debate what to do.

Finally, Mother says, "Okay, but only if you keep your mask on and be on your best behavior the entire night—especially in front of Prince Wendell. Your father and I are counting on you."

I shrug. Nothing new there. "It's a deal."

"I'm going to the ball!" Al exclaims, taking her wheelchair for a spin. She sends herself into a small fit of coughs, though she keeps her mouth closed to stifle them.

Mother tilts her head to the globe lights above us. "Hmmm…" I think she's going to comment on Al's coughing and I hold my breath. "I wonder if we should get brand-new clothes?"

My eye twitches. Okay, I guess I'm going to be annoyed no matter what my parents say. "We have plenty of clothes with tags still on them in the closet."

"Yes, Cadence, but not ball gowns. I need to look as wealthy as a viscountess—no, an archduchess. We might come out of there with you as the prince's girlfriend and Father as the king's royal advisor. We can't go in there looking like the peasants from Serency."

I scoop up another piece of candy, if only to crush it, to hide my disdain. "New clothes. Got it." There go my chances of not crying anymore today.

I should be crying tears of joy. Al and I get to leave the house, and to a ball at that! And at the royal palace! Half of my excitement is from seeing Al so elated. She wheels over to me and I give her the biggest hug I can.

"Let's pick out our jewelry," she says. "Ooh, and Mother, I want to wear a purple mask with feathers on the side."

"But of course, Allegra," Mother says noncommittally. She's staring at the ceiling, probably imagining her dress.

I ask for something pink or blue, my two favorite colors, and make sure to thank them both before Al and I return to her room to plan out our accessories.

The stories we told earlier might've been long forgotten in her mind, but as Al pulls purple necklaces from her drawers, holding one of them up to herself in the mirror, I can't help but linger on mine.

FIVE

The next day, we all meet again in the gym. This time with Dr. Sammer. With his braided hair tied in a ponytail, he might be the coolest of Al's doctors. Mother and Father have fired a couple for not finding the *right* treatments for her. But he isn't afraid to try more experimental therapies.

It seems like we're exhausting our list of options, though. First, it was tons of different medicines. Al hated the fatigue she got from them. Then spinal injections caused some nerve pain down her legs. Who knows what he'll be cooking up for her next—and the side effects my sister will suffer from it?

I sit on the mat next to him and Al while our parents stand on the opposite side, always keeping their distance from her condition—as if they'll catch it from her.

Al taps her fingers on the wheelchair's armrest. "Whattaya got for me today, Theo?"

"It's Dr. Sammer, Allegra. You know that," Mother scolds.

The man laughs and sits on the mat table. "It's okay. She can call me whatever she likes. Except for any swear words. I've heard enough of those in my years of practice."

"Don't worry. You and Dr. Hyu are my favorites," Al assures.

"Good to know." Dr. Sammer sets his bag down beside him and removes some medical devices. "I'm going to perform a routine health check, but I also want to look at your lungs a little closer since Dr. Hyu called me about her concerns. You've been having some trouble breathing the past two weeks?"

Al holds her arms out like a scarecrow. "Yep." She coughs. "I'm all yours."

I can't watch as the doctor inspects her, checking for any flaw—a crack in her progress.

I'm dreading the day he tells me everything isn't going as it should, that her lungs are failing her along with the rest of her body. I wish I could hole up in the library and read to distract myself, but I want to hear Dr. Sammer give Al a clean bill of health.

"Breathe again for me, dear." He places a stethoscope on different parts of Al's back and listens with the ear tips in. He settles on one spot and his expression darkens.

"Is everything all right, Doctor?" Father asks.

"Blood pressure's good and her pulse is normal, but I'm worried about her lung function, Lord Monticello."

My gaze cuts to Al's, and the worry in her expression breaks me. "What does that mean?"

Dr. Sammer sighs, placing his supplies back into his bag. "Respiratory function is especially important to maintain in people with this neuromuscular disease. The lungs work because of the diaphragm and intercostal muscles between your ribs. Just as muscle wasting occurs in your arms and legs, so it can occur in the muscles that help you breathe." He explains things slowly and carefully to ensure the whole family understands. It's one of the reasons I like him so much.

"So…my lungs are dying?" Al asks, her voice a bit raspier, like she's struggling to get the words out with a full breath.

"No, no." He rests a hand on her shoulder. "Nothing so dramatic. Only the lower part of your right lobe is not getting in enough air. We have to keep those muscles working so you can stay strong and get enough oxygen."

"Makes sense," she replies.

Mother starts pacing back and forth, the long trail of her dress looking ridiculous as it skims the gym's floor. "So, what's this experimental treatment you mentioned when we talked the other day?"

Dr. Sammer stands to be eye level with my parents again. "Allegra has had her fair share of therapies. I believe that's what's kept her going strong for so long. But we want to keep fighting this thing, so I'm proposing that we try an experimental treatment on her."

"Meaning?" I ask.

"My goal with this treatment is to repair her muscle tissue and reverse the degeneration that has occurred."

Al wheels herself closer to him. "As long as I can still go to the Summer Solstice Ball, I'm in."

"This shouldn't interfere with your ability to go if we start after the event. Also," he cups a hand to his mouth as if telling her a secret, "I wasn't even invited, so you're one step ahead of me."

Al beams. "Sounds good to me!"

I'm glad Al and I can still attend the ball, but it's everything that will happen afterwards that has me worried.

"There are risks once you undergo the treatment, however," he explains. "The healthy tissue could end up damaged. There's also a chance for infection or organ damage."

I scrunch my nose. It's not worth the risk of death if that's on the table. "I don't think—"

"That sounds like it'd be worth trying out," Father interrupts. "If there's any possibility it can help her, that is."

"Oh yes, it's improved symptoms in many other diseases. Because this is a rare and experimental procedure, it's going to be quite expensive." Dr. Sammer addresses my parents, though his last sentence should be directed to *me*, since I'm the one paying. Not that he knows that.

Mother waves his words away in dismissal. "Oh, that's no problem. We'll pay whatever the cost." She doesn't even ask exactly how much. It's not as if *she* has to do any work, after all.

I want to cut in, but know it will be useless. And if it can help Al, the price tag doesn't matter. As long as I'm not expected to pay it all upfront.

"Yes, let's try the new treatment," Father says.

"It's actually *Allegra's* decision," Dr. Sammer says, turning to her. "We can start next week if you'd like?"

Al bites her lip. "Um, I…" She steals a glance at Mother and Father. I can read Al's expression like a book—she might want to try something else, but she's afraid of how they'll react. "Yeah, yeah, let's try it," she says hesitantly.

Dr. Sammer smiles. "Excellent!"

"You can set up whatever you need in one of the private rooms," Mother adds.

I'll have to ask my sister what she really thinks of her new guinea pig status later. For now, I rage on the inside at Mother and Father for making decisions for us—without asking *us*—yet again.

For a split second, I consider spiting them, shoving the jewelry I'm wearing in the doctor's face, and calling it a day. But I know what happens when I rebel—even in the smallest of ways—so I hold back.

Before an ounce of weakness shows, I squeak out a quick goodbye and race out of the room, cupping my face until my hands are full of diamond tears. Al's going to need them, so I let them fall.

SIX

Thank the gods time knows how to fly. Usually, it doesn't, but this week distracted Mother and Father with preparing for the ball in ways that didn't call upon my tears. And Al's and my excitement let us forget about the experimental treatments she'll be starting next week. Before we can blink, the day—night—is finally here. The Summer Solstice Ball.

The Goldins usually host a celebration for each change in season, whether it be a concert, parade, or dance. I'm lucky they decided on a masquerade this time.

I'm also grateful Mother and Father didn't go back on their promise to let me and Al attend. But we haven't left yet—there's still time for them to disappoint us.

Our home's front hallway is one I don't frequent too often. Why would I, when I'm not allowed to just waltz outside?

Al stands beside me with her crutches. She studies the front door like she's under a spell.

I don't blame her. I'm equally mesmerized.

This space is as foreign to us as Frecochi's Bakery, the most popular spot in town for pastries and cakes. We've only gotten a taste from the crumbs at the bottom of Mother and Father's bags.

And don't get me started on the Grand Marks Theatre. Many a night, our parents come home wide-eyed and smiling from the plays and entertainment and gush about it at the dinner table. Al and I only experience it during those meals or from overhearing the maids discussing the latest town gossip.

For us, everything is always just out of reach.

It reminds me of the one time I tried to sneak out. Mother and Father had punished me so badly—the only time they ever got physical—that I never dared try again. But like those bruises, the plush carpet, paintings on the walls, and musk of unaired hallways all fade away as my focus narrows on the double doors.

A soft hand slips into mine and squeezes gently.

I turn to Al and return the gesture, flashing a smile created from the butterflies in my stomach. There are probably caterpillars and ants crawling in there, too. I'm kind of nauseated from it. To steady myself, I inhale the deepest breath I've ever taken in my entire life. Al's exhale escapes with mine as we blow the air out slowly at the same time.

"Nervous?" I ask.

Al giggles awkwardly. "No. You?"

"No," my voice squeaks, the pitch abnormally high. "I mean, no," I say in my normal tone.

We burst out laughing, but our freak-out rises to the next level when Mother and Father approach us.

My heart knocks obnoxiously against my ribcage, just like Al and I have on these very doors, wishing every day for a chance to go outside. But I guess wishes do come true since it's happening. I place a palm on my chest to settle the erratic beating.

A footman marches in front of us and pushes the double doors open. "After you, Miss Allegra and Miss Cadence."

My sister is the brave soul to move first, guiding her crutches forward and stepping into the early evening air.

When I follow behind her, I fight back tears. The warm summer wind sweeps through my long brown hair and the setting sun on the horizon appears closer than it ever has. I've played on the lawn in the past, albeit sparingly. But the grass smells freshly cut, and simply the sight of it gives me the urge to kick off these heels and wriggle my toes in them. I make out faint talking and laughing in the distance from passersby on the other side of the fence. This is unreal. This is—no, it's a reality we haven't had enough of. But now here we are, actually getting to…*live.*

I struggle to contain my excitement and quicken my pace to catch up to Al as she walks over to the carriage. It is black with silver trim, and the horses sport the same decorations, silvery feather trim along their harnesses, though their face pieces and blinders are smooth to avoid obstructing their vision.

Mother and Father had ramps installed throughout the house and leading to the front door. But after the depressing news from her doctors, Al understandably wants to go as long as she can with her crutches before she uses her wheelchair.

We climb inside while another footman loads the wheelchair into the back compartment my parents added when Al used to travel for her doctors' appointments.

Before I get inside, my attention darts back to the landscape. It's as if I'm seeing and experiencing everything for the first time, and I struggle to remember the last time I was out. The thought makes me sputter. Resentment tastes bitter on my tongue. What else have Al and I missed out on all these years?

Knowing I can't delay any longer—perhaps risking Mother and Father deciding I should stay behind—I slide into my seat and adjust the mask on the top half of my face, feeling oddly comforted and exposed at the same time.

Mother had rejected my blue or pink ball gown request. Instead, I'm sitting here wearing white—which is more appropriate for a wedding gown than a Solstice Ball.

"It'll leave a perfect impression on the prince," she'd said with a wink.

Perfect? I don't think so. Desperate and presumptuous? Most definitely. But I keep that to myself.

Despite the color, or lack thereof, it is a gorgeous piece of clothing with a sweetheart neckline and off-the-shoulder draped sleeves. Maybe I'll be lucky and I won't be the only one in white—won't stick out like a sore thumb. I ignore estimating its price tag and focus on Al. She's gazing out the window, glowing and...*radiant*.

Her face lights up with excitement at the promise of a night full of fun and adventure, and perhaps even a bit of mischief as her smile spreads into a grin I'm all too familiar with. Whatever she has planned in that brilliant head of hers, I hope it's worth it.

We may never get a night out like this again.

She's absolutely beautiful in what she asked for. Purple from head to toe. Her violet attire begins as a lighter shade in her hair accessories and mask. The top of her dress is a slightly deeper tone, and continues darkening the farther you go down, ending with a rich eggplant.

Mother and Father sit across from us, wearing matching forest green outfits with gold accents. Father usually wears fancy suits and Mother extravagant dresses, so they don't look too different from everyday life.

The driver commands the horses and takes us beyond our front garden, down the cobblestones, and to the city streets.

Forget about the ball. I could stay inside the carriage and explore Noravale the entire night. The city is also donning its summer attire, with banners and streamers strewn from streetlamp to streetlamp, peonies and daisies in full bloom along the walkways, and joyous music playing from every direction. The smell of freshly cooked meals for those not invited to the ball meets my senses.

Are the owners peering out their windows in admiration and envy like I'd be doing if I weren't lucky to be going?

I swivel to gaze out the back window. Our mansion appears so small now. Exactly how I want it—far away and insignificant. When I face forward again, I realize we have been going far too fast because I can already make out the towers of King Pontifex's palace in the distance. His castle seems straight out of a fairytale, one that Al or I could've made up from her bedroom window.

A few other carriages come into view, clearly on their way to the masquerade as well.

Mother tugs me by the arm and from my stupor. "Now, remember, girls, you must be on your best behavior."

"And absolutely no crying," Father warns, his expression stern. "Otherwise, both of you will never leave the house again."

I dig my fingernails into my palms, then release them so I don't smear blood on my virgin white dress.

"Have we made ourselves clear?" Mother asks.

"Crystal," Al says.

"Diamond," I reply.

Al stifles a laugh. "You really need to lay off the corny jokes, Cade. That was too on the nose."

I fold my arms. "I was proud of that one."

"Girls! Be serious now. The prince is searching for a mature, refined woman," Mother explains.

"Oh, so, you don't want him to marry Cadence?" my sister quips.

"Al!" I lightly punch her shoulder, and she shoves me toward the window in retaliation.

"Should we turn this carriage around?" Mother threatens.

Al and I raise our palms in defeat.

"Calm down," I reply. "We were just teasing."

Father furrows his brows and leans forward. If he wasn't buckled in, surely, we'd be nose to nose right now. "With my job literally on the line, we won't 'calm down,' Cadence. Behave, or your mother and I will make you."

"Sorry," I say hastily.

Al apologizes too, and we zip our lips for the rest of the ride.

The rest of the houses and carriages pass by in a haze as I work to forget my parents' ridiculousness. These are not the memories I hope to take with me at the end of the night.

I lean over and whisper to Al, "At this rate, we won't *want* to leave again."

My sister keeps her voice low. "Then I guess we should make tonight count."

She flashes a grin and I wink in reply.

The carriage stops soon after, and the light lilt of music and laughter permeates in the air. Lanterns decorate the veranda and a stone fountain in the center of the circular drive sends the sound of trickling water to my ears.

Flash and flair surround us. Women wearing gowns larger and more extravagant than ours stroll by, and Mother's stink eye bores a hole in them. Men donning the most intricately designed suits pass us, wearing masks as elaborate as their female counterparts.

I spot two men walking hand in hand up the stone stairs. My chest swells with pride that the kingdom accepts everyone as they are. I bet my diamonds that they'll be the cutest couple here.

Our driver pulls Al's crutches out of the back.

We exit the carriage and my legs morph into jelly.

Whoa, Cadence, I tell myself. *You'll do fine. Just smile and nod. Get in good with the prince. And. Don't. Cry. Can't be too hard, right?*

"Monticello! What a pleasure!" a man with the bushiest mustache I've ever seen approaches us. He shakes hands with Father and bows to Mother. "M'lady." He turns to me as I scratch my arm. "And what fine young women do we have here?"

"These are our daughters, Cadence and Allegra." Mother urges us forward and we tip our heads in acknowledgment.

"Lovely to meet you. Well, right this way, right this way! The summer solstice awaits you!" the man says, not even bothering to introduce himself.

It's unclear whether he's so important that everyone knows him, or not important enough for anyone to care.

I don't ask before he firmly ushers us to the palace entrance, where we join the mass of people making their way inside.

I frown, noting the lack of ramps leading to the front doors. If my diamond tears can pay for them at my house, shouldn't King Goldin have them at his? I exchange a peeved glance with Al.

She takes the reins and informs the mustache man that the royal palace should have ramps and rails installed for those with handicaps and disabilities.

He bows apologetically and promises he'll inform the necessary parties immediately. Who knows if he's telling the truth. Al and I will probably never get to see for ourselves.

The steps aren't too steep, but after we climb to the top, Al asks to sit and rest to catch her breath. She changes her mind about the crutches, deciding to use the wheelchair for the time being and save her strength for when it's time to dance.

Thankfully, one of the king's butlers has her decorated wheelchair ready for her—with flowers adorning the golden rims and armrests now colored amethyst to match Al's dress.

Are Mother and Father sure they don't want her to talk to the prince? I'm positive she'll catch the guy's eye more than I will.

My sister leads the way, wheeling herself down the hall to the grand ballroom first.

We're stopped many times by people Mother and Father work with—neighbors and, I guess, family friends. I don't know the difference at this point. They're all strangers to me. But I fake laugh, curtsy, and stay on my best behavior, even as I block out their pointless small talk.

Instead, I focus on the attire of those parading past. Some people have gems or feathers around the eyeholes, while others have huge wings or headpieces emerging from the mask, making it more of a headdress than anything else. I hadn't thought to ensure mine was up to par.

Conversations carry on around us, laughs that sound genuine, the clinking of wine glasses, and the sweeping of ball gowns on the floor. It's all so magical.

As we continue down the gorgeous hallway, I can't imagine what the actual ballroom looks like. Mosaic tapestries hang from the walls, brightly lit sconces, golden spiral columns, and a deep maroon rug signal the path ahead.

I'm also ready to gag at the extravagance of it all. But if I married the prince, maybe I wouldn't have to cry on command ever again because, clearly, King Pontifex of this country has an overflowing bounty. Al and I don't have the best impression of him because we've heard not all citizens are treated equally. And some of his laws are deeply unfair. But I tuck that hearsay to the side to enjoy the night.

I take a deep inhale before we head into the ballroom and am instantly glad I did. The room is so breathtaking I might have gotten lightheaded without oxygen. The chandeliers look as big as our carriage and the distance from the marble floor to the ceiling seems a mile tall. A live band plays soft, lilting music, complete with a piano, violins, flutes, and a few other instruments I don't recognize.

Al taps her toes to the beat on her leg rests, eager to stand and dance once they pick up the pace. Tables with lavish food and drink line a wall, and smaller ones are dotted along the perimeter for those who'd rather stuff their mouths with hors d'oeuvres than words. My type of crowd, might I add.

I'm a vegetarian, so I pass on the meat and eye the spread of roasted vegetables and fingerling potatoes until I'm tugged in the opposite direction.

Mother leads me to a circle of shiny people. I mean, people wearing shiny *clothes*.

My eyes glaze over and so do my ears—if that can even happen—because I swear, I don't hear a word she's blabbing to the other court members.

I scan the room and my attention zeros in on a dashingly handsome young man with flowing blonde hair and piercing green eyes visible behind his golden mask standing near the buttered buns. I knew I should've gone for the food. Mother's socializing could wait.

And those carbs look delicious. Who knows if they'll still be there by the time I reach them?

I pull my attention away from the buffet before my stomach decides to audibly betray me, and focus back on the guy. Except—*oh, no*—he's walking toward me and Al. And not by himself.

A herd—yes, a literal herd—of fancy-dress girls are fawning over him. I can see their drool from way over here. No introductions are needed. Only one young man here would garner so much attention.

"My father has been an Earl in Noravale for ten years now. We just bought our fifth mansion advancement," I hear one girl drone to him as they get closer.

Another hangs off the guy's arm. "You're *so* hot."

"I bet you love gold because your last name's Goldin. Get it? Gold-*en*. Ha! Bet you haven't heard that before," guffaws a third.

I roll my eyes, realizing despite hiding behind a mask, people can still see my expressions. I peek at Mother's circle of friends, but they're still chattering amongst themselves. Good. Looks like no one noticed. Well, except Al, who's been focused on me for who knows how long.

She crosses her arms. "He's quite the little heartthrob, isn't he?"

I stick my tongue out at her. "Come on, don't spoil my appetite. I haven't gotten to enjoy any of the food yet!"

"Girls, stand—and sit—tall! He's coming!" Mother nudges us, clearly having spied her prey.

I assumed my blood would rush at his presence, but it's slowing to a snail's pace. Titles and gold can be façades—just look at my parents—but I can't tell if that holds true with the prince. Is he one of the decent ones? He is handsome. I guess I should give it a shot and find out what he's really about.

"Thank you for the kind words, but I must move on," the prince says with a practiced collectiveness, bowing to the group of tagalong girls which results in a collective swoon and sigh. "Why hello there," he says, turning his attention to me.

I peer left and right. Surely, he's not coming to talk to…me? Okay, now my jitters are surfacing again. Even though I doubt it, there's a chance—that my parents have made very clear—that I could marry the prince, so I can't completely rule myself out yet. I'm just not feeling any butterflies—aside from the nervous kind. If I'm going to marry someone, shouldn't I feel butterflies? Whoever I'm with, it has to be for love, not their money or status.

"I'm Allegra Alero! Nice to meet you!" my sister exclaims, filling my awkward silence, reaching out her hand.

He smiles and bows, taking her hand and planting the gentlest kiss atop. "It's a pleasure. And…who might you be?" He switches his focus back to me, stepping closer with a curious expression.

I don't blame him. I'd wonder why a girl would be so bold to wear white to this affair, too.

Maybe Mother used her maternal senses for once and felt the uncertainty emanating from me because before I say something dumb enough to get us kicked out, she rushes in.

"Ah! Such a pleasure to make your acquaintance," Mother says with a head nod and sweep of her dress, her voice sounding disgustingly sweet. "Prince Wendell Goldin, I'd like to introduce you to my daughter, Miss Cadence Alero."

SEVEN

Iguess Mother's introduction is a good thing or "perfect timing," as Father says because two figures choose that moment to settle on either side of Prince Wendell, gilded hands resting on his shoulders.

I'm glad I kept my choice words inside before I could make a fool of myself in front of the most important people in the country.

King Pontifex stands before me like a barge, solid and sturdy. His long golden hair almost beats mine in length, and despite his thick beard and intricate mask, I easily make out his stoic expression. He's what I'd call "madly intimidating." On the other side of Wendell is his mom, Natali, the queen consort. She, too, has long blonde hair and strength in her gaze. I can't believe I'm finally meeting them in the flesh, and not just hearing Mother and Father drone on endlessly about them at home.

Speaking of Mother, I can tell she's fighting back hysterics. She holds my upper arm to steady her shaking. "Oh my, th-thank you so much for inviting us, Your Majesties." She bows and her knuckles twist against my spine, forcing me to also bow.

Al also tips her head in respect.

"It's a pleasure to finally meet you," Queen Natali says to Mother. "And…it was Cadence, correct?"

I nod and gesture to my side. "And this is my sister, Allegra."

The queen consort gives a cordial smile. "It's a pleasure to meet both of you, as well."

My tension fades slightly. Okay, the family isn't made of jerks. I shouldn't have judged them, but I'm not used to—how does one say it? Meeting people and holding new conversations and interacting like a normal teenager? Yeah, that.

The King gives me a once over, and unlike his son, his face remains hard to read. "The Aleros. Yes."

"Drinks, my king? My queen?" A masked servant approaches our group, clean-pressed and sharp-suited, holding a tray with different colored beverages.

King Goldin spreads his arm toward us. "Our guests, first, please."

The man serves Al and me, clarifying they are non-alcoholic, before handing Mother a tall glass of red wine.

I have no idea where Father has been this whole time, but he bursts between me and Mother to greet the Goldins, miraculously without spilling our drinks. "Your Majesties! Lord Monticello here. I see you've met my lovely wife and daughters."

Queen Consort Natali smiles politely as she grabs a wine glass, while Wendell keeps his eyes fixed on me.

I struggle not to fidget under his attention.

Father tugs at his lapels and clears his throat. "King Pontifex, I wanted to speak with you tonight about some very important business matters."

Mr. Apparently-Never-Smiles finally shows a bit of emotion, waving Father's words away. "Come now. Today is for celebrating another change of season—to eat, drink, and dance. Have fun and enjoy the night." The king slaps Father's shoulder then collects a champagne flute and downs it in one shot. He grabs a second from the tray before joining another crowd full of high-and-mighties.

Father's staring at the spot on his shoulder the King touched, and even though he was dismissed for now, I swear he'll never wash that suit again.

Queen Natali directs her attention to Al. "Let us know if there's anything you need, okay, dear?"

"Thank you so much." My sister looks around the room before struggling to clear her throat like there's a thick layer of mucus mucking it up or something. She settles her attention back on the queen consort. "A brand-new body would be nice."

Mother sighs and rubs her temples, but the royal laughs. "I will see what we can do." She offers a small smile and excuses herself to follow the king.

The band has picked up their pace, and the center of the ball-room is suddenly filled with both dancing souls and those with two left feet. I'm closer to the former with the right song. I've taught myself a little bit of everything with my time spent inside. What's that phrase? Jack of all trades, master of none?

I finally taste my drink, a fruity mix that bubbles on my tongue and lightens my spirits. Al takes a sip of hers too, preferring mock-tails to any alcohol. When I'm of age, I might feel the same.

A nudge at my side brings me back to the space in front of me. Mother's mouth is set in a forced smile, but her brown eyes dart from me to the prince and back again.

I bite my tongue and force my own lips to turn up as I inch toward Wendell. Mother won't leave me alone until I play my part, so let's get this over with, shall we?

"Do you want to dance? I'd love to know you better," he asks.

"I'd…" I glance at Mother who shoos me to continue. "…love to get to know you, too." And it's not a lie. If I'm supposed to marry him, I want to know what this prince is like.

He beams and holds out his hand.

I grasp it, happy to find his palm is neither sweaty nor clammy.

We weave our way around the couples already dancing, some younger, mostly older, all the cream of the crop. I'm sure the other eligible ladies are probably throwing imaginary darts at the back of my head and holding back obscenities.

I wish I could tell them they have no reason to worry. I'm here to make my parents happy and steal one night of freedom with my sis. Nothing more and nothing less. I'm an imposter in my white ballgown, but I down my thoughts like the fruity drink I just had and focus on the present moment.

Wendell wraps one arm around my waist, while mine settles on his shoulder. It feels…okay, I guess. I've never let a guy hold me like this. It's weird.

We follow the beat as the violins and piano lead into a crescendo. He's got some decent moves. I attempt to avoid his gaze but figure I can make this quick and painless if I start the conversation with something casual

"So, what do you do for fun?" I ask.

Wendell flashes his teeth and turns me for a spin. "My father, er, the king has helped me become an avid hunter. And I love horseback riding and dancing."

"I can tell about the dancing. You keep to the rhythm like you can do this in your sleep."

"Why, thank you," he says with a grin, sweeping us past another couple with ease. "You can hold a cadence yourself."

I'm not sure whether to burst out laughing or not, but he does earn a smirk from me.

"What about you? What does a beautiful girl such as yourself do to occupy your time?"

He seems to genuinely care. I don't want him fawning over me, but I'd hate to think he pulls that line on everyone. "Well…I like to read, make up stories with my sister, people-watch from the window…" That's it. I've officially become the queen of cringe. The prince looks on the verge of doing so himself.

His enthusiasm was clearly deflating with each activity I listed. I clear my throat and hope he's simply focused on not stepping on my toes.

"Oh my, you thought I was serious?" I laugh awkwardly. "My parents built a greenhouse in the middle of our property. There are over a hundred types of plants, flowers, trees, and even a pond. I've memorized all the fauna and flora! It's pretty peaceful there. And we have a giant library where I've read hundreds of books."

"Sounds…interesting," he manages. His tone says he's calling my bluff. I'm probably boring him to death, even with my exaggerating the fun I have.

I shuffle to the music, praying to the gods that this song ends soon. We dance in silence a bit too long, but I finally come up with something to redirect the conversation. "So, a wife huh?" *Really, Cadence?* But what do I care if I'm impressing him or not?

The prince studies the crowd of people standing on the sidelines of the dance floor before he realizes I've asked him a question. "Huh? Oh, yeah. Father is adamant about selecting the perfect debutante who will one day rule beside me on the throne. Feels like a lifetime away from now, but a king is never one to let anything, or apparently—anyone—slip through the cracks."

"Oh, I don't doubt it."

"Well, I'm happy he's doing this because then I was able to meet you." A smile cracks beneath his mask and I force myself not to stiffen. "I'm surprised I haven't seen you at previous gatherings. I definitely would've remembered you." Wendell is only inquiring out of genuine curiosity, but, to me, it's an attack. He's prying into my life.

"My parents…" Gods, what do I say without ratting out my secret? I totally didn't come prepared. "They usually want Allegra to stay inside because of her…condition."

I wait for a response as we step together, the bottom of my dress swishing on the ballroom floor.

His attention has again shifted to something in the distance behind me.

"Did I…say something wrong?" I ask when he doesn't respond.

Wendell sputters, shaking his head and focusing on me with a look of pity. "My apologies, Cadence. I didn't mean to ignore you. It's just…I couldn't help but notice those girls over there making fun of your sister."

He spins me around so that now I'm facing the scene. My heart crumbles at the sight of the same group of, what did the prince call them, debutantes, huddled together near one of the tall dining tables.

Al is seated on the other side in her wheelchair chatting with a girl her age. Thank the gods she's tapping her fingers and toes to the music, laughing with her new friend and oblivious to the girls' sneers, but my grip tightens on Wendell's shoulder before he spins me back around again.

"Does it bother you that they're making fun of her? Do you want me to do something about it?"

He doesn't mean any harm by it, but it still upsets me that he noticed something wrong with the situation in the first place—that the girls noticed something different about Al.

My eyes lower and I struggle to keep up with our dance. I hate how superficial some people are. "You don't have to say anything. No offense but, even if you are the prince, those girls need to learn a lot more about how the world works before they change their ways."

"None taken," he says. "Speaking of learning things, you said your sister has a…condition? What is it, if you don't mind me asking?"

I bite my lip but continue. "She has a neuromuscular disease. It affects her muscles and can lead to breathing and swallowing difficulties. It's why I choose to stay inside most of the time to help her with her therapy and stuff."

As we glide across the floor, I try to ignore the spot where those girls are. Al is having a good time, and I'd hate to ruin it by bringing attention to that group of half-brains. But it appears Al has noticed them now, their heckling obnoxiously obvious.

My sister wheels past them to grab some hors d'oeuvres then swivels quickly to return to her new friend. The girls cry out as she "accidentally" runs over their toes.

"Oops, sorry, I didn't see you there," she says nonchalantly before downing a puff ball in one bite.

I stifle a snort so as not to appear unladylike to the prince.

The girls run off, probably to the parlor room to ensure their shoes and egos aren't ruined.

I mentally fist pump at Al, but I still wish she didn't have to defend herself against people like that.

I don't know if Wendell saw. He flips a blonde lock off his mask. "I'm so sorry, to the both of you. And you can't leave the house because of her? That's a shame. I'd love to see you again after this."

I clench my teeth, unsure of what to say that doesn't involve a string of expletives. He says it like she's weighing me down, when, really, she's the only thing keeping me afloat.

He clears his throat.

I guess my unease is visible despite my masked face.

"Will she get better? Allegra, that is."

I shake my head. "It's a progressive genetic disease. She's been through a ton of different treatments to help slow down the muscle degeneration, though."

"Genetic?" Wendell's pace slows. We must've danced through a couple of different songs already. "So, it's hereditary?"

"Well, there's a genetic component—"

"I can't have that in my family."

"W-what do you mean?" I ask as we sweep past an older couple. I guess I stumble in more ways than one, nearly stepping on a woman's gown with how poofy it is.

Wendell chuckles like it's the most obvious thing in the world. "Come on, Cadence. You can't be serious. Could you imagine a future King of Soridente ruling on a wheeled throne as an invalid unable to stand before his people? It'd be embarrassing. He'd be the laughing-stock of the country."

Where was this coming from? My insides burn with a fire so intense, you'd think all the lights from the chandeliers had ignited. I halt in place and my right hand grips his tighter until my knuckles turn white. "Excuse me? My sister is not an invalid—or embarrassing. But your comments are."

41

"Calm down, Cadence. I wasn't insulting you. You're *beautiful*. But your sister…"

His prejudice makes me want to cram a buttered bun down his royal throat and call it a night.

"I'm sorry, but we can't have this disease in our family blood-line," he continues.

And I can't take it anymore.

No.

I feel my eyes start to prickle with tears.

No, no, no, no, *no*.

Don't cry, Cadence.

Do. *Not*. Cry.

This guy is just a jerk who's too pompous and cocky to know anything or act even remotely human toward someone different from him. Who isn't like everyone else.

You got this, I reassure myself. Just. *Don't*. Cry.

I try to swallow my revulsion, but it keeps bubbling to the surface. I want to run away, slip from the prince's hold—the one that now feels icky and unnatural. But how do I leave in the middle of the ballroom without everyone seeing? Without my parents seeing? Surely, I'd get in trouble.

"How can you be so cruel?" I eke out each word so as not to let my emotions—or my diamonds—overflow.

Wendell shrugs. "Next time, I'll just keep it to myself. Even though that's not what everyone else is doing."

And to think he offered to defend my sister! It must have been just a ploy to endear himself to me.

My gaze flits across the room.

An older woman is doing a horrible job of trying to hide her nosiness, but she's pointing at Al and whispering to her friend as they both giggle. And some kids are walking and pretending to stumble, one kid using his father's scepter like a cane until another kicks it out from under him.

It's too much. I can't…I can't *take* it.

They could say anything they want about me. But when they mess with my sister—it's more than I can bear.

My lips tremble and I squeeze my eyes shut, willing to keep my tears at bay. I swallow hard and take a deep breath in and out. My anger is settling and the pain in my chest for Al eases.

I finally loosen my grip on Wendell and step back as the music fades. The song ends, replaced with the thunderous pounding of my heart in my eardrums.

The faintest pain slices underneath my eyelids.

And when I open my eyes, I see a single diamond tear falls to the floor.

EIGHT

What. Have I. *Done?*

My parents are going to kill me. Even if they decide to let me live for their own selfish greed, they'll never allow Al and me outside ever again. Because now…everyone here knows my secret.

"Hey, what was that?" Wendell asks, bending to examine the floor.

The diamond is out in the open, right there between me and the prince. I want to kick it away with my foot or hide it under my dress or something, but he's in the way now.

"My diamond!" an unknown voice calls out.

My pulse jumps and my skin prickles.

A hand wrapped in black lace scoops the gem up in one smooth gesture. The owner straightens. And when our eyes meet, time stops.

If the band had struck up another song, I wouldn't know. If everyone started dancing around us, I wouldn't notice. I'm frozen in place as I come face to face with the pink-haired girl—the one I saw outside and made up a story about a few days ago!

She's wearing a black ball gown, corseted with a purple skirt and black lace everywhere. Her mask is black too, with feathers coming out of both sides. She flashes me a dark-lipped grin, clutching the diamond in her palm.

A blush settles on my cheeks, and I hope my mask can cover it.

"I knew I should've gotten a dress from a more reputable shop. Thing's falling apart faster than my mental health."

It takes me a moment before I realize she's bailing me out. But… why? And *how*?

"Whatever," Wendell says, clearly bored.

This whole ordeal is no big deal to him, while it could have been the end of my life.

The mystery girl pockets the diamond, which puts it out of everyone's minds, though the gem's image still burns in mine. "While I'm here, may I have this dance?"

Wendell sizes her up and down as if to make sure she's hot enough to dance with him. In reality, I can tell she's too good for him. "Uh…sure, I guess I'll dance with you."

"Actually, I was asking her." Her brown eyes haven't left mine.

I fight to keep my jaw from dropping.

The prince tugs at his golden cuff links. "Excuse me?"

Pinkie—as I've decided to call her—gives me a lifeline as she rushes between us, cutting him off. Her voice is soft. "Better not let a man, er, *boy* lead, so I think it's best he sit this one out."

Wendell scoffs. "Do you know who I am?"

She raises an eyebrow at him, clearly unimpressed. "Sure. Do I care?" She shrugs and turns her attention back to me. "Anyway…"

Wendell fumbles with his words, his face red from what I can see below his mask. He storms off, and I can't help but stifle a laugh.

"Thanks for saving me. How did you do that?" I ask in awe.

She shrugs. "Simple, really. My jerk radar is pretty sharp."

I laugh again. "Nice."

"So," she says in a sultry voice, "about that dance…"

My heart might be pounding harder than when I stepped into the ballroom for the first time. The look she gives me is so playful, she must've practiced that in the mirror. But it's working.

I want to avert my gaze to all the other people who might be watching us—Wendell, the king, queen consort, Mother, Father, Al. But I can't. So, I take her hand and place my other hand on her shoulder in the standard dance partner position.

When she slips an arm around my waist and pulls me close, my breath hitches.

"Who are you?" I ask.

The girl twirls me like she's been doing it her whole life. "The name's Raven. And you?"

I follow along to the melody, not the one the band's playing, but the one we've made on our own. As long as she's leading, I'll follow. "Cadence. My name is Cadence."

"It's a pleasure to meet you, Cadence."

As we dance, the faintest hint of butterflies tickles my insides, and our dresses swirl, too. A small black bag slung across Raven's chest also moves with each step. "About that diamond," I say. I'm hesitant to bring it up, but I can't leave it unspoken between us.

Raven smirks. "I thought you'd never ask." She pats the pocket of her dress where she placed my diamond tear. "I'll hang onto this, if you don't mind. A little…token to remember you by."

"I, uh, sure. But…who are you exactly?"

"I've come from very far away," she says in a hushed tone, so low I have to lean in, her breath tickling my ear as she speaks. "And I have an important message for you."

"About?"

"I know about your power."

My eyes widen and I trip over my dress. Raven rights me and sends me into a spin, but now I'm clumsy and thrown off in more ways than one.

"What!" I exclaim in a hushed cry once my vertigo settles.

"I know about your power." She says it slower this time.

"How?"

"Your diamond tear ability was a curse you got at birth. Your parents have known, but never told you. Maybe to hide you? Doesn't matter. I'm supposed to bring you back to the magi."

"Magi? Who are the magi? And it isn't a curse. I was born with this ability. And…" I scan our neighboring dancers who appear to be minding their own business. Still, I'm freaking paranoid that someone is eavesdropping, and for good reason. I lower my voice. "Can we talk about this somewhere else?"

Raven nods, slowing her pace as the song ends. "Meet me outside by the fountain in five minutes." She smiles and lets our arms stretch until her fingers slip from mine. Then she dashes away and vanishes into the crowd.

I stand there in the middle of the ballroom, stunned.

What just happened?

"Cadence!" Al calls to me. She's sitting in her wheelchair near one of the side tables, nursing a drink with now two other girls. They all clink glasses before the girls' dresses swish in their departure. "Hopefully, we'll get to hang again, and not just at the next ball," she says to them as I approach.

I hurry over to her as she puts one hand on her hips. "And who was that? I want details!"

She must not recognize Raven as the girl from my story.

"Oh, just a new friend I've made." I figured it will be better not to lie to her, but I'm still figuring things out for myself and will update her at a more appropriate time and place. "Looks like you made some new friends, too."

"Yeah, if only I knew whether I'll ever see them again."

"I hear you," I say, then lower my voice. "Did you see everything?"

Al slaps her armrest. "We watched that girl shut. The. Prince. Down! Thought I'd start coughing from all the laughter I held back."

"Where are Mother and Father? Did they see us?"

"Don't worry, they're trying to get in good with the royals. I made sure to keep an eye out for you."

I bend forward to hug her. "You're a saint! Hey, can you cover for me a little bit longer? I'm going outside for some fresh air. I'll be back in maybe ten or fifteen minutes? Not sure how long."

She swirls her drink in the air. "I'm plenty occupied, thank you very much."

I soak in her happiness, wondering how I got so lucky that the gods gave me Al for a sister.

"You don't have a lot of time. Better get going!" She winks, knocking me from my musing.

"You're the best! Thank you, thank you, thank you." I find the exit and stick to the perimeter, sliding past chatter and gossip, hugging the golden drapes against the wall. Once I assure myself that I'm in the clear with avoiding Mother and Father, my thoughts return to the mysterious Raven.

How does she know about my power, er, my curse? And who are the magi? I bite my lip to calm my nerves. Thankfully, I don't run into anyone from the royal family on my way out of the ballroom. Now that would be a disaster.

I run as fast as I can in the heels I'm wearing, down the hallway, ignoring questioning expressions, slipping in and out of the clusters of chatty royalty. I make it out the grand double doors of the palace and descend the stairs to the stone fountain in the center of the front lawn, careful to land on the stone circles dotting the path across the grass. By now, the moon hangs high in the sky, full and bright. Yet the perfectly trimmed high hedges cast shadows around the garden. The Summer Solstice Ball dissipates in the air as trickling water and chirping crickets replace the music and conversation.

"Raven?" I squint in the darkness, taking off my mask so I can see better.

She slips from behind the fountain, her mask already off and her bag at her feet.

I thought her pink curls were gorgeous when I'd spied them the other day—along with her dark eyes from behind the mask. But the rest of her face doesn't disappoint—delicate features that hold clear strength.

She breaks the silence first. "Hey. Thanks for coming."

"Of course. I kind of need answers." I tuck a strand of hair behind my ear, unsure of where to begin.

"I won't have time to explain everything right now, but I'll do my best." She sits on the edge of the fountain and pats the space next to her.

Though the moon and lights from the palace were keeping this area bright, this spot appears a little dimmer now.

"So, like I said before, you weren't born with your abilities. You were cursed."

"But what do you mean?"

She folds her laced hands. "It's not necessarily bad, but you weren't supposed to stay here with humans."

"W-what?" The world tilts and I grip the stony ledge to steady myself. That's probably why Raven made me sit. "You mentioned the magi…are they something other than human?"

"Wow…your parents kept a lot from you, huh?"

I ignore the stinging in my chest at the reminder of how little I know. Like Mother and Father haven't already hurt me enough. "Yeah, I…had no idea."

"The magi are a group of people with magical abilities like you. Problem is, non-magical humans and magi don't get along. After the last war six years ago, the king banished the magi west of the Cymber Mountains and beyond Lake Urso. The city of Kinephrus."

My face falls. "I read about those places with my private tutor, but he never once taught me anything about this city of magi."

Raven's sympathy reminds me of the looks aimed at Al inside. "I'm sorry. This must be hard to hear, but it exists. It's as real as your powers are."

"Can I get rid of my curse? Or change it somehow?"

She blinks. "You want to get rid of it?"

I nod fervently.

"I'm sure you could," she answers after a beat. "If you come with me, I can take you to Archmage Sanora. She's the leader and can give you the answers you need, including how you became a mage."

"Are you a mage, too?"

"No, but I know a lot about them. I've studied them and gotten very close."

"Archmage Sanora…"

Raven's nose crinkles as she grins, and she places a hand on top of mine. "All the magi love her, and I know you will, too. She's going to help you figure things out—both your past and your future."

My mind is whirling. I was not expecting to check this off my list of activities I accomplished at the Summer Solstice Ball. And it definitely was not something Al or I could've created a story about, though it does feel like I've landed in one of the fantasy books I've read in our library.

Is it weird to say that I hope everything Raven says is true? If I travel to Kinephrus, I can find out why someone—whoever it was—gave me my diamond tear curse-gift-thing. And if they can give the power to people, maybe there's a way for them to take it away. Then Mother and Father can't use me. The silence makes me realize Raven's waiting patiently like the statues by the hedge.

"Sorry, I'm having a hard time processing all of this. And I…I can't believe my parents would do this to me." I fiddle with my mask. "Well, maybe I can, but it's all just a lot to take in."

"Don't worry, I get it. My 'totally overwhelmed and stressed' meter is accurate, too. Let me give you some time. We can meet tomorrow night at your home." She doesn't say how she'll find it, but I trust she will.

"Other than tonight, my parents don't let me go outside. But we have a garden in the middle of our home. No one will be there at midnight. But it'll be hard since they don't let anyone waltz right in. And at the rate my parents are going, I wouldn't be surprised if they start hiring guards soon. They now have people for everything."

Raven waves it off. "Ah, it'll be no problem. I like a challenge." She winks.

I can't help but wonder if she's talking about something else. Who could have guessed how awkward I'd act with a pretty girl?

A familiar voice disrupts my ogling. "Yeah, I've never seen her before, and my parents have no idea whose daughter she is."

Raven and I peer from around either side of the fountain.

Prince Wendell is standing with his hands on his hips, clearly miffed, talking to a couple of palace guards with swords at their sides and shoulders broader than the length of the ballroom.

Raven must be in some big trouble. Hopefully, I'm not, too.

"Hey, so where do you live? Are your parents here?" I whisper.

Two of the guards begin descending the stairs, continuing their search outside.

Raven stiffens. "Sorry, I've got to go, but I'll be at your place to-morrow, I promise!"

I frown. Despite the impending threat, I kind of don't want her to go. She's the first person I've met that I actually want to get to know. But I guess her run-in with the prince—slighting him and challenging his manhood—hurt his ego enough for him to call in reinforcements. And I don't blame her for wanting to avoid an armed confrontation.

Her bouncing form fades into the distance. When I move my foot, I kick something on the ground. Her bag! I fumble with lifting it, but the strap slips from my fingers and falls to the ground.

A plethora of jewels and gold coins spill out, including a broach with the Goldin's royal insignia on it—the profile of a roaring lion.

I'm about to call out to her, but she's already gone. Literally. I don't even spy her shadow across the lawn.

I'm a little disappointed that she would steal things, though. I'm sure the king has more than enough, but that still doesn't make it right. Now I have one more question to add to my growing list.

Who are you, really, Raven?

NINE

"That was incredible!" Mother exclaims as we burst through the doors of our home, disheveled messes of sore feet and full bellies. "I wish the ball would've never ended." She fans herself as the housemaid takes her coat and purse.

I, for one, am glad the night ended quickly. I had snuck away from the water fountain and avoided Weasel Wendell and his guards. Good thing too, because they would've thought I was the one who stole the treasure. That would've been a doozy to explain.

No, that mysterious girl who's nowhere to be found and no one knows who she is? Yeah, it was her.

I hand the maid my other belongings, but not the pouch. I've hidden it under my dress, and the leather is rubbing against my skin with every step. I'm not even the one who took the royal crest, and the guilt is pummeling my gut!

Despite Raven's bombshell, I still can't believe it's almost midnight! How Mother and Father have leftover energy is a mystery.

Al and I are beyond exhausted. I guess we're not used to so much excitement. Especially me. And it's not every day you find out your parents have been keeping a secret from you your whole life.

Father finally takes his mask off, revealing his dark complexion, and rubs the back of his head. "I wish I'd talked to the king about my proposal. But I got in good with the other members of the high court, so I should get another chance."

Al yawns, slumping back in her wheelchair. "I wish I'd had the energy to use my crutches more. But that's okay. I still had fun!"

"And what do you wish had happened, Cadence?" Mother asks, taking pins out of her hair, letting her long, brunette locks fall down her back.

I fiddle with my mask at my side, wishing I'd kept it on to hide my face. "I…wish I could've talked to Wendell more. There were so many other girls he had to divide his time between." The words taste sour, but I spew them out anyway because I know it'll please her to hear them.

"But it went well? Your time together?" Mother asks. "We tried not to suffocate you two."

My eyebrows raise. That would be a first. "Oh, yeah," I say, trying to dull my sarcasm. "We talked, danced, you know, masquerade stuff." A quick glance at Al tells me I better zip my lips, or my fake enthusiasm will give me away. I yawn myself. "I'm exhausted. Can we talk more tomorrow?"

Mother nods, giving the rest of her things to the housekeeper. "Of course. But oh, I'm so excited for us! You might stand a chance of becoming Wendell's bride! The Princess of Soridente! What would that make us?" She thumbs her chin as she ponders the answer.

If only she knew the truth. "Right? Well, goodnight." I rush to my room, thankful the folds of my dress are big enough to hide Raven's bag of riches. Well, *someone's* bag of riches. Did she really steal these from the Goldins?

Once I'm safely inside my bedroom, I spin in a circle, searching for the best hiding spot. Between the walk-in closet, chests, full-length mirror, powder room, nightstands, and my four-post canopy bed, I can't go wrong with wherever I choose. I roll the bag into a blanket and push it below my bed's box spring because I have no idea if my new maid will rummage through my things to choose tomorrow's outfit. My sheets and the bed skirt drape over the side to cover the space, so I'm confident no one will go looking there.

I kick off my shoes and collapse in bed, letting the soft mattress swallow me. I'm too tired to take off my makeup or jewelry, but my mind is still active, swirling with questions I hope to have answered soon. Who are the magi, what other powers do they possess, and what do I have to do with it all?

TEN

After a late breakfast the next morning, my stomach isn't the only thing that's full. My mind is overflowing. I can't stop thinking about Raven. How she saved me from revealing my diamond tear abilities, her charming smile, and—well, I can't help it—but the way she held me when we danced.

It's weird, realizing there's an empty loneliness I didn't know I wanted to be filled. Maybe it's been hidden, always overshadowed by caring for Al, and never thinking about myself. But I can't be selfish. I need to be here for my sister.

I huff at my wrestling thoughts and switch my attention back to the agenda at hand. First, I'll figure out if Al knows anything about my curse or the magi. Then I'll see if Mother and Father will reveal anything. If I come up short, then I've got a back-up option ready and waiting—to search for any evidence in their bedroom or offices. If I have this measly bag of riches stashed under my bed, my parents must have their own skeletons in their closets.

I make my way to Al's bedroom and pop my head in to find she's not there. She's got to be in the library, then. It's her, and my, favorite place in the house. And after an eventful night like last night, she'd want to cozy up with a book or two.

It'll be the perfect place to talk. Mother and Father would never be caught dead in there. Reading? Who has time for that when you're busy faking your way to the top?

I quicken my pace down the hall, my boots moving soundlessly over the pristine carpet as I rush in anticipation.

The library's mahogany doors are open, so I push them closed once I'm inside, sealing us away from any prying ears.

Al's sitting in one of the plush lounge chairs, reading a clunker of a book, while others are piled around her on the side tables and reading chairs. Her crutches are propped against the end table.

Nothing smells better than the pages of a book. Multiply that by a hundred, and well, you'd understand the paradise I'm in right now. I need to ask Mother if this can be my bedroom when I come back—if I go with Raven. And if they don't kill me when I return.

"How'd your walk go?" I ask as I approach her.

"Pretty well. I was a little short of breath, but my legs were decently kind to me. I think they were thanking me for not wearing them out on the dance floor last night."

"Nice!" I move closer, examining the chaos of paper and binding around her. "What's this about?"

She bites her lip. "I'm rearranging them by color instead of alphabetical order to make a rainbow on the shelves. But I, uh, got a little distracted." She waves the book she's holding and laughs.

"Go figure. Want some help?"

She taps her chin and nods. "Hm…I guess I'll allow it. You're lucky I haven't reached the midpoint yet." She closes her book and sets it on the table beside her.

I wipe my forehead in exaggerated relief. "I barely made it!"

We giggle and she reaches toward the nearest pile of books.

I help her sit on the floor and join her amongst the myriad of fiction lining the built-in shelves. "So, how should we do this?"

"We'll organize them in rows here," she points to the space in front of us. "And you can pull more books as we sort each color, if that's okay."

"Sounds like a plan." I switch to a kneeling position and reach for the first pile. This one has some darker shades, brown and black, but I smile as I pull out a purple book to make a new stack. "Hey look. Your favorite."

"I've already got three books for purple," she says, pushing them my way.

After working in silence for a few moments, I get to the reason for my visit. "Hey, is it okay if we chat for a little bit?"

Al slides a book to the red color pile. "Sure, what's up?"

Oh, gods. Where do I start? I try to act casual, though my insides are threatening to upend my breakfast. "Being at the palace yesterday made me realize there's so much that we haven't experienced. It makes me wonder about all the things we don't know…and all the things Mother and Father haven't told us."

"Yeah, I thought about that, too. I had some time to myself while on guard duty for you last night."

I chew the inside of my cheek. "You could've joined the dance floor. Even in your wheelchair. You've danced with Dr. Hyu before."

"I could've, but once I was there, I chose not to. You were concerned about those jerks at the ball. I wasn't—and I'm still not. But I appreciate your hawk-like skill for picking out the rats for me."

"Anytime." I fiddle with the pages of a memoir before placing it on a tall stack of blue books. "I love you so much, Al. And I'd never want to leave you. But…what if there's a time when I'm away from home?" I quickly add, "Like if Mother lets me leave the house to buy some things for you while you have a therapy appointment or something like that? Or if we're finally allowed to make friends outside the house?"

"As long as you came back, I guess I'd allow it."

My shoulders ease, and I'm tempted to launch myself at and hug Al for how reassuring her response is. "So, this is going to sound totally random, but I also wanted to ask you about when I was born. Mother and Father said I was born with my gift, but being around such normal people yesterday made me question if there are other people like me out there."

My transitions must be smooth enough because Al doesn't react oddly to my questions and continues wiping dust off a particularly old paperback. "I was two at the time. So, as far as I know, you've always had your diamond tears. But we can only assume you've had your ability since birth 'cause Mother and Father said so. As far as anyone else with this power or others like it... I've never met anyone else quite like you. And that's even without your power."

"Stop getting all sappy on me."

She winks, then points to the book she had been reading when I entered. "Unless you count the characters in *Flames of Destiny*."

The corners of my lips tug up. "Well, I'll let you return to Furia and Elden's epic adventure." I check where her bookmark is. "Almost to the middle? You're definitely going to want to keep going."

"You're evil!" Al exclaims, grabbing the book. She lays on her back with the book over her head, already lost in the pages, the stacks of multi-colored tomes quickly forgotten.

"Don't worry, I'm not about spoilers," I say, walking toward the doors. "I can help you organize the books when you hit 'The End'!"

Her laugh fills the air, which usually makes my heart warm, but I leave the room with a mix of emotions. Mother and Father lied to Al, too. At least I wasn't the only one out of the loop. But now, I don't have any more answers than when I started.

It doesn't take long before I realize I'm not going to pry anything out of Mother and Father. Whenever I ask them about my powers, they have the same lines rehearsed. *You were born with your diamond tear abilities. It is a gift from the gods. We must keep it a secret so that others don't take advantage of you.*

I inquire about there being other people like me, but all they say is that I'm the only one they know with this power.

I push my patience long enough, finding my moment when they are both pulled into a work meeting. As a baron and baroness in the House of Nobles, they're responsible for overseeing the laws proposed by the other members before presenting them to the king's advisors for consideration.

They both head into Father's office, which is a shame because I wanted to go there first. I run back to my room and grab the mask I wore for the Summer Solstice Ball in case I need an excuse.

Then I begin by poking around in Mother's office. There isn't much to this room with a solid oak desk, chair, bookcases, and other official documents strewn everywhere. A quick flip through a couple of old files reveals they're all related to work. No mention of my name, the magi, or the Archmage Sanora. I huff, a strand of brown hair flying out and then back into my face.

Before anyone has the chance to find me snooping, I slip out of Mother's office and sneak down the wide hallway to Father's. I press my ear to the door and both of their voices ring loud and clear. I don't stop to listen to their boring babble and instead move on, taking the closest stairwell to their bedroom on the third floor.

The door's closed but not locked, so I double-check that no one's watching me then sneak inside. The walls remind me of the last time I was in there, forced to cry for them on command. I shudder, pushing the thoughts away to prevent clouding my mind and go hunting. I search the nightstands, walk-in closet, chest of drawers, and the bureau.

I come up empty and grunt in frustration. There has to be something I'm missing. I scan the room and complete a three-hundred-and-sixty-degree spin. A light bulb turns on in my mind and my pulse races as I lower myself to the floor and lift the fabric of the bed skirt up, peering underneath.

It's bare underneath. But I run my fingers along the underside of the frame all the same—and glide over something stuck in the fabric. After a bit of quick work, I manage to pull it out. What the...?

It's a pin with gold petals crossing on top of each other to make a flower design. It's beautiful. But I've never seen this pattern before. And if it's no big deal, why did someone hide it here?

Low voices and the patter of footsteps resound from the hallway, jolting me to my feet. My heart's pounding like crazy. I stick the pin inside my bra and search the room for something to use as a scapegoat. The doorknob scrapes as it twists.

It's no use. Someone's going to catch me. And with the questions I asked earlier, they'll know exactly why I'm here.

"What are you doing here?" a deep voice booms. I gulp, not realizing I'd squeezed my eyes shut. But wait, that's not Father's voice. When I open my eyes, I exhale in relief.

Thank the gods! It's the new butler who oversees all the other male servants. He's wearing a plain white shirt and black pants, along with a black and silver sash across his chest to signify he works for us. I haven't seen him around here until recently because he's always delegating tasks. It's funny because he's younger than a lot of the other staff. Still, I can't assume he won't rat me out.

"Someone must've brought my mask in here with Mother's clothes after doing the laundry. But no worries, I found it!" I hold up my mask, the stark white accessory I never thought I'd be so happy to have brought with me.

The butler nods. "Ah, my apologies. I'll make sure it doesn't happen again, Miss Cadence."

"You don't need to do all that formal stuff with me…um…"

"Malore."

"Nice to meet you, Malore." I wave my accessory again. "Well, I better put this back in my room." I rush past him but am tugged backward, his hand lightly gripping my arm.

"Excuse me, Miss Cadence, but if there's anything else you require, please do not hesitate to call for me." He speaks with gentleness and kindness, surprising me.

Most of the help keep to themselves at our parents' command. Mother and Father don't let us make friends outside the mansion. Why would they let us make friends with anyone inside, either?

"I…thank you." I can't tell if he has another message for me layered in his offer to help. But I can't think about it too long. I have to leave before Mother and Father find out I was in their room.

Back in my room, I lock the door. Then I take the pin out and examine it again. I may not know exactly where it's from, but there's certainly a story behind this item. And I'm going to learn what it is.

I pale as I picture leaving Al alone with Mother and Father. But my life is a lie, and Raven can help me discover the truth. If there's a chance this Archmage Sanora reversing my curse and finding another way to help my sister, it's a chance worth taking.

I scramble to pack a small bag with the items I'm going to take with me on this journey—if Raven returns like she said she would. She'll have to break into our house and meet me in the center greenhouse, but if she can do that without a hitch, that will be the best sign that maybe this will all work out.

I leave the bag of riches under my bed because I don't want to be caught with anything on me—that would spell disaster. Not like I'm trying to keep things cozy between me and Wendell, but it will be best to not make an enemy out of the royal family of Soridente.

I pull out a pen and paper—and I write a letter to explain why I'm leaving. I trust Al with everything I am, so I know she'll keep my plans a secret. Even though I don't know where this journey will take me and what will become of us when I come back, I tell her we'll figure it out together once I return. She doesn't need to hear it because she already knows, but I tell her I love her.

And then I cry and cry and cry. I sit on the floor, my back propped up against the bed, and let the diamonds fall silently onto the carpet until I can't take the pain anymore. It's the last bit of money I'm going to leave for Al—in case Mother and Father don't have enough. It won't surprise me if they've blown all their savings—if they ever even bothered to have any.

I fold the paper in half when I'm done, then power walk back to the library.

Al's gone now, the organized stacks of colored books on the floor waiting to be shelved, and the book she was reading sits on the cushion where she'd been, ready for her to devour tomorrow.

I slip my letter in front of the last page and smile as I notice the place she left off. She's made it to the halfway point.

I return to my room and finish my checklist in time for dinner, which now screams foreign and awkward to me, even though nothing has changed on the outside. I can barely touch my food, for all my nerves have filled me up. But I force my meal down, unsure of what the future will bring me—and how weird it'll feel facing Al after she reads my letter.

Mother and Father are sitting at either end of the dining room table, with Al across from me in the middle.

"I'm still dreaming about all the lavish food the Goldins served us yesterday," Mother says once she finishes her last bite of mashed potatoes. "I wonder if we should hire another cook?"

"Excellent idea!" Father says, raising his fork high.

More new staff? We don't need to be waited on hand and foot. "I can learn to cook some of those meals," I say, even though I probably won't be here after tonight. "We shouldn't shell out more money every time something comes up."

Mother dabs the corners of her mouth with a shiny satin napkin. "Oh, Cadence, don't be ridiculous. I'll send out a job posting to the town square in the morning."

"Why are you ignoring the priceless cut of beef on your plate?" Father asks, sawing into his protein.

I roll my eyes and stab the green beans on the plate with my fork. "I told you I don't eat meat."

"She doesn't appreciate the finer things in life, remember?" Mother speaks as if I'm not even here.

Okay, I'm officially suffocating in this huge dining room. But it's the perfect time to test my parents. To see if they will keep their promise this time. They have one last chance to redeem themselves.

I place my napkin on my plate to signify I've finished eating. "It's so stuffy in here. Can I go to the park down the block for some fresh air for ten minutes? The sun is still setting so, it's not too dark out."

Al's stare pierces me, but I keep my focus on Mother.

"Honey, you know you can't leave," she says matter-of-factly, tapping her perfectly manicured fingers on her water glass.

"But what about what you said yesterday about letting us go out again? I met Wendell, I didn't cry, and I behaved myself. I followed your rules perfectly!" I retort, even though I didn't *actually* not cry.

Father sighs, pushing his chair away from the table. "Well, Allegra starts her new treatment this week. Your mother and I don't want to stress her system with too many new things. So, we think it's only fair that we keep you both inside for the time being. We'll let you go out soon enough, though. I promise."

And that's when I realize nothing is ever going to change. I'll never receive their permission to leave. They'll always find an excuse not to give it.

Al opens her mouth, clearly ready to object in my defense, but I shake my head. I don't want to raise any red flags by drawing too much attention to the whole freedom thing.

But that doesn't mean I'm allowing them to emotionally pummel me any longer. I'm finally going to take things into my own hands. Most likely, Raven will be here tonight. And if she is, I'm going with her. If my parents won't change, I'll have to change my life myself.

ELEVEN

The garden is my and Al's little slice of heaven because it's the one place we can go to feel like we're outside, even though we're not. With high glass walls and a domed ceiling, the greenhouse seems bigger than I remember. It's only half-past eleven, but I can't wait to see Raven again. I meander the paved path and admire all the plants and flowers we've grown here over the years.

I'm surrounded by hanging begonias above me and lantanas at my feet. Butterflies circle the lantanas for their nectar-filled blooms. I've spent enough time here that I can call myself a certified botanist. I approach a row of mandevilla flowers and smile. They're purple, which is a prerequisite to end up on Al's favorite flowers list. The sweetness reaches my nostrils and I inhale deeply.

Moving on, there's a pond with elephant's ears—huge green-leafed flowers that look like their namesake. I pass it and settle on one of the many benches we have scattered throughout the garden. I fiddle with the strings of my bag. The letter I wrote to Al gives me solace that I won't break her spirit when she doesn't find me home tomorrow morning.

"Nice. You're here early."

I spin in my seat to find Raven sauntering toward me. She's no longer in her ball gown, but in the attire she probably wore under the large cloak I saw her in on the street. The short-sleeved black cloak has a long tail that fades to light blue. Her tight pants have belts looped every which way on her hips. Ankle-high black boots finish off the outfit.

"You look like such a rebel," I say, in awe of how good she looks.

She eyes my plain gray tunic and shorts. "I'll find you something just as fitting. That is, if you've decided to come with me."

"I brought my stuff." I raise my bag. "But I hid yours."

"Damn. So I *did* leave it at the fountain last night? I'm usually better than that."

"Where... did you get it from?"

She purses her lips, probably deciding whether she should lie. Leaning sideways, she sniffs a yellow flower hanging over the bench arm. "From the Goldins. They won't be missing it."

I exhale in relief. Good, she didn't lie. Still, I don't want to go on this journey only to find all of my things stolen if she is some sort of kleptomaniac. "Why'd you steal it?"

She sits beside me and crosses her legs. "That's chump change to them. But it's everything to me."

My ears perk up, and not just from the bee I have to swat away from my face. "What do you mean?"

"I *have* to steal. It's how I'm alive right now." She waves the topic away. "Listen, we can dive into the details some other time. Right now, understand that you'll be in a much better place if you go with me to Kinephrus, the city of magi, sooner rather than later. We have a long way to go."

Clearly, stealing has become as normal to her as crying has to me. Just another thing we do to survive. I decide to accept the unknown for now. It's not like she knows my whole life story, either. "Fine, but what happens if someone finds out about my...power? Are my parents actually doing the right thing by keeping me inside?"

"Cadence, please." She turns to me and grabs both my hands. Hers are smooth and warm over mine. "No one should ever be caged like this. You deserve freedom. I promise I'll protect you if you ever need to cry."

Her expression reveals both strength and comfort, but I've been burned too many times before to blindly believe someone. "How?"

"Don't worry about it. Just trust me."

"'Just trust me' is a tough pill to swallow for someone like me."

Raven stands, bending to pick up a twig in front of the bench and tossing it into the brush. "My parents abandoned me when I was ten. Threw me out as easily as that twig. I've lived six years so far doing things with me, myself, and I. I know how to survive. So, when I say 'I've got you,' I've got you, okay?"

Her words hit me in the chest. I'm always telling Al I'll take care of her. But now someone is saying they'll take care of me?

She starts pacing, searching for any other sticks or blades of grass to clear from the path. "And I see you. Your eyes reflect the prison your parents have you locked up in. Your sister—I'm assuming she feels the same?"

"Yeah." I avoid her gaze and study the stars above us, noting the silence surrounding us for the first time tonight. What would she say about Al?

"I'm sorry people don't see her worth. Her abilities. But I see hers, and I see yours, too."

My heart crashes into my ribs. Who the heck is this girl? Her understanding, her acceptance, and the way she makes me trust her by simply being herself gives me the final push I need to accept this journey. Accept the chance at freedom and change.

I finally stand and walk past her to some particularly thirsty-looking plants that caught my eye earlier—a patch of monkey flowers the color of sunshine yellow. Picking up the small watering can beside the stone edge, I water them, moistening the soil just the right amount. "I give them what they need…and I give myself what I need—freedom. So, thank you, Raven. I know we just met, but you've already helped me so much more than you can imagine."

She stands and flashes her teeth, reminding me she's a tad taller than me. "Same here."

I lower the gardening tool and meet her gaze head-on with my own smile.

"So, I have to ask. How did you get in here? And how will we leave without getting caught?"

"It's a secret." She winks. "Leave that to me!" Raven spins, her cloak whooshing and pink curls bouncing.

I laugh and spin, too, giddy with excitement and anticipation. My toe catches the can of water, sending it clattering to the ground, echoing in the expanse.

Crap.

"Hey, who's there?" a voice calls from outside the greenhouse.

"Oh gods. Someone knows we're in here," I whisper.

Raven cracks her knuckles before grabbing my hand. "This way." And like a true thief in the night, she leads me into the shadows, the trees and plants hiding us from whoever might be coming.

But who would that be? Did Mother and Father actually hire guards, or is this one of the staff like Malore?

It doesn't matter. There's no time to think as I follow after the girl who's promised to protect me.

TWELVE

Raven leads me through the other entrance to the garden, finding the quickest way from the hallway to a storage space, then to a back room in the mansion that leads outside. By the time we emerge into the cool night air, she's impressed me more times than I can count. The girl can sneak around, that's for sure.

"Damn. I'm pretty sure you know my house better than I do!"

Raven chuckles, pulling me along the perimeter of the front lawn where the hedges reach for the sky. "It's taken some practice, but I usually learn things quickly. Not as well as knowing the back of my hand, though. Don't tell me anyone knows what theirs looks like."

"True." I laugh and follow her past the last bush to the wrought-iron fence surrounding my home. That hitch in my chest returns, the same one that came when I stepped outside to attend the Summer Solstice Ball with Al.

Except my sister isn't here with me.

That tightness, it's that *no going back* kind of feeling.

Raven scales the fence like it's nothing. Does she expect me to climb over this thing? I crack my knuckles. Guess I have no choice.

Thankfully, there are enough notches in the fence pattern that act as footholds to climb onto. When my feet land on the sidewalk, my jaw also drops. Here I am…staring at my house from the other side. It's exhilarating and nerve-wracking at the same time.

"What have I done?" I whisper to myself.

Raven crosses her arms and grins. "Welcome to freedom."

I twirl in a circle, my arms outstretched as I revel in the gentle breeze, the light from the street lamps brightening my face like a spotlight. "I did it! I *did* it!"

"You're welcome. And there's more where that came from." Raven scans the area as I continue my escapades. "We should find a safe place far enough away from here to stay. I hope you're okay with traveling a bit right now? It's late, but I like the dark. I do my best work at night."

I don't know why I blush at that, but I shrug it off and stick to business. "Sounds good. I'd like to get as far away from home as possible." I cringe and try to brush that off, too. No need for her to know how much I want to run away from my life.

I guess it'll take a while for my guilt of leaving Al to subside. I have to remind myself that I'm leaving to help us both.

"Perfect. We should avoid the Cymber Mountains to the west of us. They're a beast to navigate through. The best route for us to travel is south of here, toward Tosca and Serency. We'll be able to stock up on supplies and rest along the way, so there's no need for us to stop in Jessen where the Everyfolk are. Then we'll head southwest along the trade route between Lake Sire and Lake Urso. Before you know it, we'll be in Kinephrus!"

The barrage of words makes my brain feel like I'm still twirling, even though I stopped minutes ago. "It's like you're speaking another language. It's weird, knowing that I'm about to visit places I've only read about when I've never stepped foot outside Noravale before tonight."

"Don't worry, I'll keep you updated. And if you need to stop or take a break, or if you have any questions, feel free to speak up."

"Thanks," I say, my mind eased for the time being.

We continue on our way, walking the dark city streets. Although it's hard to see, I take in every sight and sound around me. I strain to make out each detail of the homes we pass.

Raven's cloak swishes left and right in time with her steps, leaving a trail of ivory and pine, but my thoughts are still tugging me backward to Al. I know I'm doing the right thing, but I can't help worrying I've gotten myself into something bigger than I can imagine, and something that will get me into a lot of trouble. I whisk my stupid thoughts away—at least for now—and let Raven lead me for about half an hour before she stops near one of the last houses I can see for a while.

"We kept a pretty good pace there," she says.

"My legs hurt." Is this how Al feels? "Clearly, I don't get out much," I say as she studies the building in front of us.

It's a one-story home, but it seems to stretch for a mile, plus the property line goes on forever.

"Ah, we have to break in those bones, don't we?" Raven smirks.

"I guess so." I yawn, shifting the bag on my back. "Are we stopping for the night?"

"Girl, we're just getting started!"

I massage my thighs, which are screaming at me, asking me why I'm still standing on the cobblestone streets and not sleeping in my comfy bed. "How much farther are we going tonight?"

"I'd like to reach the northern border of Tosca, which is about ten miles away, so…"

"Ten *miles*?! I'm not sure I can go another ten *feet*."

Raven readjusts her hood, revealing a devious expression on her face. "Don't worry, I've got you covered. Since we just met, I haven't proven to you I know what I'm doing."

"And…what exactly are you doing?"

"Wait here." And then she's off, leaving me all alone.

I already felt awkward enough here on the streets. Like a foreigner. Like I don't belong. Now, without anyone beside me, I'm completely lost. I stand there, twiddling my thumbs—not literally, of course, because honestly, who does that? A few feet away must be the owner's mailbox, so I sit with my back against the post to rest and wait. The fresh air fills my lungs and I revel in it all.

Freedom never smelled so sweet. I can't believe I'm out here, miles away from home. Despite my fatigue, the exhilaration, the rush still jolts my senses, keeping me awake. I watch the stars twinkling overhead, time passing for an eternity before I hear or see anything.

At first, it's a slight hissing, like a balloon slowly deflating. Then a star goes out. And another. Then the darkness grows, blotting out a larger patch of the sky.

I shiver at the chill, as if the stars themselves were giving off a heat that's now been snuffed out. "What in the…?" I whisper, backing myself up, crawling like a crab on my hands and feet past the mailbox to the fence along the perimeter.

The black blob grows wider. Then two yellow half-moon slits appear like eyes from the shadows.

I stifle a yelp and try to shrink into myself to avoid detection. My hands remain sealed over my mouth until this creature—thing—turns, gliding farther north, in the opposite direction we're heading.

Rustling sounds nearby, and a scream threatens to explode from my lips. I whirl around.

The sounds are far from normal footfalls, and even if Raven were sprinting, there are too many patters on the ground for it to be her. I stand and brace the straps of my bag against my shoulders, ready to make a run for it.

But then I make out her silhouette and her billowing cloak… and the horse she's riding on!

"Did you see that thing up there?!"

She stops the horse by pulling on the reigns and it whinnies gently. The mare is midnight black, perfect for hiding in the night. "What thing?" she asks, steadying the horse in place.

"It was a big black shadow that blotted out the stars. It was super creepy. It had a face, well, eyes at least, and was searching for something…or someone." The hairs rise on my arms, and I rub them to settle the bumps.

Raven bites her lip. "It must have been a mage."

"*Whoa.*"

"Yeah, but being this far away from Kinephrus? It's pretty unheard of unless they're up to something."

I frown. "What kind of magic was that?"

Raven looks like she'll answer but then shakes her head. "Nothing I want to stick around to find out."

"It's heading toward Noravale. Do you think they're safe there? That my sister is safe?"

"She should be safe. And we'll be okay as long as we keep moving." She jumps off the saddle, patting the horse on its thick neck while keeping a solid grip with her other hand on the bridle. "So, she's how we're going to travel to Tosca in no time."

I exhale in relief, but I can't help the pinch of guilt when I glance back at the house. I don't even say a word, but this girl is on it.

"I know you're not used to this sort of thing, Cadence. But we have to do things like this to survive."

I nod. "No, no, I get it. I just have to get used to it, too, I guess."

Her brown eyes glint in the moonlight. "Well, hop on…uh, Clove was her name. I read it on her stable sign. We'll ride into the city and find a secluded spot to sleep. Then we'll be far enough away that we should be in the clear to snag you some new clothes as a disguise and stock up on supplies."

"Okay, but there's something I want to do first." I pull off my bag and grab a couple of diamonds, placing them in the iron letterbox for the owner. It's not going to replace their horse, but it's better than leaving them high and dry. "All right, now I'm ready."

Raven smiles and jumps back on Clove, guiding me to the stirrup and helping to hoist me up behind her.

I've never ridden a horse before, and the second I settle in place, I'm a kid again. This is the kind of stuff Al and I have been missing out on! She can do something like this even with her leg weakness—though I can already tell that my thighs are going to be sore after this.

"Hold on," she says, giving me a backward glance and a wink.

Raven acts like she's owned this horse her whole life, giving all the commands, and using her whole body to communicate with the horse through her movements. I wrap my arms around her torso and cling to her for dear life because, man, this girl is flying!

Raven calls, "First timer, huh?"

"*Ah!*" I yelp as she makes a tight turn. "H-how'd you know?"

"Lucky guess." She laughs.

We zip away from the city streets to the rural outskirts that separate the high life from the middle-class folk. I'll never understand why the classes are divided in where we're allowed to live, and I hate that I'm part of the hoity-toity one. But that's how King Pontifex's ancestors decided to form the cities, and he continued the separation even though he could've changed it. And we have to deal with it, whether we like it or not.

I close my eyes and let the wind whip my face as Raven guides Clove forward. Soon, my body adjusts to bouncing with every gallop. Before long, buildings pop up in the distance. Even from this far away, I can tell these homes are smaller than in Noravale. More modest. But I envy them! I'd be perfectly fine living in one of these.

I'd want a gigantic library, though. That's the one thing I won't compromise on.

Raven steers us in the direction opposite the city. We're not trying to be the center of attention right now. The horse seems in paradise as we travel through a field of grass, past crops and flower beds. Finally, the lushness fades.

"Let's check out that place!" Raven says.

I peer around her shoulder and spot a barn in the distance. "Sure, but we better make sure it's not being used."

Raven nods. "We're on the outskirts of town. Fingers crossed this baby is abandoned."

As we approach the barn, it looks like Raven's right. The windows are boarded up, and the roof has holes and broken tiles like it's one storm away from collapsing on itself. "This place is perfect!" she beams.

"Uh…are we looking at two completely different buildings? This thing is going to crush us in our sleep."

"We'll be fine! I've stayed in dumpier places than this." Raven hops off Clove, and I gratefully take her proffered hand.

When my feet hit the dirt, my legs become jelly, and I use Raven to steady myself. "Holy gods, what happened to my legs? My inner thighs are on fire!"

"Yeah…you're probably going to be sore for a while," she says apologetically, with a shrug, indicating there's nothing we can do about it.

I struggle to walk, reluctantly waddling after she moves onward. Even though this barn is as dilapidated as all the hells combined, I'm grateful for a place to stay for the night, to finally settle and rest. I'm sure Raven is, too.

She leads the horse by its harness inside first, almost breaking the creaky, dilapidated door as she pushes it open.

The darkness is overwhelming, besides the smell of manure and mold which has been festering for gods only know how long.

I scratch my arms as if I've contracted some veritable disease. Raven moves into the darkness and I dig my shoe into the dirt floor, knocking something over in the process. My legs scream in protest as I stoop to pick it up. A lantern! At least we'll be able to see the grossness of this dwelling even better now.

"Coast is clear," Raven says. She scoured the inside before I took a single step further.

"It's no wonder the owners abandoned it." I plug my nose to avoid the rancid stench, though my senses are already getting used to it.

Raven brings Clove into one of the stables and closes the latch on the door. Then we both collapse on some meager piles of hay on the floor. It's incredibly itchy and my mind is racing, so I'm afraid I won't fall asleep. Eventually, I settle in my scratchy bed amidst the lingering pungent smells.

The rush of the night and excitement for a new day help me drift to sleep.

The morning brings me achy legs and a rumbling stomach. My neck must have been bent in an awkward position last night because the left side is stiff. But I roll my neck until it pops, and it feels a little better.

"Morning," Raven says, waking up right after me.

I scratch my hair, which now resembles a bird's nest.

She has pieces of straw stuck in hers, too.

"Good…morning." I survey the barn now that it's lighter out, at the dirty and dusty space, the broken windows, the ceiling that could fall on us at any moment. "Good morning!" I say, more cheerfully this time. "I did it! I survived my first night away from home!" But just as quickly, my excitement deflates and worry takes over. "Oh, gods—surely Mother and Father realize I'm missing by now." I wonder if my housemaid was the one to pronounce my absence, how they told my parents. "What is Al thinking? Are they searching for me? And—"

"Whoa…hold on. You need to chill out a little!" Raven gives me a look that screams, *what the hell is wrong with you?* She probably regrets signing up for this, after seeing how green I am at life.

"I…I can't," I say in a huff.

She folds her arms. "Then why did you leave in the first place if all you're going to do is fixate on it? You should focus on your future and what's ahead!"

A sigh escapes me. "You're right. But it's hard."

Raven's eyes soften and her lips pout. She stumbles off the hay pile to rest a hand on my shoulder. "I can't picture what it's like to never be allowed outside. But remember, all that's in the past now. Don't let it tie you down."

Al is behind me—I will never forget her. But I still say, "Thanks." I smile and then burst out laughing when my stomach grumbles so loudly that the horse neighs in response. "Wow…was it that loud?"

Raven's laughing along with Clove. She puts her thumb and index finger so that they're almost touching. "A little. All right, that's our cue to find some grub. Let's be efficient so that we're not here too long."

"Yeah. Who knows how long it will take for my parents to get a manhunt going for me?"

We leave Clove in the stall. Thankfully, there were some bales of hay suitable to feed her in the meantime. After ensuring the coast is clear, Raven and I step into the late morning sunlight and can now fully appreciate our surroundings. There are a few other houses with barns and large yards before us.

I hold my breath when we spot the first group of people walking down the street. Worry burns a hole in me, like they know I ran away and that I have this power…this curse that they can use for their own bidding.

But Raven holds her head high, walking with surety, and occasionally interacting with the people we passed, saying hello or tipping her head in acknowledgement.

"Can you please direct us to the market?" she asks two teens approaching us.

"Keep going one more block, then turn right," one of them says, pointing to the spot.

"Perfect. Thanks!" Raven beams.

"You have a way with people, don't you?" I ask.

"Not everyone. But I usually get what I want because I either work for it or find a way around it when I can't."

"Good motto."

We follow the girls' directions and make it to the market square, which is more of a double circle, with carts in the inner circle and open windows of the shops along the outer perimeter.

I have no idea what ours looks like, so I can't compare this one to the one in Noravale, but the market in Tosca is huge. I could find probably everything under the sun here! I giggle, excited to buy food and some new clothes. An outfit like Raven's will help me shed my old self and start anew.

She scans the square. "I hope you don't mind, but I think we should get some food first."

"Girl, my stomach already told you my answer back at the barn."

We laugh and make our way to the inner circle where the food carts are. we waste no time stocking up on freshly baked bread to vegetables, spices, and fresh fruit. What makes it even better is that we can pay for everything fair and square. I eye Raven once or twice when she looks like she's going to slip something from a table into her pocket, but she refrains when she notices me watching her.

"There's no need for that. I've got enough to cover whatever we need." I pay with the Soridente coin instead of diamonds, since I'm sure gems would raise eyebrows here. "We shouldn't draw any attention to ourselves."

"Hey, I know you!" someone exclaims from behind the food booth. "You, with the cloak!"

When our gazes meet, Raven's face reflects my fear.

THIRTEEN

Raven and I whirl around, and I fully expect her to drop kick someone. Well, I'm *assuming* she can fight, since she's made it on her own out here for so long.

My companion flashes a guilty look and raises her hands in front of her, but then she quickly drops them and smiles as a lanky teen runs up to us.

He's got light brown skin like her, though his black hair is different from Raven's pink locks.

"Hey, you're Tinto!" Raven exclaims.

"And you're...Raven?"

Uncertainty replaces the near heart attack pounding in my chest. "Wait, you two know each other?"

This so-called Tinto slaps hands with Raven before pulling her into a hug. "Yep! This girl saved me from some thugs when she was passing by here last week. I knew I recognized that cloak!"

Raven tugs at the edges of the fabric and lifts her head. "Gotta love me."

"So, you're a talented fighter too, then?" My fists shoot to my hips in a pose that demands answers.

"You were going to find out sooner than later. I mean, what's a thief if you don't get caught every once in a while? The real magic is in knowing how to escape." She winks.

"So, what are you doing back in town?" the boy asks.

"Well, I'm heading back the way I came. Except now I have someone very special with me." She pulls me close, and I flash a wide grin. "But the devils know and we can't stay too long, so you better not need my help for anything, okay?"

He laughs. "No, no. I learned my lesson. I'm trying to walk the straight and narrow now." He cups his hand to cover half of his mouth and whispers, "We'll see how long that lasts."

Raven nods in approval and we're on our way again.

I'm relieved that an ax murderer hadn't spotted Raven, ready to punish her for stealing or something, but that doesn't mean someone not so nice won't recognize her and give her a piece of their mind. Like the thugs she beat up for this kid.

We scour a few more food stands and settle on a loaf of bread, peanut butter, strawberry jam, carrots, and apples, all paid for by me—the good and honest way.

Raven also picks up some beef jerky. She eyes it for a second like she is going to steal it, but one glance at me and she pulls a couple of coins out of her pocket and gives them to the vendor.

I smile and we settle onto the cement steps of a shop that's currently closed and dig into our haul.

"This is harder than I thought," she says after swallowing a bite of beef jerky.

"Well, it *is* dried meat. Before I became a vegetarian three years ago, I'd eat that stuff like candy, but it's super tough to chew."

"I meant *not stealing* is hard."

"Oh!" I laugh. "Never mind then. You don't have to worry about not having money to pay for things because…" I peer around to make sure no one's eavesdropping, even though I'm smart enough to not say the words out loud. "You know."

"So? I'm not going to use you for that. And I've been doing it this way for so long, it's pretty fun. It's a game. One I like to win."

My eyes almost well up automatically.

I'm not going to use you for that.

Here's this girl, a stranger, who doesn't want to use me for my diamond tears. And there Mother and Father are, squeezing me until I'm dry. It makes my muscles relax and bones settle beside her. "I…really appreciate you saying that. It goes against everything my parents warned me about."

Raven sips a canister of water. "Yeah, I learned pretty early on that parents aren't always on your side. Sometimes, you're better off on your own."

"Well, the offer is on the table. But I should have enough for now." Huh…I never thought I'd say that to anyone but Al. I tear off a chunk of the bread, which is warm and soft, and slather a bit of peanut butter on it before devouring it.

We eat until our bellies are full and stash the rest of the food in our bags for the journey ahead.

"Outfit time?" I study my meager clothes then Raven's. "I'll…get whatever looks like yours."

Raven grabs the edges of her cloak and twirls before striking a pose. "How do I look?"

I blush and fumble over what to say. "Uh, like a fierce rebel I wouldn't want to mess with?"

She laughs and gently grips my shoulder before walking past me. "Putting up with your parents, I'd say you're already just as resilient without a cloak. But you're also cute too, so…"

I realize I've been low-key crushing on this girl when I don't even know if she likes girls back. Sure, she danced with me, but that could've all been a ploy to get close enough to talk to me about my curse. Still, she could've pulled me off to the side. I'm not courageous enough to outright ask her about it, so I give an awkward giggle and follow her to the market's outer circle with all the clothes and other goods.

Beautiful dresses in an assortment of colors hang from clothing racks, light and flowing to match the start of the summer solstice. Although they're pretty, they don't match Raven, or my definition of fierce status. If I need to run or ride a horse, I'd like to be comfortable. That means pants for me.

Even though I feel like an imposter beside her, I want to look cool like Raven. I guess I'll have to look the part before I own it?

She's searching through a stand of shirts, tunics, and tank tops. She pulls a blue tank top with gold trim from a pile and holds it up to show me. "How's this?"

I take it. "Ooh, I love it! Are there matching pants?"

The shop owner must have overheard my inquiry because she lights up and ushers us over to where the pants and shorts are. There I find blue shorts with the same design. Good enough. I also buy some brown and gold fingerless gloves and matching boots. Now the lady is beaming with the sale she's about to make. I gladly pay her with the coins I have.

She puts everything in a bag, and I thank her. When I turn to leave with Raven, she's nowhere to be found.

"Did you…did you see where my friend went?"

The shop owner rubs her chin. "Hm…not sure. I thought she was here this whole time."

I search the immediate area and can't find her anywhere. Of course, my initial reaction is to freak out. Despite her dark clothes, with her hood down, her pink tinted hair is striking and unmistakable. I should be able to spot her no matter how far away she is, but I can't.

Clutching my purchases, I push past people, following along the circle of shops, frantically scanning the crowd. Beads of sweat form on my brow—and not just from the summer heat. I can't do this alone. I don't know where to go or what to do. I need her!

I see the bounce of her curls and the last bit of her cloak disappear into an alleyway. I run after her, whipping around the corner into the shaded space. "Raven!"

She whirls around as if she'd expected me. "Hey, Cadence!"

I stop in my tracks. "Where…where did you go? I was worried."

She twirls a bag like she didn't almost give me a panic attack. "Sorry, I was picking something out for you!"

I eye it and then glare back at her. "Did you…pay for that?" I ask, saying each word slowly.

"Of course." She waves away my words, but she doesn't sound very convincing.

I guess old habits die hard? What am I talking about? My parents are living proof of that.

"Well…what'd you get me?"

She sticks out her tongue. "You'll have to wait until we get back to the barn!"

"What are we waiting for? Let's go!"

She smiles. "We have those carrots for Clove, too. I'm sure she'll be happy to see us."

We speed walk back out of the market to the city edge, across the plain field to the abandoned barn. Thankfully, everything is just as we left it.

After feeding Clove her carrots, I pull my new clothes from my bag. "I'm going to change. I'll be right back!" I head into the empty stall next to the horse. It's like shedding old skin, the old me who was cooped up inside. As I slip the tank top over my head, a pang of guilt hits me. It's not like I'm off on a vacation, being reckless and having fun away from home, but I still can't help the pull to go back home to see how Al is doing.

She should be starting her treatment sometime this week. Did she finish the book already? Does she hate me?

I shake my head to clear away all my toxic thoughts. *Come on, Cadence. You know why you're doing this. For Al.*

I finish changing into my blue and gold attire and lace up my boots, which go up to my mid-calf. I clear the hair from my face that I messed up while changing.

Do I look like a hot mess?

Where's a mirror when you need one?

When I emerge from the stall, I stride toward Raven, who's crouched, drinking some of the water we got at the market.

When she notices me, she stands slowly and whistles. "*Wow.* You look awesome. I mean, those clothes hug your body like…" She flashes an approving sign.

I tuck a strand of hair behind my ear and avoid her gaze, though I can't hide the rush of blood to my cheeks. "Uh…thanks."

"Here, now you can have your present!" She runs behind me and pulls something out of her bag.

Before I know it, her hands wrap around me as she drapes something over my shoulders.

Then she stands in front of me, tying a knot and stepping back.

"My own cloak!" I say after I survey the gift. It's black like hers but fades to gold at the bottom instead of blue. And it comes with a hood, too. I pull it over my head and strike a model pose as she did earlier. "How do I look now?"

Raven grabs the hood and pulls it back down, studying my face. "Still awesome…and still cute."

Okay, this is so not fair. I can't hold this in anymore. I've never been able to focus on my love life. That phrase doesn't exist in the Alero household. So, it feels weird to have these thoughts about Raven and to experience these reactions that are so…so automatic. "I…uh…"

"What?" Raven says playfully before turning to sit on a wooden box off to the side.

"You know what." I settle on a bale of hay by the box and stay silent, examining my new gloves.

"Hah. Okay, you must be thinking, two can play at the cryptic game, huh?"

"Yep." I draw the word out.

Raven leans back, propping herself up on her elbows. "I don't mean to be so secretive. I try to live my life with no apologies, you know? I'm myself and people have to deal with it."

"Yeah...I don't know what that's like."

Raven's face softens. "I'm sorry. I've seen so much of the outside world and experienced so much, I've learned to do what I want for my happiness. 'Cause that's all that matters."

I frown. "You mentioned your parents abandoning you when you were younger. I'm sorry."

"Eh, don't be. If that's how they were going to act, I don't wish they were with me a second longer. I miss having a family, but not one like that."

"You don't have any other family members?"

"Not that I'm aware of. I was a part of a group of orphans who banded together. We called ourselves The Prowlers because we liked to work at night. They were friends, and...kind of my make-shift family."

"Were? Whatever happened to them?"

"It's a long story." Raven sounds depleted from even the quick mention of them. She doesn't expound on the subject more, so I don't press.

It's not like I want to reminisce on the days I spent locked in the house and crying diamonds on command.

Raven sighs. "Anyway, it was the best thing that could happen because now I've got all the independence a girl could ask for. I embrace it all. I like girls. Guys, I couldn't care less about. I like money. I don't mind doing what I need to get it...Yeah, so, that's me in a nutshell."

She said it!

I don't say anything, but my expression must give me away, because she smirks at me.

"I thought that was pretty clear from night one."

"I-I guess so. But I'm not good at reading people. I've never had to. I like to make up stories with Al about the citizens we see outside. So, I guess I wanted to make sure I wasn't making things up or hallucinating."

"Well, you did let me dance with you, so I'm assuming I'm not all that bad, huh?"

Clove neighs, startling me from my musings.

Raven laughs. "See? Even Clove agrees."

I give a half smirk. "Hm…" I pause, pretending to be deep in thought. "I guess not."

Raven curls a lock of hair behind her ear, sending my heart fluttering in response.

I can't take it.

We need to get a move on to Serency before I decide I'm perfectly fine with staying in this dirty old barn with her for the rest of my life.

FOURTEEN

Traveling with Raven is going to make me nocturnal. After napping for a few hours, she wakes me up in the middle of the night so that we can hit the road. In my sleepy haze, I gather my things, hop on Clove behind her, and we're off.

Clove gallops at a record pace. She's had a long day of rest, so she's ready to go as well.

I barely remember the trip through Tosca. I saw more of the outskirts of the city instead of going straight through. If that one kid recognized Raven, who knew how many other people would? The only thing that keeps me going is when I glance at the sky now and then, ensuring no stalking magi are snuffing out the stars.

My cloak flaps behind me in the breeze and the cool night air keeps me awake. The memory of my achy thighs after the last long ride stays at the forefront of my mind.

"Now, I'm sure you know," Raven calls to me, "But Serency is where the lower-class citizens of Soridente live. I didn't stay the whole night there on my way to Noravale, but we might have to settle there to rest."

"No worries. We just slept in an abandoned barn. I'm up for anything at this point."

"Got it. There's a forest coming up that separates Tosca and Serency, so we can always camp there. Other than stopping somewhere in the city for food, we won't need to stay long."

We race through the fields, shielded by the darkness and protected by the gods. Before long, the sun starts peeking over the horizon, revealing a slew of treetops in the distance.

"We better stop here for a break," Raven says, slowing the horse to a trot as we enter the forest.

"Sounds good. I need to stretch my legs."

She grabs the reins to tie Clove to a tree branch, but I take them from her. "Here, I've got it." I make a loop around the branch, then grab my ankle and bend my knee back to stretch the front of my thigh, holding the tree trunk to brace myself for balance.

Raven lies in the grass, munching on some food and taking a swig of water.

I follow suit, savoring the quick break. Birds chirp all around me, and the scents of pine and moss give me smells I've never encountered even in my giant greenhouse back home.

"You know, I keep thinking about that dark blob in Noravale, and Tinto's warning. Now that the allure of being outside and exploring such cool cities isn't so new, I've realized the world can be a scary place."

Raven props herself onto her elbows. "It's completely normal to feel that way. The world is vast. But you can't let fear stop you from exploring it. Freedom, remember?"

I flash a small smile. Fear would've kept me stuck at home. Fear would've kept me away from Raven. "Right. Freedom."

I finish with a few more stretches in silence before we're ready to head back on the trail.

Nearby, a twig snaps. I freeze.

Raven takes a readying stance, legs and arms spread for balance, searching around the myriad of trees and foliage in a circle.

A deer leaps through a pair of tall bushes and runs past us. I stumble back and almost fall on my butt, but Raven catches me.

Clove rears back on her hind legs, her front legs thrashing. And I must have done a crappy job of tying the reins to the tree branch because the knot slips loose and our ride goes running in the opposite direction of the deer.

"Come back!" I exclaim.

Raven scoops up our bags. "Hurry! We have to catch her!"

We rush through bramble and brush, jumping over tiny rocks, weaving around trees and bushes. Sure, Raven picked a midnight black horse so that she'd remain undetectable at night, but that makes Clove harder for us to see even in the daytime.

My lungs burn and I'm sure I look like a madwoman, but I'm glad I'm wearing decent footwear for the mad dash—including flexible pants. Eventually, I lose sight of the horse, and Raven and I ease to a stop. "I think she went this way!" I say, pointing to the left at the exact moment Raven points to the right.

"I thought I saw her go this way…" Raven says, chewing her lip.

"Crap…" My shoulders droop in defeat. "How far away from the city are we?"

"We're a mile or so away, so we should be fine walking. But I'd really like to find her. And if we can find another horse to help take off the load when we're traveling, that would be ideal. Or even another way of traveling. Otherwise, it's a lot on us."

"I hear you." I wipe the sweat from my brow. "Well, which way is the city?"

Raven points to the right.

"I guess we better head that way then and hope we run into Clove on the way," I say.

She agrees and we start in that direction, searching for clues along the open pathway, for any prints in the dirt, trampled grass, or broken branches. If there is a deer in this forest, then there are many more where that came from, along with other critters to stir up the forest floor. This *sucks*.

Despite not finding Clove after fifteen minutes of tramping through the forest, through the trees lining the distance, I spy the beginnings of small buildings and homes.

"Is that Serency?!"

"Yep!" Raven says.

I continue marching forward, but Raven halts and whips her head to the side. "Wait a minute. I hear music…"

I guess I was so focused on moving forward that I hadn't even noticed. Or maybe my ears aren't trained to pick up minute sounds like hers. But when I close my eyes, the faint lilt of music, of strumming guitars, and singing fills the breeze. It's late morning, so the party must not have ended last night.

"Follow me," Raven says, heading in that direction.

"Is everything okay?"

"It should be. I'm curious where it's coming from."

We stay silent and slink through the trees in the morning light. We both lift our hoods over our heads to stay a bit more concealed.

The music grows louder as we stalk toward the source. It's jovial and uplifting, definitely something people need in the mornings for an extra spring in their step.

We tread around a cluster of trees and find ourselves face to face with a small building that looks like a restaurant or pub. The sign hanging above the door reads, *Better Days*.

"Hah, maybe Clove was sick of us and wanted a drink?" Raven winks as we stride closer to the building.

"Should we go inside? Check if anyone has seen her run by?"

But my answer comes in the large wooden door swinging open and a group of men ambling out. Some look like they've been drinking all night, slumped over each other, hiccupping, and stumbling, but others have their wits about them.

They're from Serency, wearing torn and tattered clothes, muted colors of brown and tan, meager pouches at their sides, and the corral on the side of the bar is empty. I pick up the scent of ale even though they're a decent distance away. One man shifts his weight to one side and folds his arms with a devious grin. Another shoves his hands in his shirt pockets.

I'm worried about what he's hiding in there.

There's a malicious look in their eyes that I don't appreciate. I know it all too well. It's the greedy glint Mother and Father had when I cried for them.

"Well, well, well, what do we have here?" one of the pub customers says, the others sidling up behind him.

Crap. Just our luck.

"Where y'all from? Surely, not from around here," the man asks when we don't say a word.

My limbs are paralyzed. I couldn't lift a toe if I tried. What in the devils do I do? I never have to interact with strangers aside from at the Solstice Ball. Apparently, this journey is determined to make me an expert really quick.

Raven folds her arms and tips her chin up. "None of your business. We're looking for our horse, though. A black mare. Might've passed by this way."

One of the other patrons hoots and hollers, slapping his thigh. "Ooh, check out the mouth on that girlie. She's somethin'."

"Can't say the same for you…" Raven blurts out.

I pull her back by her hood and whisper, "Girl, don't get on their bad side."

"I think both of their sides are bad, so…"

I sigh and hold my palms up in front of me, addressing the crowd. "Listen, we're only passing through. We want to find our horse and get on our way."

"Aw…" A woman steps out from behind the men, whipping her dirty hair over one shoulder as she takes a mocking stance. "She's trying to play nice."

"But look at those expensive clothes…" the first man says. "And if they have a horse, what other goods can they…share with us?"

Raven steps in front of me with an arm out to protect me, though I'm pretty sure *I'm* the one who needs to step in front of her—if only to stop her from starting a fight.

"You better leave us alone," she spits.

"Or *what?*" the woman says.

Raven's ready to either attack them or defend us, but I can't help but sympathize with these people. If I didn't have my curse, my family and I could be in their exact position.

"Or else, yer 'bout to take my boot to yer arse for scarin' away potential customers!" A short man with a bushy beard emerges through the front door. He ambles toward us, sending the other men scattering like mice. "And two lovely lookin' missies you'd be scarin' away, at that."

"Aw, c'mon, we were only having a bit of fun!" the woman groans, shifting her weight to one leg and pouting.

My shoulders dip from my ears, but I don't let down my guard completely. "T-thank you, sir. Are you the owner of this place?"

The stout man tips his head. "Yesiree, yer lookin' at him. Gunder McGee, the owner—er, I mean, what do the rich folk call it? Ah yes, the King of Better Days."

Someone in the crowd opens his mouth points a finger at his tongue, fake gagging. "*Blech.* Don't mention the *king* around here!"

Some of the other men throw their hands in the air in disgust.

I turn to Raven, and she shrugs.

"What did he do to piss you off?" she asks, genuinely curious.

"Hah! What hasn't he done is more like it," Gunder spouts.

One guy aims a glob of phlegm into the dirt. "Pontifex and his men haven't been around these parts in years. He leaves us here to waste when resources have dwindled. We don't have enough to repair and replace what's breaking down in the city. This forest and this pub are the best thing we got."

"I'm sorry Pontifex hasn't treated you the way you deserve," I say.

"Thanks, missy. And your names are…?"

"Oh, that's right! Raven," my companion says, tipping her head.

"I'm Cadence. And if it makes you feel any better, the king is kind of on our hit list, too."

One of his eyebrows rises, and the customers surrounding him become silent.

I'm not sure if I made the right move divulging that information, and hold my breath.

Gunder tilts his head. "Where did you say you were from again?"

Raven inches closer to me. Thankfully, she takes the lead, because I have no idea how to dig myself out of this one. "Up North. But we're on our way to a better life, the same as you're looking for. After we find our horse, we'll be on our way."

"What's in it for us if we let you?" One of the women reaches for something behind her back, leaving her hand there.

"We don't want any trouble." I gulp, raising my palms in defense again. I thought we were past this, but clearly not.

"'Xactly! I dun want no trouble in my pub!" the owner harrumphs, crossing his arms.

"But we're outside of it…" a man retorts.

"You know what I mean." Gunder turns to me and Raven. "So, are you runnin' away from the king or toward something else? Besides the horse, that is."

I bite my lip, unsure of what answer he's searching for. A breeze sweeps past us, rustling the leaves on the trees and sending strands of brown hair flying in my face. I use that window to pause and curl a piece behind my ear as I ponder my decision. Our best bet is to be as truthful as we can, without giving everything away. What's that saying about white lies? "The king hasn't been kind to us either, but it's my family I'm escaping. Well, my parents, to be specific. Raven is helping me search for answers to my past. And we need our horse to get there."

Murmurs rise up from the crowd. I can't tell what they're saying but at least no one is threatening us at the moment.

Gunder strokes his beard. "Search for answers to yer past? Sounds all woo-woo and stuff."

I laugh. "You're telling me, Beardy."

"Beardy?" he asks in confusion, shaking his head before a smirk spreads on his face at the nickname. "Alrighty then, we'll help ya search for yer horse."

"*Hmph.*" The ornery woman from earlier folds her arms. "I'm not helping them. If *they* ain't got nothing to give, I ain't got nothing to give either."

Raven nudges my arm.

I meet her gaze and understand her silence.

Must be all that woo-woo stuff going around. I nod and clutch my bag at my side, stepping toward the woman.

She takes a step back in turn.

"As we said, we don't mean any harm. We'd appreciate all the help we can get. I know what Pontifex may think of you all, but that's not what we think of you. Serency is full of good people."

The woman appears thrown off by my response. She turns to her friend, who scratches the back of his head.

"I take it all you want is enough money for your city's resources, for food…" I tilt my head in the pub's direction. "And some delicious drinks."

That earns me some chuckles and catches the group's attention, including Beardy's.

The woman raises a brow. "Go on…"

Raven's lips remain sealed, allowing me to take the lead. It's both weird and natural. I've been helping people my whole life, so this should be a walk in the forest.

I swing my bag around and dig through it. There are still plenty of diamonds from when I cried in the past, saved up over the past week from the emotional whiplash I've endured. But if I give them just the diamonds, I might make things worse.

The other townsfolk will wonder if they stole such precious money, and I don't want to make more trouble for these people. It'll be less suspicious if I only throw a few into the mix. So, I pull out diamonds, copper and bronze coins, and other gems.

I cup the money in my hands, which feel so full I'm afraid they'll start falling out of my grasp.

The pub goers stand stark still as I approach them with a smile.

They're taken aback by my non-conventional approach, presenting both curious and guarded expressions.

Raven eyes me with inquisitiveness. No doubt she's wondering how the Serency citizens will respond.

"Open your hands," I say.

The group look at each other and back at me with puzzled expressions. But no one moves to follow my gentle command.

"Open your hands," I repeat.

Beardy is the first to do so, placing his palms together, face up.

I open my hands and let some of my small treasure fall into the man's hands.

After that, the rest of the group quickly cups their hands, in turn, their eyes wide and mouths open.

But the sparkle in their eyes aren't greedy or malicious. These are...thankful. *Grateful.* And of course, surprised.

Once I'm done dolling out the money, I move back in line with Raven. "If you help us, there's more where this came from," I say softly. "Even if you don't, that should last you a while. I hope this helps you live," I read the pub sign, "better days."

Beardy seals his hands around his fortune and scans his customers. Then he locks eyes with me...and smiles. "Wow...I...thank ye. No one's e'er done this fer us before."

Wait. Are those tears forming in the corners of his eyes?

A curly-haired woman hugs her arms to her chest. "Usually passersby take things from us, try to steal money and goods that we already don't have enough of. But you...you *helped* us."

I dig my boot into the dirt. "You need it more than I do."

The skeptical woman from earlier lunges at me. "Yeah, and we need more!"

I yelp in shock.

Raven immediately steps in front of me to block the attack, arms splayed out. "Don't you touch her," she snarls.

I can picture her furrowed brows and intense glare.

Beardy rushes to the woman's side, squeezing her arm as he holds her back with one mighty fist. "Hey! What're ye think yer doin'? Is that any way to thank 'er?"

"She's got money. Why show her any mercy?"

Beardy scowls. "Because we ain't the savages the king thinks we are. We ain't playin' that game."

The woman stops struggling in Beardy's grip but still narrows her eyes at us—*me*.

Raven fakes a lunge in her direction. "We're not either."

The woman finally backs down. "I see your point."

"You'll behave?" Beardy grips her arm tighter, clearly not trusting her.

"I promise," she vows. Her expression becomes contrite. "I'm sorry I rushed at you."

Raven lets the apology slide off her, not acknowledging it before she whips around, frantically looking me over with a worried expression even though the woman didn't lay a finger on me. "Are you okay?"

"Yeah, yeah, I'm fine." I'm grateful Raven stepped in to protect me, but I hate that I need protecting. I wish I was strong enough to defend myself, but I'm not there yet. With my curse being diamond tears, I'm not sure I ever will be. "Just a bit frazzled."

One of the men in the crowd pockets his newly-gifted stash from me and rubs the back of his head. "Sorry for all that commotion. So, uh…since you're against the king and all that, I don't see why we can't help you find your horse."

The others nod in agreement, Beardy and the previously skeptical woman included. Relief floods my insides.

Raven grabs my hand and smiles. "You did it, girl." Her touch is soft, yet as electric and shocking as I'm sure the coins and diamonds felt to the people before us. I let her warmth sink into my skin and savor the moment before she lets go.

I quickly mask my disappointment.

Beardy adjusts his belt, oblivious to my silent plight. "Alrighty then, missy, we gotta horse ta find!"

FIFTEEN

The forest is bustling with chirping birds, while the scent of pine and sweet flora permeates the air.

We weave through trees, stumble over shrubs and branches, and sprint over rocks in search of Clove.

My feet crunch on pine needles that litter the ground, while squirrels and other critters upturn leaves and plants in their scurrying. As I move forward, other boots crunch on the same pine needles behind me. Branches snap and it takes everything in me to remember I don't need to watch my back. It's weird for tons of other people to surround me when it's just been Raven and me for a few days now. I pull my nerves back from the edge.

As I search, the foliage is a welcome change from the walls of my home. But when I think of home, I can't help but think about Al. What's she doing right now? What's she saying about me? Gods, you'd think I've been gone a week for how much of a sap I am. But I can't help it. When we've always been together, even a day apart feels like a lifetime.

"Clove! Where are ya, girl!" Beardy yells, as if the horse were a dog that would come when called.

I know nothing about horse mannerisms, so maybe it's a thing?

One of the men studies a cluster of trees in the distance. "I might have seen your horse earlier. A black blur ran past that clearing where there's a small pond. Maybe she wanted some water?"

My hopes rise, and Raven immediately stalks forward. I follow her to the pond along with some other people in the group, while the rest search in a different direction. We make our way deeper into the forest, and the smell of rainwater tickles my senses as the pond comes into view.

And there is Clove, drinking her fill! There's even a deer on the other side drinking, too. Maybe the one that sent her running in the first place.

I hold my hands out and keep my voice calm and low. Raven does the same, stooping so she looks un-intimidating.

The pub goers hold back so as not to scare her.

Clove lets us approach her, seeming to recognize us, and holding an apology in her eyes for fleeing.

When we reach her, I stroke her thick neck, the hairs somehow both bristly and smooth at the same time.

At our presence, the deer runs away, but the good news is that Clove doesn't.

Raven pets her nose and gives her some carrots, which she gobbles up. Raven studies her in silence before sighing. "I feel bad now. We need another way of traveling to Kinephrus. I journeyed for weeks across Soridente to find you, Cadence, but we don't have the luxury of time on our side."

"Yeah. If Mother and Father search for me, they could probably travel in half the time. I wish we had my family's carriage."

"Hm…" Raven ponders. "I wish we did, too. If we had one and an extra horse, we could go much farther and put less strain on Clove. But even if we could find one here, no one would give up or even sell their horse or carriage. If they even have one in the first place."

"Um…" I kick at some pebbles at the edge of the pond. They fall into the water with a plop, sinking like my hopes. "Is there anything else that can help us?"

Beardy makes his way past the crowd and claps, interrupting our considerations. "Ah, there she is! Wow, she's a beaut!"

Raven glances at him and the Serency citizens, who are now folding their arms and shifting restlessly. She tilts her head toward them and leads Clove by the bridle.

I follow suit.

"Heard your dilemma about wanting another horse or a carriage," the previously ornery woman says as we draw near. She rubs her arm sheepishly. "I might be able to help you out. My neighbor was looking to sell their horse—said something about not being able to take care of it anymore? I can see if they'll part with it."

"Really? That would be so helpful!" Raven says.

"Can we go there now?" I ask, patting Clove's flank.

The woman turns to her friends and bites her lip. "Not sure if that's the best idea. We know you're against the king, but the rest of Serency doesn't."

Beardy approaches me and slaps me on the back. "Why don't you stay at the pub for a bit to rest your bones and down some grub? Can't pass along any ale, but we've got plenty of drinks you young ones can have."

My stomach grumbles, my tongue turns to sandpaper, and my leg muscles scream at me at the same time. I never notice these things until someone mentions them! I look at Raven and she nods her head. "Yeah, sounds great."

A couple of the men laugh and high-five each other, already making their way through the forest back to the Better Days pub.

The woman starts in the opposite direction but I tug on her shirt sleeve to stop her. "Wait, here's some extra money for the horse." I drop more coins—and diamonds—into her hands.

"I...thank you."

"No, thank you!"

She smiles. "I hope I can bring you the steed. I might be gone a while, but I'll return as soon as possible, okay?"

"Okay." And it's the truth. I trust her as I have with the rest of these kind folk.

I follow Beardy as Raven leads Clove onward.

I'm able to admire the forest a lot better when I'm not searching the foliage in a panic. Now the bird's chirps sound melodic and not frantic, and I notice a ton of different plants I didn't see on the way to the pond. From trillium to blood roots, the colorful array of petals reminds me of the greenhouse back home, where I first chose to leave with Raven on this crazy adventure.

Before long, we've reached the pub.

We tie Clove in the stable yard right beside the tavern, which according to Beardy, is usually empty.

He fills up the water and scrapes the bottom of a bucket for the last crumbs of grain, dumping them into a trough.

Clove starts eating the meager offering, so Gunder unlocks the wooden doors and ushers us through the entrance.

Smooth wooden tables and chairs dot the pub's open area.

Like any tavern, there are barstools lined against the bar with a myriad of alcohol I won't be able to try for a couple of years. It doesn't matter what time it is to everyone else. Bottles are being popped, caps opened, and liquid is already freely flowing to fill these customers' bellies.

The people who helped us in our search are ready for their meals, too. They push their way inside like water bursting from a dam, hopping into seats as if on command. They must be regulars if they have designated seats.

Raven and I stand in place near the doorway, taking in the scene to not accidentally take one of their spots.

A hand rests on my shoulder and I turn as a woman ushers us toward the barstools.

After checking out the menu, we don't have to wait long for our order before we fill our bellies with sweet peppers, a perfect grilled cheese sandwich, the best onion soup I've ever eaten, and a delectable ice cream parfait to top it off.

Who knew pub food would taste so delicious?

Raven orders the same food as me, though she also has some sort of sausage dish. It smelled good, but I still wouldn't eat it. I joke with her that when I don't eat meat, it leaves more for everyone else. And I smile when it makes her chuckle.

We make sure to pay them generously for our meals before we move to a table that has chairs with backs on them to lean into so we can let our food settle. Only then do I realize the jovial music of a man in the corner, playing away on his fiddle, filling the air with carefree whims.

After talking with Beardy and the others, hearing both stories of heartbreak that almost had me shedding a diamond tear, and jokes so funny my cheeks hurt from laughing so hard, he shows us up the stairs to the sparse but nice spare bedroom he owns. One he sometimes rents it out as an inn for traveling folk to earn some extra coin.

"Ye two missies can stay here for a bit before gettin' on your way," he says, a smile showing through his bushy beard.

Like the downstairs area, this bedroom is modest and homey, with wooden furniture, a small rug in the center of the room, and bare walls save for one piece of wall art featuring clanging beer glasses. The simplicity is a stark change from my room back home, but it sure beats the hay we slept on yesterday.

"Thank you, Gunder."

He closes the door on his way out, leaving us a moment to breathe at last.

Raven plops on the bed and props herself up on her elbows. "So, now that we're alone…"

My heart skips a beat at her forwardness. "Uh…"

"I wanted to go back to what you asked before about whether we can get any other help if we can't find another horse or carriage."

I scratch the back of my head and feign ignorance. Nope, no silly thoughts running through my head at all. "Oh right, that!" I chuckle awkwardly, finding my way to the sofa chair beside the bed. "What about it?"

"Well…there is another way we can travel faster. But we won't be able to get there for a while."

"What do you mean?"

"Remember, you're not the only mage in the country. *And* your power isn't the only kind that's out there."

"Wow…" I draw the word out. "I've had so much to worry about, that didn't even cross my mind." I laugh at my stupidity.

"Hey, you learned about the magi four days ago. No one's blaming you," Raven assures me. "So, there are magi called Transport Magi. Pretty self-explanatory, but they're literally able to teleport from one place to another. And the stronger you are, the farther you can travel—and the more people you can take with you."

My mouth drops. "Whoa. That's so cool! But how are we going to find a mage like that? Don't they live *in* the city of magi?"

"Well, I've never been there before, but we might be able to make it to Jessen. I only know two things about it. One, it's a city that's kind of built like an island, with an ocean to the south and a river running around the rest of the town. So, it's difficult to reach."

"And two?"

Raven flashes that signature wily grin like she's gotten away with stealing something. "It's rumored that tons of magi live there."

"So, if we can reach Jessen, we might find a Transport Mage to take us the rest of the way to Kinephrus?"

"See? You're a natural." She fluffs up one of the pillows beside her. "Though Transport Magi are hard to come by since their power is in such high demand. Hopefully, we can find one. We just have to get to Jessen first."

"At least we have Clove back. And we might be able to get another horse!" I say as raucous laughter echoes from downstairs. The group sure knows how to have fun.

"Yeah. But we've still got a long way to go. I heard about the leader of the magi there. His name is Bidyzen. Supposedly, he's like their messiah, helping them escape from Goldin and his goons."

"Then he sounds like someone I'd like to meet, too." I tap my chin. "And that's three things you know about Jessen." I wink.

Raven smirks. "Nice. I see I'm rubbing off on you." She opens her mouth again but quickly closes it, as if taking back what she was going to say. "You know, out of all the people I could've met in Noravale, or anywhere in Soridente, for that matter, I'm glad I met you."

Damn it, I'm sure I can't hide my flushing cheeks. My shoes toe the tassels at the edge of the rug. I'm not used to compliments. Unless it's something like, *Good job crying for us today, Cadence.* "I…"

She fiddles with a particularly curly strand of her pink hair. "Sorry. Not trying to go all sappy on you. But I tell it like it is."

"I already knew that." I laugh awkwardly. "But why? Are you glad you met me, that is?" I feel the same about her, but don't quite have the guts to say whatever's on my mind. After years of living with my parents, I've learned to keep that inside.

"I mean, look at how you helped out the Serency folk. I'm so proud of you for taking the lead and finding a way to make it work for both sides. It shows your soul deep down and how much you care for others."

I'm ready to cry right now. She notices me. Not my diamond tears—*me.* "Thanks, Raven. That means a lot to me."

And *you* mean a lot to me.

But I'm not ready to say that.

She appears indifferent to my lack of reciprocal admiration. Raven can probably read it all over me, anyway. She scoots over and pats the blanket. "Do you need a quick nap before we're on our way? I could use a bit of shut-eye myself."

My focus darts to the single bed and back at her. "Um…"

"I'm well aware that there's only one bed here. Hence," she says with a smirk, tapping the spot next to her again.

My palms grow sweaty and my heartbeat pounds my eardrums. I block my mind from any irrational thought and stand on sturdy legs, ready to sit…and lay…beside Raven.

A rumbling from downstairs knocks me from my foundation. "What the—?"

Faint yelling resounds from both inside and outside the pub. I grit my teeth as Raven and I exchange furtive glances. We sneak to the door and inch it open a crack, hoping it's nothing but a bar rumble between customers.

But it's not.

SIXTEEN

With our ears pressed to the door, Raven and I hold our breath as voices reverberate from downstairs.

"Captain…searching…by order of the king…"

I can only pick out bits and pieces of the message, but my eyes widen at the words I hear. I keep my voice to a whisper. "What the…? Captain? What's the captain of the King's Guard doing here?"

Raven furrows her brows. "I have no idea…" She strains to make out more. "I can't hear! I'm going to get closer."

"Be careful!" I whisper as she slowly cracks the door open enough to slip through.

Thankfully, there is a large landing at the top of the stairs to keep us hidden from those below, but we still have to make sure not to peer too far forward in case they spot us through the wooden slats of the railing.

Together, we investigate the unwelcomed guests.

Two guards stand in front of the pub's doorway. They're wearing silver armor with gold trim to signify they serve Pontifex Goldin. And in between the two guards? Donning a red sash and more medals than Father could wish for is Captain Rioza herself. I've only heard about her since he wants her advisor position. I think she was there at the masquerade, but I'd been too preoccupied with the pretty girl currently crouching beside me to notice or care at the time.

One of the guards holds up a poster.

I squint to make out its features.

And my jaw drops open when I can see it clearly.

The paper has my face on it and my name is in bold black capital letters across the bottom with the word *Missing* at the top.

They can't be serious right now. The king sent the freaking Captain of the Guard...for *me*?

As if on cue, the other guard holds up a different poster.

Raven...oh *no*.

This one has her picture on it but without a name. Since she'd snuck into the Summer Solstice Ball and remained undetected by anyone when she came to get me at my house, she never revealed her name to anyone but me. The picture they have of her is way less accurate, a cruder drawing based on whoever might have caught a glimpse of her. But hers reads, *Wanted*. Do they know she stole some of the king's riches? Or do they want her simply for gate-crashing the party?

"My cheeks aren't that puffy," Raven whispers to me with a pout and folds her arms.

I press one finger to my lips to silence her. Something big is going down, and I don't want to miss a second of it.

All the customers have stopped eating and drinking, frozen in place like we are.

One guy's gripping his mug so tight it looks like shards of glass could burst from his palm at any moment.

The captain points to the posters. "We have reason to believe this thief has kidnapped this girl from Noravale and is hiding close by...possibly inside this tavern."

Gunder strokes his beard from behind the bar counter. "Aye? And what reason is that?"

Rioza smirks and tilts her chin up. "You've got a mighty fine horse tied up in the stable yard out there. It looks very well taken care of."

Clove! They better not hurt her, especially since we just found her. And we need her to get out of here.

I study Beardy, hoping that she and Raven left a fine enough impression on them to remain on their good side and avoid being ratted out. After all, they did say they hated the king and his cronies. And well, the captain and her guard are *exactly* that.

Gunder clears his throat while a knot forms in mine. "Pardon me, uh, Captain, but how do ya know it ain't my horse?" He spreads his arms wide. "I've got the customer base to warrant as such."

Rioza chuckles and folds her arms. "Between me and the King's Guard, I think we've got enough brains and brawn to put two and two together." Her boots crunch as she saunters around the room, eyeing the decor—and people—with clear disgust. "I doubt you'd be able to scrape together more than a few measly coins to keep this place going."

A few of the customers grumble and mumble, clearly holding back what they want to say. I'm sure they've got the same choice words I'd like to use on this woman right now.

"Well, well, well…what is this?" She bends forward and plucks something from a table laden with beer mugs, cheese curds, ciga-rette butts, and napkins. She rolls the object between her thumb and index finger as she holds it up to her eye.

A single diamond.

"What do you make of this?" she says in a voice, smooth like a snake ready to strike.

Great. Beardy tried to keep things on the down low and someone just had to let one of my diamonds slip through the cracks.

But wait—that means my parents told the captain, and therefore the *king*, about my power.

Why would they be so reckless with their knowledge after all this time?

Raven rests a palm on my shoulder. "You trust me, right?"

"Of course," I say without hesitation.

She smiles, then replaces her expression with fervor and focus. "Okay, then I need you to go down there and pretend to give your-self up."

"W-what?" Okay, maybe this whole trust thing is going to be harder than I thought. "But…I don't…"

"You only have to *pretend.* I'll take care of everything, and we'll get out of this mess."

I bite my lip and turn my attention to the first floor. How is she seemingly unfazed by these bulks of metal?

"Serency may be worse off than you snooty rich folk, but that don't mean we can't build our own wealth," Gunder spits out.

Rioza narrows her eyes and walks back to the front door, an iron grip around the diamond.

One of the customers starts to kick her leg out to trip the wom-an, but decides against it, sliding it back right on time.

"Seems like we're both asking for a little trust here," the captain says with faux calmness.

"Ha, what makes you think we'd trust you?" Gunder says, his tightening fists turning his knuckles white.

"My thoughts exactly. I don't believe you'd have anything more than coal for money in this place."

My pulse skips a beat. So, she doesn't know about my power!

Gunder snaps, clearly done with this woman parading around as holier than thou. "King's Guard? More like the king's *filth.*"

"Guards," Rioza commands, pocketing my diamond tear. "Search the place."

Two more enter the pub along with the two who'd held up the wanted and missing posters.

I watch in horror as they start flipping chairs and causing un-necessary damage to Gunder's property.

Guess it's time for me to deescalate this situation and put some of that trust to work. There's no time to uncover what Raven has planned. All I know is, it better work…for all our sakes.

I straighten and march what's hopefully not to my demise down the stairs, a couple of the steps creaking under my pressure. They sound like cracking whips as the whole room becomes silent and everyone notices me, and those with their backs to me turn to investigate the scene.

The guards stop their pillaging and stare hard.

I lock eyes with Beardy, whose expression is one of surprise and confusion. I can't help but offer a measly shrug.

"Cadence Alero?" the captain almost snarls my name out, even though *I'm* not a criminal.

I make it to the bottom of the stairs, but before I can even say a word, the guard directly to the captain's right speaks up. "It's Cadence Alero, all right."

Okay. I thought my mouth couldn't drop any further, but now my jaw is completely unhinged. Standing there is someone I thought I'd never run into here or anywhere—my family's freaking butler.

"Malore!"

His chiseled features anger me, his very presence mocking my independence. He watches me with...what is it? Sympathy? *Pity?* "So, you remember," he says, rubbing the stubble of his freshly shaved beard.

"Of course, I do." *I thought you were one of the good ones.* "What are you doing here? Did my parents send you? Did—"

"You ask too many questions. Why would your parents want you back?" one of the other guards spits.

"So, my parents *did* send you!" *I want to return for Al, but not yet. Not when my journey has just begun.* "How did you find me?"

"We have ways of...tracking you," the stupid-mouthed guard says. His eyes flick to Malore for a split second, but I notice.

"It doesn't matter how we found you. You're here, and now you have to come with us," Captain Rioza booms.

One of the customers sitting closest to me pushes his chair out, ready to take a stand against the captain.

I hold my palm up to signal him to refrain. I don't want to cause an all-out brawl.

But Beardy doesn't take the hint.

It worries me, to see this man trying to intimidate King Pontifex's most highly ranked guard, the captain who he entrusts so much that she's also his advisor.

"You best leave this missy alone! We won't have none a' this in Serency," he says, spittle sticking to his thick beard.

Rioza studies him before exploding into laughter. "Surely, you and your...friends...don't want to get on the king's bad side. We have orders to apprehend these girls."

A customer spits on the ground, while another pats an empty beer bottle in her palm. And still, others growl in contention.

Beardy scowls even further. "Pontifex ain't our King. Ain't done nothin' fer us or our people. But these missies here...they helped us. They didn't judge us. So, you don't have to threaten us about getting' on ole Crabby Crown's bad side. He's already on ours."

My heart hurts for these people.

Serency is still a city in Soridente, and therefore, under the king's rule. Clearly, he likes to keep things divided. If I have any say in it someday, I'll have to change that.

"You don't have a choice. *She* doesn't have a choice. These are the king's orders. We are to bring back the vagrant thief and the girl whom she kidnapped."

"*Kidnapped?* I went with Raven of my own choice!"

"So, Raven's her name, huh?" Rioza asks slyly.

I groan at my mistake but quickly divert the conversation, hoping they won't realize she's not here with me—yet. "Why are my parents using the King's Guard to find me? And why are you helping them?" I direct my attention to Malore, fighting to hold back my tears. I want to curse him.

He was probably the one who was in the garden the night Raven came for me and ratted us out.

I thought he was okay, letting me go when he caught me in my parents' bedroom. I glare daggers at him.

He averts his gaze.

"If you don't come with us willingly, I'll make you." Rioza unsheathes and brandishes her long sword, blood red at the hilt, the blade a stunning silver—a threat to Raven, Al, me, and my future.

My beating heart could have reached Noravale for how loud it sounds. I'm not ready to go. I can't go. I haven't gotten my answers. What will my parents do to me if the King's Guard brings me back?

And what will they do to Raven if they think she's to blame? Where *is* she, anyway?

The customer who'd been slapping the beer bottle against her palm smashes the end of it on the edge of the table, sending shards of glass flying out. The jagged edges gleam in the lamplight as she holds it up menacingly.

Another man spits at them. It lands just shy of Rioza's boot.

My eyes round in fear of what the captain and the guards—including Malore—will do with these acts of disrespect. Turning to the stairway, my insides squirm as Raven's still nowhere in sight.

"Captain?! Captain, where'd you go?"

I whirl around, finding confusion painting the guards' faces and what has surely overcome my own expression.

Rioza is nowhere to be found. But where did she go?

"What are you on about? I'm right here, you fools!" the woman yells, seemingly from the same spot she'd been moments ago.

But no one's there. The guards start forward, crouching and waving their arms in front of them to feel their way around and catch her.

"What the devils is going on? She…she disappeared!" Beardy exclaims, his complexion turning a ghostly white.

A few of the customers rise from their seats and start walking around, too. The woman with the broken beer bottle leads with the weapon, jabbing the air to find her with a mighty stab.

"I see you! Why can't you see me?" Rioza shrieks, exasperation spewing from her.

I step forward, only to be tugged backward. I twist to find my cloak is flowing out as if someone is pulling it—pulling *me*. Is it the invisible captain? But a recognizable scent of ivory and pine leads me to concede. Wait, is that…?

Soon, I'm led past the fumbling and bewildered guards through the entrance. My boot catches on a divot in the ground and my legs buckle as my arms shoot out to catch my fall. My palms skid into the dirt and I cough and sputter as a billow of dust kicks up around me. I push myself up so I sit back on my knees, wiping myself off.

"Cadence, are you okay?!"

I swipe at my brow to find Raven standing beside me with a sheepish smile, a hand proffered. I cough as she helps me to my feet. "What the…where did you come from?"

Raven winks. "I told you I'd get you out of this mess. Come on! We're not done yet!" She keeps her hand clasped around mine as she leads me toward the stable yard where Clove is hopefully still tied up.

My brain is trying to process everything on overdrive, so I'm glad Raven knows what's going on because I feel as lost as Rioza was in the tavern.

She pulls me back onto the paved path to the east side of the pub before stopping abruptly.

I nearly collide into her as I spot the source of her distraction.

The Serency woman who had gone into town to find a horse for us jumps in place in front of the stable yard, waving her arms high. "Over here!"

We sprint toward her, Raven a touch ahead of me. As we draw nearer, I'm sure I'm not the only one who's pleasantly surprised.

One of the King's Guard lays sprawled in the grass face down with a red mark on the back of his balding head, with a giant barrel settled beside him.

"I don't know how I did it," the woman says in a huff, resting her palms on her knees to catch her breath, "but I knocked this goon out before he realized I was here."

"So, what now?" I ask between gasps.

"You said you needed another horse, right? I couldn't find you one in town, but…" She points to what the man had been guarding, what they must've used with the captain to travel here.

Another white horse is in the corral next to Clove, pawing the ground. He's hooked up to a carriage behind it that looks more like a prison wagon than an everyday traveling cart, with vertical black bars making up the windows. Was it meant for me and Raven?

Clove blows air from her nostrils, her tail swishing. She's frustrated like us.

I pat her side in reassurance and try to stand tall, swallowing back the tears that are eager to make their way to the surface.

"Take 'em before it's too late!" the woman sputters.

Raven places her palms together and bows in thanks not just to the woman, but to all the pub folk from Serency for their protection and kindness. "Thank you."

A rumbling on the ground startles us from our gratitude. Clove starts backing up, but I keep a hold of her bridle to steady her as Raven hooks her up to the carriage.

"Hurry, hurry, hurry!" I urge Raven on, my feet dancing as if on hot coals.

The ruckus inside has now made its way outside, with some of our brave allies fending off the king's goons. Unfortunately, the magic trick has finally faded.

Captain Rioza is visible again—and angry.

She's on her horse, which must have been somewhere else than the stable. She sneers at us, turning her steed in our direction, and raising her sword threateningly. "Get away from there!"

I wish I had a blade of my own or something, but all Raven and I bought in Tosca was food and water. Why didn't I think about buying a weapon? Raven has a small knife or two on her person, which would be quite handy right now, but I don't know how to use it. And I never would've thought I'd need to protect myself from the King's Guard.

"I won't fail the king!" Captain Rioza yells, rushing toward me on her snow-white steed. She slashes her sword downward.

I swear she's trying to cut my head off.

Yelping, I barrel roll out of the way, becoming a tumble of brown hair and limbs on the forest floor. I sputter in the grass and dirt as I lift my cloak out of my face. "Hey! The poster said *missing*. Aren't you supposed to bring me back alive?"

She scoffs and scowls at me. "Fair enough. But no one said you couldn't come back with a few scratches on you."

I scramble out of the way just in time to avoid her horse's hoof slamming onto my arm. What in the devils is this woman on? She's got bloodlust as badly as the girls admiring Prince Wendell.

I scan the scene and find the Better Days crew is holding their own. Thank the gods there aren't more guards. Otherwise, we'd be in some deep shit. I guess the king—and my parents—didn't expect two girls to cause them this much trouble.

"Hey! Stop that right now!" a guard yells. He's waving his hands high and running toward Raven, who finishes hitching up the horse.

"Git over there with ya friend, missy. I'll take care of these crazies!" Beardy calls from the front post.

I breathlessly thank him before sprinting back to Raven, quickly hopping into the prison, carriage—whatever it is.

"Go!" Raven commands Clove and the other horse forward.

I slide into the wall with a thump as the wheels bounce over a hole in the ground.

Soon enough, the ride has a steady bump to it as the horses run at full speed out of the circle of fighters and out of the forest.

My muscles relax as we find Beardy and the pub crew still holding off the guards. I hope that they all make it out safe and sound.

It's one thing to risk my life for my own agenda, but I'm not about to put others' lives on the line.

A thud from the back of the carriage rattles my bones.

I rush to peek out the hatch to find one of the guards is clinging to the side lip.

He's the one the Serency woman had knocked out.

Gods, don't these guys ever let up?

I open the back and thank Raven for buying me these thick brown boots because with one stomp I smash his fingers.

He yelps, but somehow holds on with one hand. "I won't let you get away with this!" the guy shouts.

"Raven!" I call. "Raven, go right!"

She must've heard me because the horses turn right and the carriage swerves, knocking the guard off balance. With one more sharp turn in the other direction, he loses his hold and goes flying onto the grass. His form grows smaller and smaller as we speed farther away. He'll have a few good bruises to remember us by.

I close the back door and blow out a sigh of relief.

As we travel onward, all I can think about is why my parents got the king involved and if we'll have any more chance encounters. I can only hope that Beardy and the Better Days crew are okay. I'd hate to hurt any more people—all over a handful of diamonds.

SEVENTEEN

I thought steering one horse was hard enough, but somehow Raven easily commands the reins and whip for both horses pulling this freaking carriage. I offered to help her, but she said it'd be too hard—and dangerous—to teach me in such a short time, so she remains the one in control.

I remember learning horse commands in a book from my library, but that doesn't translate to being able to do it in real life. Plus, if I had to apply my skills—or lack thereof—in such a tense situation, there's no doubt I'd be setting myself up for failure.

But I'm grateful for the carriage we have, and take the opportunity to rest my bones. My muscles scream at me for the beating I've given them on this journey so far. It feels good to get a bit of a reprieve from the earlier rumble. After Raven took a quick cat-nap, she led us from the edge of Serency to the barren land of the Ivory Sands, a field of dusty plains. Here, there are no trails, only random tracks every which way from random animals and humans—and maybe magi too, traveling to and from their rural dwellings to the urban cities.

I also appreciate Raven's generosity and care as she takes us to safety. Her, Beardy, and so many strangers who have come to my aid—they warm my heart.

But then I taste sourness thinking about Malore and Rioza. Their presence—their hunt—can only mean that the king and my parents are working together to get my diamonds back. And I don't like it one bit.

I switch my focus back to Raven. Her charm, her wit, her smarts. She's that breath of fresh air, that cold drink of water, that shade on a hot summer day. Her image takes over my vision as I curl up in the cart.

I don't remember drifting off to sleep, but I swear it's the best I've had yet. It leaves me well-rested with pleasant dreams on the tip of my memory.

After riding far enough to ensure that we weren't followed by Captain Rioza or anyone else, Raven stops seemingly in the middle of nowhere. It's a desert out here, but the summer heat is dying down as evening approaches.

She tiptoes around the back, thinking I'm asleep, trying to stay silent as she pulls her bag from the back and noshes on some food.

"Hey, don't eat all the food," I say with both eyes closed.

"Shoot. I was trying to be quiet."

I laugh and sit up. "Girl, nothing can get past me anymore. You've helped me learn to sleep with one eye open."

She scratches the back of her head. "Go figure."

"How did you do that back there? Make Rioza disappear?"

She waves my question away with a hand. "Just a cheap parlor trick the Prowlers taught me."

"Well it worked, so it isn't cheap." I joke. She doesn't say more so I don't prod.

We let our legs dangle off the back of the cart, eating our fill after tending to the horses.

"The new guy's named King," Raven declares of the guard's white horse.

"'Cause he's way better than our current one?" I chuckle.

She winks. "Read my mind."

I'm silent for a moment as my thoughts return to recent. "I gave my diamond tears to strangers because it was *my* choice," I muse, "went up against the king's head honcho, and well, now I'm here."

"You'll have many new memories from where those came from."

"So, where do we go from here?"

Raven scans the distance. "We're a good thirty miles outside of the edge of Jessen. We're on the outskirts of the desert oasis. I've never been across the river that surrounds the city, so we'll have to play it by ear once we get there."

"Sounds like a plan!"

"Speaking of a plan, I know you managed your own out there against the guards, but I think that was a bit of beginner's luck. Seeing how you fought, girl, I have to teach you some basic hand-to-hand combat if we're to get through this alive."

I stand, placing my hands on my hips. "I thought I kicked ass!"

Raven folds her arms, smirking. "And almost made yourself look like one."

I laugh, playfully punching her in the shoulder.

"See?" Raven asks with a chuckle. "Weak. We have to beef up those arms."

I stick out my tongue. "Oh, yeah? You mean like yours?" I move to grip her bicep. My fingers tingle at the sensation of her smooth skin. My gods, why did I do that? Apparently, I can't trust myself because I'm doing stupid things in the name of a crush. We're so close now, like we are when we ride on horseback, but it's different this time. More…intimate. And her hair still smells like the pine of the forest.

"Will you help me get stronger?" I finally ask.

Raven looks at my hand on her arm, gazing back up at me with a twinkle in her eyes. "Sure, but only if you make it worth my while." She keeps her gaze locked on mine.

My cheeks burn in embarrassment, so I back away, coughing as I kick the dusty ground.

She clears her throat and curls a stray pink lock behind her ear. Are her cheeks as pink as her hair now?

I smile faintly in relief that I'm not the only one affected. "So, uh, where should we begin?"

"Huh? Oh, right," she says, wiping her palms on her pants. She pulls out a dagger from the small leather scabbard wrapped around her thigh. With ease, she flips it in the air and catches it at the hilt before turning it again and handing the hilt side toward me. "Let's get you used to this beauty, why don't we?"

"*Beauty*. Got it," I lie. Can a blade *be* beautiful?

"So, first things first, you want to hold the dagger like this." She takes my hand and curls my fingers around the hilt. "Now, show me your fighting stance."

I blink at her and try one from the books I've read, holding the weapon in front of me in one hand and raise a fist with my other.

I'm tempted to clamp a hand over Raven's mouth at how loud she laughs. I'm sure the King's Guard, wherever they are right now, can hear her. "Come on now, it wasn't that bad, was it?"

Raven wipes a tear from her eye. "Sorry, sorry. It reminded me of when I was ten years old and my friends taught me how to fight. I swear my arms and legs were limp as noodles."

I laugh at the image now gracing my mind.

"But if I could learn, so can you. Now, widen your base of support," she says.

I take a step back to broaden my stance.

"A little farther." Raven's hand slides down the outside of my thigh and pulls it back.

The spot where her fingers hold me sparks a pulsing heat in other parts of my body. I just hope she can't hear my heart pounding in my chest.

"And your arms…" She stands up behind me, holding each of my wrists to adjust the rest of my posture. "You want to be like this."

My breath hitches when her body presses against mine, my back feeling her every curve, her breath tickling my neck.

"Like that?" I squeak.

Raven smiles and I swear her words come out like a purr. "*Just like that*."

I turn my head slightly, wondering if she's going to kiss me, or what would be to my surprise if I kissed her.

But her body seizes up, and my hopes sink in disappointment.

"Is there something wro—"

Raven cuts me off. "What the *devils*? Cadence, look!"

My focus follows her pointing finger to a spiral of sand sweeping across the dusty plain before us. The sand swirls upward, from a tiny point on the bottom and becoming wider at the top. It spins like a top across the sand, uprooting the sparse trees and plants as it circles like a tornado, growing larger and wilder, zigzagging in an unpredictable pattern.

"Damn it!" I scream, shoving the dagger back into Raven's hand.

Combat practice will have to wait because this little knife isn't going to do anything against the impending twister.

Clove and King rise on their hind legs, neighing in obvious fear as their front ones kick wildly like the storm.

Raven rushes to pat their muzzles and calm them. Her hair and cloak fly every which way like mine as the wind picks up speed. "We have to find shelter!" she yells through the deafening roar.

I struggle through the sand, running as fast as I can to help her hold the horses, holding onto their bridles. Squinting, I strain to make out the surrounding area despite the setting sun. "I don't see anything for miles."

"And we're nowhere close to Jessen."

I press my lips together, fighting to ease my racing heartbeat. "Our only option is to outrun it."

Raven's expression drops. "I...I don't know if we can do that."

"We have to try!" I hop into the front seat of the cart and grab Clove's reins.

Raven settles beside me and does the same with King's.

I try to speak again, but sand flies into my mouth. I sputter, tasting the gritty grains that make my throat like sandpaper. A huge gust blows in our faces and I shield myself with my cloak. Once it dies down, I point forward and to the left, where the sandstorm is waning slightly.

The whole scene looks testy, but it's our best chance of making it out alive.

The horses' muscles tense in protest at our command.

I scream as another flurry of sand shoots past us. Like a whip, the threat jolts the horses and they're ready to roll, breaking out into a gallop. They trample over the few small plants growing in this desert and send the carriage to the right with a jolt, almost tipping us over.

I can barely see five feet in front of the horses, but we try to steer them around the eye of the storm. The sand tornado moves like it's chasing us, and I direct Clove to pick up the pace. But we're still going too slowly.

"Maybe we should ditch the cart?" I yell, hoping Raven can hear me over the whooshing, dusty maelstrom.

"There's no time!" she calls back.

I swivel to find the natural disaster keeping up with us. "It's gaining on us!"

"Keep pushing!" Raven shouts, spitting sand out of her mouth.

King and Clove are now running at full speed, and it seems like we might avoid this thing if we can keep the same pace. But out of nowhere, another sand tornado kicks up, cutting across our path.

Predictably, the animals rear back on their hind legs.

The momentum knocks me back and I'm thrown from my seat. My arms flail, trying to hold on to the side of the cart, but the sand makes it hard and my hand slips.

I land hard on my right elbow, making it throb. I grit my teeth and work to stand. A blur of white and gold flashes across my vision as the distant neighs of the horses echo in my ears before I collapse into darkness.

EIGHTEEN

When I come to, I see a bright light on the other side of my closed eyelids—I'm dead. How many times have I almost died since starting this journey? And now I have before I could get any answers?

But—wait a minute—I'm alive. I'm thinking. I'm breathing.

My fingertips curl around the comfort and cushion of soft linen and I realize I'm lying on my back. I can't hear a raging sandstorm, so that's a good sign. But then less happy sensations creep in. Sand particles stick to my tongue, and my elbow aches.

When I open my eyes, a cream-colored domed ceiling greets me.

"Cade!" Raven rushes over to me, filling my vision with her own concerned brown eyes.

I scratch at my hair and try to sit up. "Wha...what did you call me?" I ask in a stupor.

"Oh, Cade!" She helps me up, propping some pillows behind my back before hug-tackling me. Or is it tackle-hugging?

Either way, I don't mind it one bit. I'm only thrown off by her nickname—exactly what Al calls me...

"Where...are we?" I survey the one-room home. I'm on a bed. Raven must have been on the couch, where a rumpled blanket and a dented pillow lie.

A small kitchen sits in one curve of the building, and next to that are a chair and a table. The space is barely furnished, but the decorations make up for it. Gold and silver trinkets, sculptures, and knickknacks adorn every inch of the dwelling.

"We're still on the outskirts of Jessen, but far from the Ivory Sands—and the sandstorm. Are you okay?" Raven brushes a lock of hair out of my face, curling it behind my ear.

If I didn't die from the storm, I probably will now from her tenderness. How am I supposed to survive the rest of this trip?

"I should be fine." I rub my arm. "Elbow's a little sore, and there's sand in places that never see the light of day, but nothing a little cleaning and resting won't fix."

"Good." Raven sighs in relief, too concerned to react to my joke. "And what about you?"

"Eh, I'm fine. I've got a few bruises, but as long as you're okay, that's all that matters. Anyway, Aura should be back soon. She's searching for any other travelers that need help out there."

"Aura?" I blink.

Raven grins. "She saved us. And get this..." Her grin widens. "She's a mage."

NINETEEN

A tall, toned girl bursts through the doors as if on cue. Her dread-locks swing as she walks, gold bangles jangling along with them on her wrists. She's like a desert spirit, wearing a white cloak with a turban head wrap and with skin darker than Raven's.

That attention-grabbing presence Raven has? Well, this Aura girl has it, too.

"Oh, good! You're up!" she says, marching over to me and kneeling. "Are you hurt?" She doesn't wait for my reply, instead inspecting me for cuts or bruises.

"I'm a little sore, but I'll be okay. Thank you," I respond in awe.

This girl just saved us from a freaking natural disaster, after all.

"You're very welcome. I'm Aura. Raven told me you're Cadence?"

I nod.

"Did you find anyone else?" Raven asked.

Aura shook her head. "Thankfully, no. It's as if the sands were only after you two."

I push myself upright more with my right hand and wince in pain. I forgot I have to take it easy. "Could a mage have sent it?"

"I don't think so. Never seen any magi power do that," Aura replies. "Why would you have a mage after you?"

"I would put nothing past my parents. But if a mage can't do that, it definitely can't be their or King Pontifex's doing." I sigh, settling in my seat.

Now that I'm more alert, I have a better look at my surroundings. It's clear Aura lives alone. The place is like Beardy's bedroom—one bed, couch, and dresser. But this space is much nicer than the pub. Each piece of furniture has white with gold accents, matching the girl's attire. The knickknacks I examine look like animals—cats, birds, and...horses!

"Oh, my gods, what about Clove and King?" I ask, snapping back to the moment at hand.

Our host scrunches her face before her features soften in realization. "Ah, you mean your horses. They're outside, safe and sound."

"What happened?" I ask as Aura straightens and walks to hang up her cloak on the back of the door. "How did you save us? And Raven...she says you're a mage?"

She spins around and places her hands on her hips, head held high. "Loud and proud. I don't care what the king says. We're allowed to exist."

My eyebrows rise. So, the *king* knows about the magi. What, does the whole freaking country know about them but me and Al? "And...so you used your curse to save us?"

Aura laughs. "Curse? Oh no, this is our power. If mine were a curse, well, then I wouldn't have saved your lives, right?"

"I, uh, I guess I never thought about it. I thought mine was a gift until Raven told me someone cursed me. But my abilities have helped me out quite a bit on my journey."

Aura's dreadlocks fall to one side as she tilts her head. "You... you're a mage, too?"

A sinking feeling falls from my chest to my belly. Oh, my gods. I just revealed to someone about my power. Not the specifics, but still. My eyes dart to the door and I'm tempted to run away. Mother and Father always told me to keep it a secret. Apart from Raven, who already knew, no one outside of my family knows.

I must do a poor job of hiding how distraught I am because Aura rushes over to me again and grabs my hands. "Oh, I'm sorry. Don't be afraid. I'm a lover of both magi and Unremarkables. If you want this to remain a secret, my lips are sealed."

"Unremarkables?"

"Humans. Non-magic folk," Raven answers. She fiddles with a crooked trinket on the wall, adjusting it before traveling her hands along the wall back to her couch bed.

"Okay. Good to know. So, how did you save us? And why? You didn't have to." I don't want to be annoying and ask so many questions, but we were in a sandstorm one minute, and now I'm here. Surely, it's not too much to expect some answers?

"I try to aid travelers across Soridente, especially on the outskirts of Jessen. Usually, it's people trying to enter the city."

"Is it true there are magi in Jessen?"

"Yes, but there are humans, too. There, they aren't called Unremarkables. In Jessen, there is no difference between those with magic and those without. Everyone lives in equality and peace. They are the Everyfolk."

"That sounds awesome."

Aura smiles. "We are. Partly thanks to Bidyzen."

I bounce on the bed, nearly jumping in recognition. "Bidyzen! That's…didn't you tell me about him, Raven?"

She nods in response, grabbing one of the stone pieces off a shelf. Does she ever not have something in her hands?

Aura flings a dreadlock behind her back. "Now *there's* a king if I've ever seen one. Bidyzen is everything Goldin is not. He's kind and understanding, but also strong and assertive. He doesn't rule with a…shall we say…*golden* fist?"

I squeeze the pillow with each word she speaks, my anticipation rising. "Wow. Can I meet him someday?"

"Definitely! Even though we are equal with Unremarkables, we magi stick together and confront each other's challenges!"

"So, what kind of mage are you?" Magi etiquette is a mystery to me, so I hope I'm not overstepping any boundaries by asking.

Before I know it, Aura's no longer beside me. Instead, she's standing clear across the room by Raven.

I blink to ensure my vision hasn't betrayed me. Maybe I hit my head during the sandstorm, too? "What the—how did you…?"

Then the girl returns to my side in the blink of an eye. "I'm a Transport Mage. Goodbye, dangerous sand tornado. Hello, home sweet home."

My nerves act electrified with how giddy I am, like when you shiver, but not from the cold. "That. Is. So. Cool!"

"And what are you?" Aura asks naturally.

"I uh…I'm a Diamond Mage? I…uh…I can cry diamonds." The words come out jumbled and awkward. They're not used to spilling from my tongue as it's not a question I have to answer every day.

"Well, blessed be the gods. You're a rare one, aren't you?"

I turn to Raven for solace, every part of me a ball of nerves, but she's still focusing on her latest distraction.

"I didn't know. I…hope you don't mind if I don't show you? It's pretty painful."

Aura shakes her head. "Oh no. Not at all!"

I'm grateful, though I plan on leaving some diamonds under her pillow before we leave as thanks for saving our lives.

"What other powers do magi have?" I ask, hoping to direct attention away from me.

"Oh, there are so many. Too many to count!"

"You'll discover plenty of them, soon enough, Cade," Raven assures, finally speaking up and placing the stone back on the shelf.

Aura walks to the kitchen counter and pulls out three cups and a pitcher of water for the three of us. "You're from Noravale, correct? You two are a long way away from home."

Raven's serious expression tells me I shouldn't correct Aura that only *I'm* from Noravale. I don't know why she would want to keep it a secret—hells, I don't even know where home is for her. I guess it's nowhere and everywhere at the same time.

"Yeah, but we're traveling to Kinephrus. I need answers about my power."

"Aren't you in luck, then?" Aura hands us each a glass of water.

I chug mine in one gulp.

Raven does the same.

"Not sure how many drinks it'll take to remove this sand from my mouth," Raven says, smacking her lips in disgust.

"Maybe there's a mage for that?" I joke.

Aura laughs and Raven covers her mouth to stifle her own amusement at my quip.

"So, Aura," I change subjects. "Is your power enough to bring us to Kinephrus?"

"If that's what you want. Transport Magi with weaker powers can only teleport short distances by themselves. But I've been practicing since I was in the womb. Literally—that's how I was born. My mother didn't have a natural birth or any intervention. I just popped right into the doctor's arms."

"Wow. That's, uh, impressive," Raven says, raising her eyebrows.

"Yeah, so even though I'm only seventeen, I can take…about five people at a time with me across cities. I'm still working on distance and increasing my carrying capacity. So, thanks for the practice."

I chuckle. "You're welcome, I guess."

"It's pretty late out, and no one in Kinephrus will be up, so it's best if we go in the morning—if that's okay with both of you?"

Raven purses her lips. "I prefer traveling at night, but I agree with you."

"It's settled then!"

I'm starry-eyed that she's a mage at all–the first one I've met besides myself! It's crazy to realize.

After Raven and I take turns washing in the bath, we both feel a little more human again. We help Aura cook dinner and choose to sit in a circle around the center of her home since she has one kitchen chair. We eat our food and talk. Once yawning takes over the conversation, I'm kind of sad because Aura's been pretty cool, and I've gotten to learn a bit more about Raven.

I'd still like to learn more. I hope she wants to know more about me, too.

At my insistence, Aura takes her bed back while Raven and I sit on the couch, talking deeper into the night. We keep our voices down so as not to stir our host. I don't know how much sleep a Transport Mage needs, but more is probably better, right?

"I can't sleep. I'm too excited about tomorrow!" I kick my legs like a giddy little kid.

Raven crosses her legs and smiles. "I am, too."

"So…" I turn serious now, staring at my hands in my lap. "There's been something I've been meaning to tell you. But I'm nervous."

"Well, you *have* to tell me now."

"Only if you tell me a secret about you."

"That's not fair!"

I lightly shove her to the side. "It's *only* fair."

She raises her arms up in defeat. "Okay. You've convinced me."

I bite my lip. Gods, I'm too anxious to speak now. "You go first."

"What? No, no, no. That's not how this works."

"Please? I *promise* I'll tell you."

Raven gives a dramatic sigh, though the corners of her mouth lift. "Fine. This is a pretty big thing. Not many people know about it other than the other Prowlers. Well, and my parents."

"Is it okay if Aura overhears?"

A light snore proves she's still sound asleep.

Raven rubs the back of her head. "Sure, it's okay. I'm just like her, after all."

I cock an eyebrow before both rise high on my forehead. "Wait… what? You're…you're a Transport Mage?"

"Girl, you think I'd have tormented myself on this journey if I could've teleported us to Kinephrus? I'm a Shadow Mage."

"Didn't you tell me you weren't a mage?"

Hurt tries to settle in my chest, but I realize it's dumb to get upset with her secrets when I've kept my own. And at least she's telling me now, right?

Raven fiddles with the end of a pink curl. "Yeah. But, like I said, not many people know. It's how I'm such a successful thief. You wondered how I got into the royal palace. How I prevented us from getting caught by Captain Rioza and the King's Guard? I used my powers. It's why I work at night. I've got all the darkness I need."

I stare at her in silence. "It all makes sense now," I finally manage. My jaw must be permanently unhinged at this point. I'm constantly learning new things that shock me into silence. "So…you can create shadows or something?"

"Or become a shadow myself. It's pretty fun." She grins, but it quickly fades. "Except…that's why my parents abandoned me. I was a normal human baby when I was born. But then the War of Humanity happened between the magi and humans—Unremarkables—whatever you want to call them…magi infiltrated our town, and my parents fended off a couple, but one touched me and gave me my curse. It has to happen in the first week of life, or they can't pass magic on."

"Is that what happened to me?"

The light ticking of the clock on the wall fills the small moment of silence.

"It must have. In my case, my parents didn't know it at the time. I didn't start using my power until I was ten. It freaked them out. And when the Goldin War happened, the magi came and destroyed our town. My parents lost everything." She stands, fists clenched. The low light creates a halo around her silhouette. "They couldn't afford to care for me, so they abandoned me. But I knew it was because they feared my Shadow magic."

I hold back the choice words I'd like to use and say, "That's horrible." I want to reach out and settle her, but my nerves keep my hands in my lap.

"Yeah. But then I never would've met the Prowlers. They found me failing to steal some fruit from a marketplace and raised me in their band of thieves."

"They're like your real family, right?"

"Yeah. Not sure if we'll ever come back together again. But yeah, so…" She sits, slapping her hands on her thighs. "That's my secret."

"Thank you for sharing that with me. I never would've guessed. I don't even know about all those wars and stuff you're talking about."

"No worries, Cade." She rests her palm on mine.

I revel in her nearness—all of it—her breath, the scent of ivory soap on her skin, her very being down to the rawest parts. My cheeks burn as her touch pulls me back to earlier in the day. When I wondered if we'd kiss. "So, you've heard me call Allegra by her nickname, Al. What you don't know is that she's the only one who calls me Cade. It threw me off at first when you said that…but I don't mind it. It's like having a piece of her with me."

"Well, you can call me Rave, Rae, whatever you want. And hey, that wasn't your secret, was it?"

"Okay, I'll call you Rae. And no, that wasn't my secret, but I wish it was." I laugh, adjusting the couch cushion behind my back to hide my shyness. Gods, this girl is everything. She's easy to talk to and she understands me. It's given me enough confidence to push me to continue. *Here goes, Cadence. You can do this.* "Okay, so, you know how you told me before that you're into girls?"

"Yep."

I smile at her casualness. She's not nervous or scared or ashamed. I'm definitely not—I'm just not used to embracing this part of myself. "Well, I'm into girls, too."

Raven squeezes my hand. "Girl, that isn't a secret! I couldn't miss your googly eyes at me if I tried."

We stick out our tongues at each other before snickering.

"But I'm half and half—or maybe three quarters to one quarter? I'm not sure. I haven't been able to do anything about my feelings."

"It's totally cool that you like both genders," Raven reassures me. "As long as you're into girls in any capacity, I'm happy. And I *guess* I'll accept that as your secret."

I bite my lip and twist my head away, trying to hide my flushing face. "Good, because, I really, really like you. A lot."

Raven inches closer to me on the couch, then she cups my cheek, turning my head to face hers. With a voice both sweet and seductive, she says, "Well, what do you know? I really, really like you, too. Like, a *lot.*"

And then her lips are on mine. They're soft and tantalizing, and I swear I'm melting right into this couch right now. Her lips are warm, kissing me tenderly, and I kiss her back with all the yearning I've built up this week. I slip a hand around her waist and pull her in, eliminating any distance between us because right now, I can't get enough of her.

Her arms wrap around my neck in response. The parts of my bare skin she touches with her hands tingle in pleasure, electrified. And it feels. So. *Right.*

When we reluctantly break away, I'm sure I'm all sorts of hot and bothered. But I love the sensation. "I'm not scared anymore."

"Of what?" she asks, as breathless as I am.

"Of us…this…"

Raven leans in and plants a shorter but equally enticing kiss on my lips. "You're the best thing that's ever happened to me, Cade."

I fall asleep in her arms for the rest of the night, nuzzled into her side, safe and secure. I've never slept beside another girl—or guy—before. Not like this. And it is absolutely remarkable.

TWENTY

The next morning, I wake on my side, my head snuggled into Raven's shoulder. Her arm drapes around me, the weight of it comforting me down to my bones. I'm probably wearing the goofiest smile right now, and I turn to watch her sleep—but not in that creepy way.

Soon enough, her eyes flutter open. At first, she acts confused.

A spark of worry hits me, and I wonder if she regrets our kisses last night.

But then a huge grin spreads on her face, melting my insecurities faster than spring does winter.

We sit up on the couch in a tangle of limbs.

"Morning, lovebirds," Aura says from the kitchen, less than ten feet away.

I blush, unsure how to respond.

Raven hooks an arm around my shoulders. "Yep, aren't we the cutest?" She flashes her pearly whites.

Aura smiles. "You are."

I admire Raven's openness. With time, I hope to be as forthcoming, letting my outside reflect all that I feel on the inside.

Aura moves on, as if this is an everyday thing for her. "Remember, today you meet the Archmage."

"I can't believe it!" Nervous energy swells in my chest and I inhale deeply, slowly blowing out my breath to calm myself.

"I'll make sure you're prepared for the adventure ahead." Aura opens a small cooler, searching its contents. "Does oatmeal, eggs, and bacon sound good?"

"Well, I—"

"Cade's a vegetarian, so no bacon for her. But I think we're good on the rest, right?" Raven asks.

My heart warms. Raven's learned so much about me in such a short time. It makes me appreciate her all the more. I rub her arm which naturally settled on my shoulder like a glove. "Yeah, that sounds great."

Aura whips up the meal and serves us at the couch while she eats at the table.

"This is delicious," I say between spoonfuls of oatmeal that I doused in brown sugar. "Thank you again, Aura."

"Do we *have* to leave?" Raven laughs before scooping scrambled eggs into her mouth.

"My pleasure." Aura raises her glass of juice, and we raise ours in a toast. "To adventure?" she proposes.

I smirk and turn to Raven. "We've already been on one. So, here's to our next adventure."

"To our *next* adventure!" Raven clinks her glass against mine and we drink and eat to our hearts content.

After breakfast, we quickly packed up our belongings, now even more eager for the day ahead.

Aura searches the drawers of a side table. "You'll find plenty of goods in Kinephrus, so you should be set for now. But let me know if you think of anything else you need."

"What about the horses?" I ask.

"You shouldn't need them once you're in the city. It might be hard to maneuver around with them given how the city is built," she explains.

"Really? How so?"

"You'll see," Raven adds with her signature wink.

I sling my bag over my shoulder. "Okay. Thanks for the tease." I chuckle, then turn my attention back to Aura. "Is it okay if we leave them with you for the time being? I'm expecting to return home after all this, so…" The thought of Al being so far away from me still hurts, but knowing I'll be back with her with answers makes this whole journey worth it.

Aura nods. "Sure, I'd love the company!"

"I'll be right there," I say.

I wait until the door shuts, then quickly hide some diamonds under the pillow as a thank you before I exit her home and follow them. They stand next to another house near Aura's, one of a few smaller, domed ones. Our temporary dwelling's exterior is a smooth cream color—but this is my first time seeing it, since I was passed out when we were rescued.

"Aw!" This must be a barn or stable because the half-door is closed on the bottom, and Clove and King's heads are poking out of the open top. I pet both horses on their muzzles, and they nudge their heads into my hand in return. Could I take them home with me when I go back? Maybe I can give them to Beardy and the Better Days crew.

Outside, it doesn't look like a sandstorm hit the night before. There aren't many trees to shade the area, so the sun still beats down on us, but lush plant life surrounds us. It's weird to have the warmth on my skin because we've been working at night because… Raven's a Shadow Mage.

What other magi powers there are out there? I guess I'm going to find out soon. Will I find the other answers I've been searching for? Like how I became a mage? Can I get rid of my power? Can I help Al another way? I squint to make out the edges of a river in the distance, and that must be what's separating us from Jessen. Maybe I'll visit one day, but right now, I'm focused on only one thing. *Kinephrus.* The city of magi.

"Are you ready?" Aura asks.

"I'm ready!" Raven says, pumping her fist.

I shake my head from my musings. "Yeah. I...what if I don't find the answers I need?"

Raven plants a kiss on my cheek. "You will."

"Okay, then I'm ready." I say, beaming.

Aura stands between me and Raven. "All I need is a physical connection for my power to work. May I?" I have no idea what she's asking permission for, but I nod and Raven does the same. The Transport Mage places her hands, warm like the rays of the morning sun, on our shoulders. "All right, girls. Let's go to Kinephrus!"

An odd sensation ripples through my limbs, like I'm having an out-of-body experience but also feeling every part of myself at the same time, every nerve, vessel, tendon, sinew, and bone. And, in the blink of an eye, I'm no longer standing outside Aura's house.

I shield my vision from the same sun that's somehow brighter now. A grassy plain filled with the tallest towers I've ever seen lays before me. They stretch far higher than even the royal palace's spires. Colorful patterns on the walls and roofs break up the white of the buildings. They look like tall mosaics, some reflecting the light as if they're made of mirrors, others illuminating paintings that could tell a story. Midway up and at the top of each tower, walkways span from one building to another.

My eyes round, taking in the sights and sounds. Squinting in the sun, I make out tiny dots moving on the paths above us. They're people. No. *Magi*.

"What do you think?" Aura grins, folding her arms.

"It's more than I could've imagined." I knew Al and I were missing out on so much by being locked up inside, but I never could've guessed something like this existed. I fight the urge to dance around in excitement and turn to Raven.

She doesn't look as enamored by the city as I am. Expected, since she's seen this place before. Still, there's something in her expression I can't quite read.

Aura pulls her dreadlocks to one side, letting them drape over one shoulder. "Because you're both magi, you should be allowed in without a problem. There should be guards at the bases, Transport Magi in fact, who will let you up the towers."

"Why couldn't you transport us straight up?" I ask.

"The Archmage has rules here to protect her people. These," she gestures to the tall architecture, "prevent unwanted visitors and allow the city to thrive undisturbed."

"Got it."

"Is there anything else you need from me before I let you go?" Aura asks before I can inquire further.

Raven drapes her hood over her head. "Nope, we should be good. Thank you for saving our lives." She hugs Aura, and I do the same.

"You don't know how much this means to me. I hope we've done enough to repay you," I say.

"Repay me? No need for that. The Everyfolk are happy to help." And with that, she's gone.

I stare at the spot where she disappeared for a moment before turning back to the towers ahead—and Raven, who still wears a cryptic expression. "Is everything okay?" I ask.

"Huh?" she says a little too quickly.

Did she flinch, too?

"Oh, yeah, I'm fine," she continued. "It's just weird being back."

"Well? Come on! What are we waiting for?" My elbow feels a little better from yesterday, and I'm grateful the sandstorm didn't injure my legs when I sprint to the base of the nearest tower.

A woman with short, wavy blond hair and green eyes steps out from behind the tower. She's wearing a blue and silver short-sleeved robe. Clasped in the center is the same emblem I found under my parents' bed—the one that looks like overlapping flower petals, making a new and intricate flower design.

"Well, who do we have here?" she asks, folding her arms behind her back.

Even though I still don't know Magi etiquette, I bow as a sign of respect. That can't be wrong, right? "I'm Cadence Alero. I've come from far away to get answers about my past from Archmage Sanora after finding out I'm a mage last week."

The woman clasps her hands to her chest. "Oh my, I'm so sorry to hear. It's not the first time a new mage has come here, either because they never knew they had their power until only recently, or they knew about them but were finally ready for answers like you are now." Her sympathy drops as soon as she whips her head to Raven. "And you?"

My normally confident friend—and maybe more—tugs on her hood to better hide her face and clears her throat. "I've helped her on her journey. I'm Rae McKae."

The woman narrows her eyes. At last, she blurts out, "Cute name! My parents thought Cessi would be nice, but I so wish they'd named me Cassia or Celine. Oh, well!"

Raven keeps her head tilted down, and I find it odd that she gave them a nickname instead of her full name. In fact, I don't even know if McKae is her last name. Seemed like such a minor detail compared to everything I've been trying to catch up to speed on. And I've been too preoccupied to ask.

"So, why do you live in these towers?" I hope that's not a dumb question to ask, but I want to focus on getting more information instead of Raven's odd actions.

The guard's face falls. "Ever since the Goldin War, we were banished from the rest of Soridente. This is all we have. To keep out Unremarkables, and stay safe, we live up high. The only way to get up here is with a Transport Mage. Like me!"

"Oh, I'm glad that works out then."

"Well, you came at the...shall we say, perfect time? The magi have decorated every inch of Kinephrus for Tor's Celebration of Life." She looks up, admiring the streamers and strips of flowers dangling from the walkways.

"Tor?" I ask.

"Oh, my…" Cessi appears ready to rake her hand down her face in exasperation, but for my sake, she refrains. "He was Archmage Sanora's husband and died almost fifteen years ago. A real tragedy. She was never the same after that. So instead of getting hung up on the sorrow, we celebrate his life, and how we knew him before. And not for one day, but a whole week. Today is the beginning of it."

"That's really sad." My eyes itch as if they'll well up with diamond tears—which I guess would be okay in the city of magi. Still, I take a big gulp and try not to think about it too hard to avoid it. Raven's unusually quiet, so I ask, "Isn't that a shame, Rae?"

"Huh?" Raven raises her head to meet my gaze, looking as spacey as the moon. "Oh yeah, a real shame," she says in a monotone voice.

My forehead creases. What's going on? She didn't even acknowledge that I didn't call her Raven! *Whatever*. It must be weird to be back with her own kind. The heritage her parents had shunned.

I take her hand and give it a gentle squeeze. "Hey, it's okay."

When she still doesn't speak, I follow her gaze up the tower.

"Come on, let's climb!" the guard exclaims. She's got so much pep and excitement—I wish I could be as eager to use mine.

I'm glad I experienced the teleportation with Aura because traveling with Cessi is the same. She places her hands on our shoulders, zapping my whole body like every nerve is firing, and we're suddenly at the top of the tower.

Good thing I'm not afraid of heights. I haven't had enough experiences to get scared about things like that. The third floor of my home is as high as I've been until today.

I step out of the small alcove to the walkway. Decorations, lights, and more—just like back in Noravale when we celebrated Summer Solstice—fill the space. But these colors were much prettier. Do they have mages for this?

Up here, the air is fresher than on the ground—clean of pollution and the past. Standing here…it feels like starting over.

Cessi's cloak sways in the wind, her hair bobbing as she leads us to another set of guards. "These magi would like to meet with the Archmage. Cadence here only recently found out she's one of us," she chirps, pointing to me.

One of the guards, dressed like Cessi, steps forward. "And what are your powers? It is a requirement to reveal it before we take you to the Archmage."

I'm about to speak, but another guard cuts me off. "Hey, I think I know you!" He points to Raven.

She stiffens and suddenly looks like a corpse. I've never seen the color drain from her face so quickly.

"I-I'm Rae, a Shadow Mage. I've brought Cadence here with me. She's a Diamond Mage." She loops an arm around mine, but it seems more protective than loving.

Everyone's focus immediately zeroes in on me—wide, disbelieving, and in shock. Some of them whisper to themselves while others remain silent, unblinking. "Is there…something wrong?"

"We've got this from here, Cessi. Thank you," the first guard says. Cessi turns around and heads back where she came from, back down, I assume, to continue her duties.

As we stand there, some magi walk toward us. They're wearing beautiful headpieces and wraps, cloaks, jewelry, and belts, similar to Raven's attire but less dark. As they pass us by, their eyes linger on us for a while, curious as to what's going on. Though clearly, we shouldn't be cause for a spectacle?

"I'd like to present her to Archmage Sanora, please." Raven tilts her head up, but I catch the quiver in her bottom lip.

The second guard lumbers over to us, his arms covered from his wrists to his shoulders in tattoos. "Of course. Right this way." He sweeps his hand out for us to continue, so Raven pulls me by the hand to follow. I glance back at the guard marching behind us, catching his broad shoulders. When I face forward and study the two guards in front of us, I feel like a pig being led to the slaughter.

"Why are they acting like we're prisoners?" I ask, unease settling in my chest like heartburn. I wish I was a Transport Mage to leave this creepiness behind.

Raven waves off my concern. "Oh, don't worry, Cadence. They want to ensure we stay safe on our way to the Archmage."

"I'm meeting her right now?!"

Raven nods, keeping her focus straight ahead.

I frown. I don't know what's going on, but I don't like it. Still, I trust her. It's the only thing I can do. My trust is all I've had to go on this entire trip, since Raven first plucked my diamond tear off the ballroom floor to the kisses and fears and dreams we shared last night. And so, I let these guards lead us across the walkway. A couple of towers away, there's a tower that's thicker and fancier than the others, with a taller peak and more guards lined outside the perimeter. It must be where Sanora lives.

The silence is killing me, so I speak up. "So, Rae, you finally fulfilled your end of our deal. You brought me here to Kinephrus. I wish I'd brought the king's, er, *your* jewels, but I left them back in my room. Do you want diamonds instead?"

This time, Raven seems to notice I've used her nickname, but she doesn't say anything. "Oh, no, Cadence. I don't want any of that." She quickly swipes at her eyes.

"Are you…crying?"

"No, it's this wind. Altitude, am I right?" She chuckles nervously.

I thought my worry for Al was too much to bear, but this is pushing me over the edge. "You know you're one of the few people I can trust, right?"

"Yeah. Same here." She keeps walking, dismissing my concerns.

She leaves it at that, so I do, too. But I can't help feeling like this dread isn't all in my head. It's too familiar, but what can I do? I've traveled here with the promise of answers, and I'm finally about to get them.

TWENTY-ONE

I wish I could appreciate all the cool sights Kinephrus has to offer, but all I am is a bundle of nerves. I never thought to ask Raven anything more about the Archmage. I'm not sure if she even knows much about the Magi Queen, but it's too late now.

Before long, we reach the end of the walkway. Painted blue and gold swirls adorn the edge of the doorframe. It's mesmerizing. I snap to attention when the five guards there step to the side, allowing us passage.

"Show the Archmage respect," the tattooed guard commands—his tone threatening and not simply a gentle reminder.

I gulp as they push open the large double doors.

Inside, braided spiral columns dot the grand expanse, giving the room a whimsical feel. A cobalt blue rug underneath a tiled floor greets me, stretching from the entrance down a long hall. There are a few stairs where it ends. At the top, Archmage Sanora sits on her throne, which appears to be made of pure gold. I'm sure King Pontifex would like it—his might even look similar.

She stands when she notices our presence, sauntering forward with poise. As she saunters closer, I study her features. From her dominating presence to her extravagant attire, she looks every bit like a formidable Magi Queen.

She has brown skin and light brown twists tied into a braid draped over one shoulder. Gold beads sprinkle her hairstyle, matching the accents on her cobalt blue and black dress and cuffs around her upper arms that hold up a cape of a similar fabric. I'd admire her radiance more if she didn't scare the crap out of me.

"Who might you be?" she asks when she reaches us. Her voice is high but commanding and strong, the same as the strength in her toned arms.

The tattooed guard steps forward, gesturing to Raven. "This is Rae." Then he points to me. "And this, Your Majesty, is Cadence Alero—a Diamond Mage."

There it is again with the Diamond Mage bit. Is it *that* special? And isn't this supposed to be a curse? "Uh…" I swallow my nerves. "It's nice to meet you, Your Majesty. I've come a long way to get answers about my…power." My gaze flits to Raven to ensure I didn't speak out of line, but she misses the silent message, keeping her focus on the floor.

"That's a pretty bold move, coming back here, *Raven*," the Archmage spews.

She knows her real name? Obviously, they have some history— and it doesn't sound pleasant.

"You…know her?" I ask, still confused by what's happening.

The Archmage narrows her eyes and her lips press thin. "I wouldn't call it that, but I certainly recognize her as the little thief who tried to steal Tor's crown and escaped from my prison."

"What?" My stomach twists and I turn to Raven. The guards who brought us in tightly grip her arms. "W-what did you do?!"

"I'm sorry, Cade. It's all true."

She looks defeated. I've never seen her like this.

"But…why?"

"The jewels. I wanted to become rich."

My heart is threatening to burst from my ribcage. "W-what do you mean? I thought you didn't want my diamonds?"

Raven's face is impassive as she answers me. "And I don't. I was offered something better."

"Can we pick up the pace here?" Sanora asks no one in particular. "Raven is the least of my concerns." She focuses on me now, and I can't quite read the look in her eyes. But it reminds me of Rioza's expression—wild and crazy with reckless abandon.

"Not yet, Your Majesty. I need the money you promised as a reward for bringing the Diamond Mage to you," Raven says, not even looking at me. She should at least have the courage to face me when she's breaking my heart.

But I guess it doesn't matter because it's cracking down the middle whether she watches or not.

I can't help it. I'm crying now—Absolutely bawling. Diamonds clink to the floor, onto the tile, rug—everywhere. But the pain from each gem's cut is nothing compared to the sharp stabbing in my chest. "What deal? I...I'm so confused."

I stifle a sob, trying to get answers at the same time, but the Archmage cuts me off when I try to speak again. "*Tut tut*, this is what Raven wanted. Guards, can you please escort her to the parlor room for her reward?" Her voice is so cold, an icy imitation of our country's distant winter.

No one is who I thought they'd be.

"Wait, I need to talk to her!" She can't leave until she explains. I lunge for her, but the tattooed guard thrusts a hand toward me.

I can't move. I'm frozen in mid-motion, yet he hasn't laid one finger on me. Every muscle in my body is tensed, more than they already were. "Don't take her!" I cry out, still able to speak.

But Raven simply turns to me and shrugs, devoid of emotion. "I want to go." Then she turns around and lets the guards lead her to a set of doors on the right...and leaves me alone with the Queen of the Magi.

Once the double doors close with an echoing thud, I can lower my arm and leg. The mage who left must have been the one controlling me. I move freely, wiping at my eyes to compose myself. But it's *difficult*. This cannot be happening right now.

"Ah, there we go," Sanora says. "I'm sorry about the Trap Mage, but I couldn't let you leave when we have so much to talk about."

Clearly, she believes I'm not enough of a threat to need guards. She's probably right. What can diamond tears do to her? And she is the Archmage, after all. She must be powerful. I wonder what her power is?

She circles me, examining every angle as she talks. "Finally, the girl I've been looking for…"

I frown. "I came here for answers about my past and—"

"And answers you will get. I would never skip the chance to tell you what the Unremarkables have done to the magi—and all the horrible things your family has done to mine."

I fight to untangle the clues of my life to uncover what they could have done. Sanora's malice is undeniable, but it's not all directed at me.

I stand here as vulnerable as ever, wrought with heartbreak for Raven leaving me for some reward, but also, for whatever pain I may have unknowingly caused to the Archmage and my own kind. "What did my family do to you?"

Reminiscence transforms her expression.

I read sorrow and pain and anger.

"I doubt your parents told you," she sneers.

"You're right. They told me nothing, Archmage." I try to speak with respect, even though I'm hurting and angry, myself. "Last week was the first time I heard I was a mage. They told me I was born able to cry diamonds."

Sanora narrows her eyes. "Lies. My late husband, Tor, *gave* you that power."

My mouth drops. "W-what?"

"It was a power I wish he'd never given you…"

"Power? Raven told me it was a curse."

"She isn't wrong." Sanora's expression turns somber. "Power is both a blessing and a curse. Magi used to roam and live amongst the Unremarkables. We wanted to spread the gifts we were given to increase our population. But King Pontifex saw this as a threat and began the Goldin War."

Her expression hardens. "It ended in a stalemate. So, we agreed upon a treaty that he would leave us alone if we stayed within eastern Soridente and didn't meddle in human lives outside our city." She fiddles with the beads in her braid. "Despite our agreement, Unremarkables still regularly and secretly worked with magi. Your parents were—maybe are *still*—among them."

A pit forms in my gut, the same kind that does when I'm forced to cry for Mother and Father. The same one I got every time Al's symptoms worsened. I know where this story is going. But I keep my lips sealed so I can find out the truth.

She stalks around the hall, weaving around the tall silver columns scattered throughout the room. "A mage must cast a spell to bless a human during the baby's first week of life, otherwise the power won't transfer. Your parents asked Tor to do this when you were born. They were only supposed to benefit from your skill for a short time, a year at most, before they had to give you back to the mage who blessed you—my husband."

"Wait...my birthday is in a week. And that's..."

"The anniversary of the day he died. Your parents accepted the price. However, when my husband came to collect you on your first birthday and bring you back to Kinephrus—and me—they killed him." Her voice trembles.

It isn't glaringly obvious, but it's enough for me to know that she hides her sorrows, and stuffs her pain deep inside. Just like me.

"I'm...so sorry..." But the words come out as a puny mumble, as if I'd never said them. I wonder if the magi emblem my parents kept was Tor's. "Am I a Diamond Mage because Tor was, too?"

"No. He only imbued you with the gods-granted power of the magi. What skill manifests in you is entirely up to them," she explains, almost gently.

Curiosity gets the better of me because I haven't heard anyone talk about a royal consort or anything like that. "Did you remarry?"

"Of course, not! What kind of mage do you think I am?" she exclaims, as if the notion is absolutely ridiculous. "I would never betray Tor. I never graced an Unremarkable with my power after that either. No one deserved it because *he* didn't deserve to die."

For a moment the way her bottom lip trembles and the glistening of her eyes make me think she's going to cry. But then she turns her attention to a statue next to her throne.

I can only guess it's a bust of her late husband.

"And you know what part hurt the most about what your parents did? Tor was a Sentinel Mage. He built the city of Kinephrus with his own hands. He created every tower, every wall for our protection. But the part of his power that stings the most, is that he could make himself as strong as steel, too. So, when your parents killed him, it was worse—because it shows how much he *trusted* them."

I never thought I would cry my diamond tears so willingly and out in the open. The pile building on my boots will never repay Sanora and doesn't act as reparations, but it has to be worth something.

"And so, from that moment on, I made a promise that anyone who found the Diamond Mage, for whom my husband died, would receive not only a reward of riches but also one thing they desire. Any request. I swore it on Tor's grave. I tried to use my magic to find you, but that Shadow Mage held a veil of darkness over you so I could not."

My thoughts immediately zero in on the weird shadow bird I'd seen in the sky when Raven and I escaped from Noravale. So, it *was* a mage—and the queen at that!

"Archmage Sanora," I say softly. "There's nothing I can say to bring Tor back or to make up for the pain my family has caused you. But I'm going to apologize anyway. I'm so, so sorry."

She doesn't even acknowledge my words. I'd hoped her grudge hadn't extended to me, but now I'm not too optimistic.

"Tor deserves to have his killers pay for what they've done. And that brings us to why you're here."

I gulp. "Which is?"

She grins deviously. "You're going to help me enact my revenge." She stalks forward and I back up with each step, stumbling when my boot catches on the edge of the cobalt rug. "If you hate them, then you won't mind me using you to get back at them."

"But...if you wanted revenge on them, why didn't you go after them in the first place?"

The Archmage *tsks*. "I won't be the one to break our treaty. If I could kill every Unremarkable as retribution, it still wouldn't make up for my loss. But more importantly, I refuse to leave my people behind. They are my family...my *only* family. I won't risk Pontifex ambushing our city the second I leave. I don't trust any human, let alone a *certain* mage."

I silently curse Raven for her stupidity in adding to the queen's ire and let the Archmage continue.

"And I needed you as proof. I figured your parents kept you hidden away for their selfish needs. It's why they broke our deal— broke their promise to my husband."

I want to run behind one of the swirling columns in the room, to hide from Sanora's rage for eternity. But my feet are glued in place as if that Trap Mage from earlier still has a hold on me. "Archmage, I hear you. I hear you and I'm sorry. But like your people are your family, my parents are still *my* family. They are all I have. I don't want you to hurt them."

"Don't worry, I won't be hurting them directly. I'll be hurting you instead. Surely, that would hurt them, wouldn't it?"

"Please don't." I raise my hands in defense. "I hate my parents as much as you do..."

"Well, then you're about to hate them even more."

I wipe at my cursed diamond tears. I don't even try offering them to her. I know she'll only accept blood for blood. My mind races and

148

I say the first thing that comes to my mind. "Raven's going to come back for me."

Sanora's laugh rattles the walls. "You're still hung up on that girl? She *used* you. She was in it for the money. She got what she wanted, and now she's gone."

I can't argue with her.

Raven showed me she doesn't care, loud and clear.

Still, I don't want to believe it. "How do you know?"

The Magi Queen wraps a finger around one of her beaded braids, like she's trying to wrap me around her finger, too. "No magi power in all the land can save you from what I have planned."

"W-what are you going to do to me?"

Sanora steps over the treasure I cried on the floor and looms over me. "Oh, you'll see, little Diamond Mage…"

TWENTY-TWO

Vertical prison bars fill my vision, and behind that, a gray, stone hallway, while I'm stuck in this tiny chamber. A stale stench of mold and sitting water fills the air. I'm surprised I haven't needed to swat away any flies in this festering waste hole.

The woman meant to be the answer to the mystery of my life turned out to be my worst nightmare, punishing me for others' actions. A whole journey…just to be trapped in another prison. Lovely.

Needing to burn off some anxiety, I start pacing.

All the new information shakes me down to my marrow. The queen's husband gave me my cur—power.

No wonder my parents called it a gift. It was a gift—from Tor.

And they murdered him. All because of their greed. If they were like that from the start, no wonder nothing I did or said changed their minds. *Nothing* could tip the scales in my favor.

Tired of walking the short width of my cell, I settle on a cloth cot I'm afraid will break under my weight. Despite my situation, I snicker, thinking this place isn't too shabby. After all, back in Tosca, Raven and I slept on dirty bales of hay in a dilapidated barn. The memory jolts me back to Raven's betrayal.

I lie on my side, facing the wall, trying to forget all the hurt she's caused me.

Another prisoner bangs against their bars. A mage guard yells at them to stop, but they don't.

I want to drown out the noise and my thoughts, but with what? Without an effective distraction, I can only worry how Archmage Sanora plans to use me against my parents.

Is Raven long gone by now with her reward? I guess that's why she didn't mind losing her stolen treasure from the Goldins, and explains why she never asked me for a single product of my power. But instead of simply taking a couple of diamonds from me, she took so much *more*.

Raven said I was the best thing that's ever happened to her. Was it because she actually liked me or only because she was going to turn me in to the Archmage for money? I bite back tears at the thought of whether it was all a lie.

Gods, how could I have been such a fool? I've read about stupid romances in books. Al and I made up plenty of stories about the couples we'd see walking outside our home. All heartache. All drama. I should've known it wasn't all just fantasy. The tropes came from *somewhere*.

Guess my parents were keeping me safe from *something*, after all.

I groan and roll onto my other side, again facing the bars. Why couldn't I have become a Transport Mage so I could bust out of this prison?

Hold on. Raven escaped once before, right? But she's a freaking Shadow Mage, and I only cry diamonds. There's no way I can use my power to escape. I puff out an exasperated sigh before an idea hits me. The plan plays in my head perfectly. I just hope it will work.

I spring to a sitting position, my eyes tracking the guard when he walks past my cell.

I stand and run to the barrier, my fingers wrapping around the bars. Then I peer left and right, down the empty corridors. Good. He's all alone. "Guard? Excuse me? *Guard?*"

The guy stops and backs up until he's in front of me again. He's younger and looks to be in his early twenties, so maybe he's new. His uniform is the same as all the other guards I've seen, but also has a visor. Abnormally purple hair sticks out from underneath like a fern. "What do you need?" he says with a gruff. "Lunch isn't for another two hours."

Okay, not the brightest of responses, but he isn't opposed to talking, so that's a good sign. "I...I only want to talk. I just found out I was a mage last week, and a Diamond Mage at that. I was so excited to meet my own people, well, and now...this." I twist to show the depressing cell.

"That's not my problem. I'm not supposed to talk to prisoners."

I pout, my fingertips curling even tighter around the bars, willing my desperation to reach him. "Oh, okay. I wish I knew that magi were bad. I would've never come here..."

"Hey! We're not *bad*. Not any worse than those Unremarkables you've lived with for years."

I hold my hands up in defense. There's no need to lie to him, and every word I speak next is the truth. "I didn't say they weren't. I know how evil they can truly be—even to those they call family."

At first, it appears I've struck a chord with the guard, maybe jolted some memories that he can relate to, but he narrows his eyes at me and takes a step back. "Good thing you aren't anywhere near them," he says, twirling a ring of keys on one finger. "Now, that's enough with the sob story. You don't think that's been used on me before?" he scoffs, scowling at me. "Best shut your trap before I find a mage who'll do it for you."

"I only figured you'd like some diamonds for all the trouble I've caused here."

The young guard shifts his weight onto his heels and crosses his arms. "Trust me, Sanora's paying me plenty to keep the likes of you locked up. And besides, she specifically put me here because of my power. If they think I can't use it correctly, I'll lose more than just my job."

"What's your ability?" I ask, wondering if he'll humor me with a response.

"I'm a Trap Mage. *I'm* keeping all of you inside your cells," he proudly declares.

"Whoa…that's…crazy. How does that work exactly?"

His tense muscles ease slightly as he remembers he's the one in control. "It means we don't need bars, or even doors at all."

"Damn, that's intense."

"Exactly," he says. "So, don't even try it—whatever '*it*' is. As long as I'm here, you're not going anywhere." Then he walks away with a whistle on his lips and a new pep in his step.

I shuffle backward further into my cell and huff out a breath, sending the hair in front of my face upward. So much for that.

I plop onto the measly cot and lift my knees to my sternum, burying my head between folded arms. Familiar, pathetic desperation settles like heartburn in my chest, a nagging, searing pain I can't get rid of. Usually, it likes to manifest into tears, but I'm surprised to find my eyes are dry, like I've got no tears left to cry after Raven's betrayal. I squeeze my eyelids closed until the burning dissipates.

After a while, I awake on my side, one knee bent over the side of the cot and one arm flung over my head. How I managed to sleep even a wink is beyond me. My grief must have made me so exhausted that the whole Better Days crew could've been drinking and laughing outside my cell and I would've still been snoozing and drooling like a baby amidst the hopelessness of my present situation.

I stretch my limbs and rub the back of my neck, which feels stiff from sleeping at a crooked and awkward angle. My muscles tense again at the sound of voices in the hall. They sound like they're coming from a couple of cells down, but I can still make out the words. I press myself against the stone wall and sneak closer to the door.

"But between us, I'm quite intrigued that she's a Diamond Mage. She's the only one I've met!"

It's the guard I spoke to!

"Really?" a young woman, from the sounds of it, says. "I wish I wasn't put on the northwest tower. Gods, no one ever goes there. It's like all I'm doing is keeping myself from falling asleep. I figured I'd stop by to see some excitement on my break."

She must be another guard. I lower myself to the floor. I need to pretend that I'm sleeping and not eavesdropping on their conversation in case they pass by.

The Trap Mage seems eager to have someone to talk to besides us conniving prisoners. "There have only been a few in our history. She's rare. Kind of royalty."

Man, how is he so enamored by my Diamond Mage status but not enough to let me go?

"Yes, that's true," his companion answers.

Boots clop against the stone floor, but it sounds more like pacing back and forth.

"But you'd think Sanora would appreciate the girl for having one of the rare abilities," he continues.

"What do you mean?"

"It's interesting—any human given power by a magi is essentially seen as their child. And the Archmage is barren—that's why Tor did it so much."

"Wow. So, what does that make this girl—whatever her name is? Is she…?"

"Her adopted daughter? Yeah."

I clamp my hands over my mouth to stifle a gasp.

"And, apparently," the guy continues, "she's the only one left. Sanora never remarried after Tor died. And she has never imprinted on a human out of distrust. Supposedly, the other magi Tor made died during the Goldin War. Tragic."

"Oh…then that means…"

"This Diamond Mage is the long-lost heir to the Magi Kingdom."

If I hadn't been sitting, surely, I would've stumbled backward and collapsed. This cannot be happening right now!

If what the guards say is true, then the Archmage can't keep me in this cell until I rot. She can't kill me as revenge for my parents killing Tor, right? I press my fingers against my temples and rub them to stop the throbbing in my skull, a feeble attempt at composing myself.

The guards are still talking but their words are hazy, like fuzz in my ears through my shock. It's like trying to listen to someone speak underwater.

Think, Cadence, think.

Aura lives on the outskirts of Jessen. She says magi and Unremarkables live as equals — the Everyfolk — there and that it's better than being kept apart. Maybe I could take Al with me.

Al.

I can't stay here sulking. She's waiting for me back home. Whether I'm Sanora's daughter through magic or not, I refuse to leave my sister alone with our parents a moment longer. And that's why I can't let these stone walls be the last thing that I see.

TWENTY-THREE

I have no idea what kind of mage the female guard is and what sort of curse—er, power—she possesses. But I have to work with what I've got. And what I have are diamonds. The few I was able to cry are still lying on the cot amidst the sheets, which are still wet from my runny nose. I snatch some of them up, shake them in my balled fist like dice—and you could say I'm taking a gamble here—and toss them into the hall. Aiming in the opposite direction of the guards.

The jewels clink on the stone floor as they scatter. The sound echoes exactly as I want them to.

"What was that?" the woman asks.

"Who's there?!" the Trap Mage calls out.

Their clothes rustle as they move closer to investigate.

I back up against the wall and pretend to sleep, keeping one eye slightly open to spy them rushing past my cell.

Then I fling a few more diamonds in that direction, using as much force as I can to throw them. Those clank against the wall, as if someone's actually there.

"Hey! What's going on over there?!" the woman exclaims, frustration clear in her voice.

I scatter the remaining gems right in front of my cell door and wedge myself between the cot and the back wall, draping the sheet over myself. I cross my fingers, praying to the gods that my plan works.

"Diamonds!" The Trap Mage gasps. "The Diamond Mage!"

Footsteps bound closer to me before the cell swings open. I stifle my breathing as best I can and wish I could make myself smaller—that I could disappear like Raven with her shadow magic.

"W-where'd she go?" the female guard asks.

The Trap Mage curses. "We can't lose her! Come on, let's follow the trail!"

I stay as still as a stone statue until I know the guards are long gone. When I finally slip out, my heart somersaults with joy in my chest. The cell door is open! But is the Trap Mage's magic is still in place? I slink toward the opening, praying to the gods for a stroke of luck. My hand stretches toward the open doorway, one eye open as I reach past the doorframe, expecting a blast of magical sparks to keep me contained within the cell.

Nothing.

I sigh in relief. It's *gone*. I peek my head out and peer left and right down the hallway to ensure the coast is clear before stepping out into the dank passageway. Freedom seems so close yet still so far away.

I haven't thought of a way out of Kinephrus after escaping the prison cell, which is pretty stupid of me, but my mind can barely hold all the new information I've learned since coming here—about Sanora, my parents, and the magi. There isn't *room* for anything else.

I sprint down the hallway, trying to formulate a game plan at the same time, but my mind is reeling. What if the Archmage catches me? What if I never make it back home?

What if I never see Al again?

My only hope is to find that first Transport Mage—*Cessi*—and hope I made a good enough impression on her that she'll be on my side. At least to send me to Aura's home, if not all the way back home to Al. Because, right now, that's the only place I want to be. With my sister.

I don't make it too far down the dank passageway before a sound prickles my skin and halts me.

"Why'd they put her in a cell next to mine?" a boy's voice echoes throughout the chambers. "I don't wanna catch Raven's toxicity and, clearly, her bad luck!"

My ears perk up. Did that kid just say what I think he said?

Another boy's voice, a little higher but similar to the first says, "Oh shut up, Tambor! At least she's where she belongs — back in here with us."

"She can't even talk to and face us. We know you can hear us, Raven!" the first boy yells.

Raven.

I don't understand why my stupid brain — heart — whichever is making the decisions right now is choosing to listen to the commotion instead of moving on and getting out of here. But I can't leave Raven behind. Not because I need her, but because I need *answers.*

I won't let her get off that easily.

Creeping forward, I reach the cell of the second boy. Even though I just took a few steps, I'm breathless — panting as if I'd run all the way here from Noravale.

He's sitting on his cot, hands draped over his knees. A too-large long red robe and black hood hang off his frame. His hair is shaved on the sides, though red and slicked back in the center. He looks to be about fourteen or so, way too young to be locked up in here.

"Wha — who are you?" he asks when he notices me.

I poke my fingers through the openings in the cell bars and cling to them, pressing my face close. "Raven's here?"

The boy looks taken aback by the fact that I ignored his question and mentioned Raven.

"Y-yeah?" he manages out in his confusion.

I rush to the next cell, where I reach the boy who had first been yelling about her. Tambor, was it? The first thing I notice is the tattoo sleeve on his right arm, snaking up to his neck.

He's grumbling to himself as he rakes his hand, wearing a black, fingerless glove, through his messy hair. Like the first kid's, it's shaved on the sides. Their physical similarities and the way they were bickering with each other make me think they're brothers.

The teen raises an eyebrow. "Can I…help you?"

"Raven. Where is she?"

"Uh…" He stands and walks closer before hiking a thumb to his right. "Is she finally gonna get what's coming to her?"

My gut reaction is to curse at him for bad-mouthing Raven, but I can't blame him. "Not quite," I say, then hurry to the next cell.

I scan the space, which looks different from the others I've passed. Instead of bars, there's a solid door with a window in the center. I peer inside but there's no one there. I check the next cell over, but that one holds an old man who's currently asleep. I back up to where Raven should be and check again.

I scrunch my nose and press against the window, wondering if my eyes are deceiving me. I'm ready to grumble in annoyance until a realization hits me. A smile spreads across my face. My eyes *are* deceiving me.

"Raven!" I whisper. "Raven, I know you're there!"

Sure enough, she appears, her curls frizzy and frazzled. She's huddled in the corner, in the space between the cot and the wall. She must have been using her Shadow magic.

"C-Cade?" she whispers.

"How could you do that to me?" I exclaim, unable to hold back my accusatory tone.

She rushes to the door, tears spilling down the cheeks of her beautiful, soft, face.

I bite my lip to keep back my own tears. I don't need a diamond trail giving me away. Despite my efforts, a few jewels fall to the cement floor with a clink.

"I'm so, so, sorry! You're in here because of me. I can't…I can't believe…" Raven looks like a hot mess. I've never seen her so distraught. But how could she be making a complete one-eighty from her coldness in the throne room?

"Why did you do it? Try to steal Tor's crown, bring me all the way here? Was it really for riches? For Sanora's reward?" My lips threaten to tremble, but I stay strong and prevent my emotions from showing.

Raven shakes her head, palms slapping the window. Her fingers flex, trying to tear through the glass to me. "I wanted the riches, but only at first. Listen, once we went on our journey together, everything changed. I told you that you were my everything, and it's true."

My anger starts to melt away. Well, not all of it, but the Raven I was catching feelings for is still in there somewhere. Deep down, I know it. And that's who I'm happy to see and who makes my heart leap from my chest, though my resentment hasn't subsided yet.

"Okay, but you still turned me in. You still acted like I was nothing but dirt at the Archmage's tower!" I try to keep my voice low, but it's hard. "How could you leave me like that?"

"No! I didn't leave you!"

I sigh in frustration. "We don't have time for this. We need to get out of here before they catch us." I figure those two boys can hear us quite well, but I'm hoping I've deterred the guards enough that they'll stay gone for a while.

"Not yet. Not before I explain myself." Raven's voice breaks. "I was going to take back everything I thought I wanted. I turned myself in and told Sanora to let you go free."

I frown and my eyebrows scrunch together. "No, you didn't."

"Yes, I...Oh, no..." Raven's hands slip away from the window. "What is it?"

"Oh, my gods...Sanora...I know what kind of mage she is. I never knew until now."

No wonder she never told me. My nerves are getting the better of me at the sight of Raven's distraught expression. "Well, what is she?"

"She's...she's an Illusion Mage."

I'm not sure what that is, but it doesn't sound fun or fluffy to me. At my quizzical expression, Raven continues.

"They're rare, kind of like Diamond Magi. But they're also incredibly powerful. No wonder she's the Archmage…"

"What can she do?"

"She creates illusions to make people see what she wants them to see. There's not a lot known about the power, but I heard she can show someone their inner demons and reflect their fears at them."

Raven shivers while a chill crawls up my own spine.

"So…" I start, slowly piecing together what happened. "She showed me a scene of you running off with your reward, leaving me behind, when really you were fighting for me?"

"Yes!" Raven says breathlessly. "Cade, I…I could never do that to you. You're the family I want."

One of the boys, I think it's Tambor, yells from his cell. "And what are we? Chopped liver?!"

"Guys, I swear I didn't know you'd been locked up with me back then. Maybe it was Sanora playing her mind games," Raven explains.

"Or maybe it was *your* mind games," the other one spits back.

"Come on, Xander, we're a different kind of family. Well, you guys are actually family. They're brothers," she says to me.

"I guessed that," I note.

"Are Garit and Kya here, too?" Raven asks the boys.

Tambor, the tattooed brother, sighs. "Haven't seen them since we were captured. It's been, what, three? Four weeks?"

"What's going on over there!"

Damn it, I pressed my luck by staying too long.

The shadow of a guard grows larger as he rounds the corner, lumbering down the hall. He's neither of the two guards who were here earlier. I can tell by how loud his feet thud on the cement floor that this guy is a beast I don't want to mess with.

I inspect the door, keeping Raven inside. "There has to be a way for me to bust you out of here…"

She shakes her head. "Nope. They didn't know my power before, so I escaped by becoming a shadow and slipping through the bars."

She knocks on the window of the thick door. "That's why I'm in a solid enclosure this time. And, in any case, you have to let the other Prowlers out. Forget about me."

"These are your thief friends you were telling me about?"

One of the boys laughs. "Hah, friends? That's a good one! We used to be, until she screwed up our mission. Got caught with Tor's crown, landed us all in this prison, and then busted herself out while leaving us here to rot. But if that's your definition..."

The guard's steps are growing louder.

"We have to hurry! Do you have any magic that can help?" I ask the boys.

"We're not magi, otherwise we woulda used our powers and been outta here a long time ago," Tambor says somberly.

I don't have time to respond before a hulking brute of a man steps forward.

My eyes flit between him and the two younger guards I'd tricked earlier coming up behind him.

"It was her!" the Trap Mage guard says. "The Diamond Mage tricked us with her magic."

If only I had left when I had the chance. But *no*, I couldn't leave Raven and her friends behind. It wouldn't have been right. It might as well be murder. But what can I do now?

The youngest guard swoops behind me and locks my hands behind my back as if I've got handcuffs on. Despite it just being his power imprisoning me, I still feel something biting into my skin, as if actual chains were wrapped around my wrists.

The big metal chunk of a man glares at me and studies his comrade with the same intensity. Then his head snaps to Raven and her comrades' cells before he narrows his eyes back on me. "I sense that you're lying."

My sweaty palms slip against each other from behind my back. I didn't want to get in even more trouble, so I make quick work to formulate an alibi. "W-what? No, I didn't mean to—"

The guard folds his arms, his biceps bulging. "Come now, I'm a Psychic Mage. I can't read your thoughts, but I can read your emotions. And yours right now is fear. The girl's aura is the same. I'm going to have to turn you in to the Archmage."

Shoot! I fight to clear my brain since the Psychic Mage can sense my plotting and scheming.

Raven bangs on her window, rattling my bones and causing both guards to jump. "Hey! I need to speak to Archmage Sanora."

"What makes you think I'd ever let you do that?" the Psychic Mage grunts.

I want to kiss Raven. Even imprisoned, she is using her wit and smarts, figuring out a way to save us.

But even I couldn't have predicted her answer.

"Because it involves a promise she made to me...and Tor."

TWENTY-FOUR

The renewed chance at a successful escape warms me to my core. I can't believe it worked—the beefy guard actually listened to Raven. He must have used his power on her and sensed that her request was serious enough not to be shrugged off.

Promises must be of high importance to the Archmage. My parents didn't keep their promise to Tor, so she could just as easily hold it against me. I guess I'm about to find out if she'll still keep the ones *she's* made.

I remain silent, swallowing all my emotions as the guards lead us up multiple stairwells until we emerge through a large wooden door and out into the hallway right outside the Archmage's throne room. Of course, the Trap Mage holds both mine and Raven's arms behind our backs with his magic the whole time, but even that doesn't discourage me.

Sanora looks like she's been waiting for us all day. She's sitting on her throne, legs crossed, leaning to the side with one elbow on the armrest. It's a casual stance, but she has a haunting glare. In other words, she's still freaking pissed at us.

I don't need a mirror to tell that Raven is the complete opposite of me. She's proud, assured, and confident, her head held high despite being held back by the guard's enchantment.

"Well, look who's back," Sanora says in a monotone voice. Clearly, she's unimpressed by our presence.

The burly Psychic Mage steps forward. "Archmage, we found the Diamond Mage outside of her cell, trying to break out the Shadow Mage and her crew."

Can't he call us by our names? We're more than our curses—powers—aren't we?

Sanora chuckles. "And? Throw them back in jail where they belong. I'm done with them for now." She waves us away as if the very movement would magically remove us from her throne room.

Raven narrows her eyes. "Well, *I'm* not done with you, Sanora."

"I-I'm sorry, Your Majesty, but we brought her because she went on about a promise you made to her and Tor." The Trap Mage, purses his lips and tightens his grip on the folds of his robe like he's straining to keep his hold on her. Maybe he has to work extra hard to prevent her from shifting into a shadow?

The Archmage doesn't seem bothered by the new information. "Oh? And what might that be?"

Raven's voice is solid. "You're breaking the promise you made on Tor's grave! I brought Cadence to you—the Diamond Mage. You swore you'd give the person who did one wish—anything they desired—not throw them in jail." Her fists are balled so tightly they look like they'll explode.

Sanora rolls her eyes as if she's bored. "So, you wish to free yourself? Leave with your rags to riches story?"

"No."

Well, that wakes the Archmage up. She straightens in her seat, all ears.

Raven takes a step closer to the throne, and I'm afraid she's going to attack the woman. But she replies, "No, I wish for you to free both me and Cadence."

The Archmage's laugh is a punch to my gut. "I cannot go back on my promises, either, you know."

What? My attention darts between them. "Raven, what is she talking about?"

The Archmage answers for her as if Raven isn't worthy to have the answer spill from her lips. "Anyone who commits a crime must be punished under my rule. It's the law. It's how we've kept Kinephrus safe. A utopia of sorts, free from the taint of greedy and selfish Unremarkables beyond our towers."

"Fine." Raven's head falls in defeat like she's bowing to the queen in submission. "I don't care if I have to stay here, whether that's in a jail cell for the rest of my life, or dead in the ground. If it can't be both of us, then my wish is for you to let Cadence go free."

"Raven, no!" I object. This cannot be happening. I've finally reunited with the best thing to ever happen to me, and she's sacrificing herself to save me. In so many ways, she's saved me. I can't believe I ever doubted her.

"Now don't forget" the Archmage says almost gleefully, "the punishment for your crimes is death by a Poison Mage."

Raven tilts her chin up now, eyes unblinking. "I understand."

"Please don't do this!" I shout. Diamond tears clink to the floor in my hysterics, and not once do I feel the normal stinging pain. It's all being overpowered by the slicing in my heart. Not a dull ache, but a sharp, seething cut that sends my mind whirling.

Raven gives me a somber look. "Cade, I love you too much to drag you down with me. You need to get back home to Allegra. Please, go."

"But Raven...I'm not letting you die..."

"You're not, Cade. I am."

Her words shred me, but mine aren't getting anywhere with her. There's no way for me to change her mind.

But maybe I can change Sanora's. "Wait!" I scream, desperation coating my throat. "What about me being your adopted daughter?"

The Archmage's shoulders tense. "What did you say?"

"I know I'm the last remaining heir to the throne...the last surviving human gifted with Tor's power."

Sanora narrows her eyes. "What of it?"

The Trap Mage keeps my arms bound but I still fight to gain some control. "You were never going to hurt me. So, Raven's wish should be granted to save herself. I shouldn't even be part of this."

"And you're not." She flings a bunch of braids over one shoulder. "Raven's reward is null because of her crimes. She will not be granted pardon."

My heart sinks. I'm afraid now. Of what the Archmage will show to me, to Raven. How will I know what's reality and what's not?

Sanora motions for the young guard to lead us to her.

We walk with labored steps in a long march until we're face to face with evil itself.

I lower my head in defeat, angry at the Archmage for taking Raven from me. My parents took her husband from her, but I would make any reparations I could to make up for their offense. Because clearly, "I'm sorry" will never be enough.

Sanora's ice-cold fingers hook under my chin, and she lifts my head until my gaze meets hers. We study each other in silence, before Sanora asks, "How does she read, Pavi?"

The Psychic Mage closes his eyes for a moment. When he opens them, he says, "She wants to return home if she is freed. She will not harm our people."

"*Hmph*," Sanora says, releasing me. "You're lucky I never go back on my word, especially not on Tor's grave. He was too good of a man to taint his soul. You're free to go, but the Shadow Mage stays here. Go home like you want to, but if you ever return here, you'll be dead in the ground with poison in your veins like your little thief friend."

The invisible binding disappears and I gasp, even though I've been able to breathe normally this whole time.

The Trap Mage also seems relieved. Like maybe he was having a hard time maintaining his hold on both me and Raven.

At least there are limits to his magic, too.

I rub my sore wrists, which ache and throb from the magical chains. "I…I never got the chance to ask my questions. On whether you can take away my power, or find a way to help my sister. She's sick with a genetic neuromuscular disease. My parents have been torturing me all my life to cry diamonds for them to pay for her treatment, but they use me for their own selfish gain. I...I thought you could help me."

"I'm afraid I can't. Unremarkables, traitors, *killers*, that's the whole lot of you. Kinephrus is the only pure place left in this country." There's no sympathy in Sanora's eyes, just an air of sweet justice. But shouldn't my parents be the ones suffering?

I return my thoughts to the matter at hand. Raven's plan worked. I'm free. For now.

I rush over to her. I need to hug her, kiss her. I need to say goodbye, and she needs to understand that it won't be forever. I want to tell her I *will* be back for her, no matter what anyone here says.

"No." The voice comes hard and firm, freezing me in place.

I thought what halted me was the young guard's hold on me again, but it's Sanora—and not her magic, but her voice. "What do you think you're doing?"

"Please, I want to say goodbye." Goodbye. It's the final chapter. Goodbye means *The End.*

"I *need* to say goodbye," I say more firmly this time.

The Archmage scoffs. "Your parents stole my love from me. Do you think I'd let you have yours? You don't get to have the kiss I'll never have again."

Raven's face falls. It's the look of wondering what my life will be like without her. It tells me that everything we've been through was worth it for a couple of stolen glances, touches, and kisses. It breaks me. She's stunning and beautiful and I want her forever.

"Please?" I say through trembling lips. Cold diamonds form in the corners of my eyes. "This is the last time I'll ever get to see her..." I add, though I pray to the gods my words are a lie.

Sanora's expression turns blank, and she walks back to her throne, assuming the same position we had found her in. "How nice. Now you know how I felt. Have fun asking mommy and daddy why they're murderers. Now, get out of my sight."

At her command, Raven and I are ripped apart.

The Trap Mage leads her back to the prison hold, while the Psychic Mage ushers me toward the end of the hall that leads to the tower's exit.

I cry and cry, diamond tears falling with every step. I can't do anything else, terrified as I am by the realization that I'll never see Raven alive again.

TWENTY-FIVE

I'm escorted to the transport tower on a walkway which now feels miles long. I dread the moment when I'll finally confront my parents about how they killed Tor, and why they've lied to me for sixteen years. The devils know, I'll bring them to Sanora myself if it will get her to let Raven go. But I have to hurry. The threat of the Poison Mage sends my mind whirling, and I stumble, afraid I'm going to fall right off this strip.

It's late afternoon, and the sun is starting to set to the west. The sight of streamers and lanterns hanging everywhere churns my stomach. This city that should have been my home is now a tainted prison. It's the only memory I have to take with me about this place. Other magi eye me with disdain, whispers, gasps, and glares. I don't think they realize their Archmage just let the mythical Diamond Mage go, but I'm sure they sense something's off.

Cessi, the peppy, blonde Transport Mage who had first led me up the tower, now has a frown painted on her face. She avoids my gaze and focuses on the guard. They talk briefly about what happened between me and the queen, but I tune them out. Instead, I look down, feeling like all my progress is lost.

I couldn't get rid of this stupid curse. It helped me along my journey, but it was ultimately useless. I'm in the presence of magi who can change what I see, control my movements, and sense my intentions. And I can cry diamonds? *Awesome*.

"This is the end of the line," the Psychic Mage says to me. "Heed the Archmage's words. You'll be wise not to return to Kinephrus."

My words have done nothing for me here, so I silently nod and trudge up to Cessi.

She places a hand on my shoulder, but I barely feel her there. My body is too numb for me to notice the zap through my limbs before I'm already on the ground.

I glance back up the tower, tracing the path across the walkways to Sanora's tower. Where could Raven be? I stare, trying to imprint it in my mind.

Cessi fiddles with the ends of her short curls. "I…I'm sorry, but you must leave now."

I turn and look past the plants now surrounding me to the world beyond. It's a lush plain, but I don't want to return to if it means I'm leaving alone—without Raven. I trudge forward, with no idea where to go or what to do. I spin on my heel, but Cessi is already gone.

I walk through the grass, feeling more alone than I ever have before. Raven's been with me this whole time, and before that, Al was always by my side. Gods, I miss her so much. I wish I had some way of contacting Aura, but I didn't think I'd need to when we parted.

I dig through my bag, which I forgot I had on under my cloak, only to huff when I discover all my diamonds and coins are gone. As if the Archmage doesn't already have a billion to fund this city.

I grumble as I search through my bag for anything useful, finding some crumbs from the food I'd eaten. Then my hand curls around a folded piece of paper. I pull it out and unfold it, elation quickly replacing my frustration. Yes! Raven had said she would draw a map of Soridente for me. And here it is! It's no Gio Amario painting, but it isn't chicken scratch either. I kiss the scrap with its crudely drawn landmarks. Except, holy moly, Aura's place is far.

My hand falls to my side and I grip the lifeline harder. Looking ahead of me, I sigh louder than I ever have in my life. It's going to be a long journey. But I trudge forward all the same.

What did Al use to say to herself when she was in rehab?

Oh, right.

Suck it up.

I think my legs are going to fall off. My thighs are burning, and my calves are as tight as my balled fists. Even my back aches. I've cried…how many times since I left Kinephrus? I don't even know, but the fact that my bag is now stuffed to the brim with diamonds says it's a lot.

The greenery has ebbed away, but I take it as a good thing. I must be heading in the right direction. Though that means I'll be approaching the desert—and I really don't want to outrun a sand-storm. *Again.*

I find one of the few trees left in this barren land and collapse on the ground, slumping against the tree trunk. I close my eyes, imagining vultures encircling me from above like I'm a carrion. Of course, the sky is clear of any crazy creatures, but who's to say it won't happen? After all, I finished the last of my water during my last break. It isn't looking good.

Night overtakes me.

I awake in the early morning refreshed, but now super hungry. I dump out the diamonds in my bag and pick at the crumbs that had been at the bottom. Crusty old bread or crackers? I'm not sure. But all the nibbling does is make me hungrier. My stomach's screaming, *Okay, but where's the rest?* I'm ready to turn around and head back to Kinephrus, to wave my white flag and beg for mercy, when a tree branch snaps.

I spring to my feet and whirl in a circle. There's nothing around me except for the tree I slept next to, so what could it be?

I must be hallucinating.

Another snap sends goosebumps up and down my arms. I tip my head back as I look up, fully expecting vultures to be perched high, ready to swoop down on their prey. But nothing is there, either.

When I bring my focus down, I yelp and stumble backward, falling flat on my butt.

Someone's standing there. And it's not Aura, but my freaking butler. Even if he's not wearing his uniform. His clothes look flowy and light, loose and casual. Clearly, he's off duty.

"M-Malore!" I exclaim, scrambling to my feet and wiping the dust off myself. "What in the devils are you doing here?!"

He folds his arms, flashing a smile that doesn't reach his eyes. "I'm here…for you."

I tilt my head to the side. "Uh…okay…but how? And why?"

His toes tap the ground like he's impatient. "I can explain later. We have to go." He starts toward me.

"Whoa, whoa, whoa, hold on there." I back up, holding my hands in front of me. "There is no way I'm going anywhere with you until you explain yourself. You sold me out to the royal guard and tried to capture me, and now you're here—over halfway across the country—telling me you'll explain later? Guess again."

Malore rubs the stubble on his chin. "Okay, okay, but I'm going to try to make this quick because we don't have much time."

He pauses like he expects me to say something, but I gesture for him to hurry up and continue. I clutch my bag and position my body slightly away from him. He's got to earn my trust, and he's not doing a good job so far.

"I'm not just your butler. I'm a mage. A Tracker Mage."

My jaw drops. "W-what? But…how? You're living with my parents. You're in cahoots with the king. Doesn't he despise the magi? I was told there were a ton of wars."

He rubs the back of his neck. "He doesn't know. Rioza doesn't, either. I had to make up how I knew where you were."

"But my parents?"

"They know what I am. There's a whole black market for humans to hire magi to work for them."

"I-I had no idea. So, you…you wanted this?" I sputter.

"It was the only way for me to feel useful with my power. I didn't want to work for Archmage Sanora."

I throw my hands in the air. "Oh great, *now* somebody warns me about her."

His eyes round. "You met her?" He shakes his head. "We can talk specifics later. Listen, trust me when I say I'm on your side, but I had to pretend like I wasn't. When you went missing, your parents knew they could use me to find you. I had no choice in the matter. But once the fight happened between the citizens of Serency and the guards, I led the latter the wrong way even though I knew you were headed toward Jessen. We regrouped back in Noravale."

"So everything's fine?"

His expression darkens in the early morning light.

I don't like that reaction one bit. "What is it?" I demand.

"It's Allegra. She's...not doing well."

I thought my whole world was falling apart before, but now, getting eaten alive by hungry birds is the least of my concerns. "What... is she...will you...?" I can't even form a coherent sentence.

I find the same sympathy in Malore's eyes as I'd witnessed back when he'd been with the King's Guard. "The new treatment isn't working. She's...getting weaker, having a harder time breathing. She's going downhill fast. I knew you would want to be with her."

I close the distance between us and tug at his vest, struggling to stand. "Please, take me back now! I...I need to see her!"

"Don't worry, we'll go."

I glance around us, almost whimpering. "But how are we going to get there? How did you get here? You're a Tracker Mage, not a *Transport* Mage!"

"That's where I come in."

I yelp in surprise and spin to find Aura here, too. I've never been so happy in my life for someone to sneak up on me.

"Oh, Aura!" I run to her and she takes me in her arms. Jewels sparkle in the sunlight as they fall to the ground. Her presence is another comfort, showing me I'm not alone when I feel like I could've been stranded in this desert forever. Without Al or Raven by my side right now, that wouldn't have been such a terrible option.

Aura fiddles with one of her dreadlocks. "Malore tracked you across the desert to my home. When I told him where you were, he was planning how to infiltrate Kinephrus. When he sensed your presence outside the city, I sent him here, and well, here we are. I can take you back home."

"Yes, please!" I eagerly agree.

"Come on, let's get you home." She touches both my shoulder and Malore's.

In the next moment, we're back in Noravale. Well, almost. We're on the outskirts of the city. It's more desolate, yet there are homes further away on plots of land, like the one Raven had stolen Clove from. I'm glad Aura was smart enough to bring us here. It would be a little odd for people to see three magi appear out of nowhere in the middle of broad daylight in a town of rich humans.

"Please reach out to me if you ever need me," Aura says, glancing around to make sure there weren't any passersby.

"How can I? Is there a mage for that?" I ask, half-joking.

"I'll let one of my messengers stay here with you." Aura holds her palms in front of her. She closes her eyes and whispers an incantation I can't make out. And then, it appears.

A huge, beautiful falcon, flapping its wings before landing on Aura's arm with its massive talons. It cocks its head and stares at me with its beady, black eyes.

She lifts her arm and the falcon flies into the nearest tree, watching us from a low branch.

"You sure she's not going to peck my eyes out? Ever since I thought I was going to die, birds and I are getting a little iffy. Except for Raven, I guess." I regret the words as soon as they come out.

"Kazi will do you no harm. You didn't get to meet him before since he was out on a mission. He's happy to help with any task I assign him. There's a pouch tied around his neck for any messages you want to relay to me. I'll get them and respond promptly, okay?"

I say okay even though I'm not ready for Aura to leave. But at least I have Malore. "Thank you, Aura. For everything. How I can repay you?"

She rests a hand on my shoulder. "You don't have to. By the way," she says, lowering her voice and her stance, "thanks for the diamonds. You shouldn't have." She straightens and winks.

"Duly noted." I chuckle and wipe at my nose. "I...I should get to my sister."

"Of course. Well, if you need Kazi for anything, whistle and he'll be there in a pinch." And then, she's gone—no magical twinkles or glitter left in her wake.

I turn to Malore, whose face likely matches the resolve in my own. I take a deep breath and exhale, focusing down the streets that I walked on what feels like forever ago.

The magi don't want me. Maybe my parents don't either. But I'm going back to the one person who, wherever she is, will welcome me home. "Let's go. I can't wait another minute to see Al."

TWENTY-SIX

I kind of forgot about the whole missing persons thing. My face is everywhere—and Raven's is, too. Her cheeks are still as puffy in these as they were in the previous drawings, which Raven won't be happy to hear. But it means that her Shadow magic worked and the royal guards never saw what she looked like. But her name *is* slapped on there in black fat capital letters thanks to my blabbing. I push thoughts of her aside because every part of me is focusing on only one girl right now.

Al.

Malore leads me down the cobblestone streets, past the rows of houses that I used to have memorized. Now, everything is foreign. The smiling faces, the music lilting in the air, the fashionable couture, and the perfectly presentable lawns and front walkways. *All fake.* Tainted by what I learned. Wars between magi and humans, a secret black-market for hiring magi, and who knows what else!

I shield my face from the passersby as we enter the hustle and bustle of Noravale. People might recognize me or Malore, but I don't care. My focus is on my home.

"Oh, it's such a shame. She's such a beautiful young woman," someone says as I pass.

"Right? I'm sure the Baron and Baroness are devastated. First, one daughter gets kidnapped, and now the other is very sick. The poor things," another responds.

I freeze, and it takes Malore a few steps before he realizes I've stopped. The world tilts and I grab the wrought iron fence beside me to keep from falling over. Hands grab my shoulders.

"Come, Cadence," Malore says quietly. "We should go."

"But…they're talking about Al!" I whimper, my feet plastered to the sidewalk.

"I know, but you'll see her soon. Come on!" He nudges me forward and I'm on my way.

As we approach the fence and the hedges I've stared at from the inside way too often, my stomach churns. Sure, I'll see Al again. But that means I also have to face my parents. And I'm not sure I'm ready for that yet.

Malore keeps his hand on my shoulders until we reach the front gate. A guard is there, and what shocks me isn't the fact that we've never had a guard at our gate before, but that he's dressed like the King's Guard—a red and gold suit and a sheathed sword at his side.

"Who goes there?" the man asks.

I lift my hood off my head and place my fists on my hips. "I'm Cadence Alero, and I live here. Who in the devils are you?"

At least I earn some sort of satisfaction from his surprised expression. He hadn't expected the *kidnapped* daughter to return. He straightens and stumbles over his words. "Oh, yes! Right this way!"

"I'll bring her to the Baron and Baroness," Malore says, following me inside after the guard unlatches and swings open the gate.

We make our way up the long driveway.

Either my parents were watching from the window, or the King's Guard has some way to report things directly to them. Oh, I know. That guard is probably a mage they secretly hired. In any case, before I even make it to the bottom of the stairs, my parents rush out the front door.

Father has one arm around Mother, who's cupping her hands to her chest. They run down the stairs and I'm swallowed up in their arms, though mine are glued to my sides. Their tears hit me as they smother me. Yeah, I'm sure they're really glad I'm back. Now they can maintain their high and mighty lifestyle.

I maintain an impassive face.

Do they expect me to be happy I'm back here? It's only because I was almost killed by the widow of the man they killed. And their crime has made it so that I'll never find their actions genuine—ever.

"Oh, Cadence! We thought we'd never find you!" Mother cries, finally releasing me from her grasp. Or is it her clutches?

Father dotes over me, kissing me on the head multiple times. "Are you okay? Are you hurt?"

I resist rolling my eyes. I'm sure they don't want one scratch on their money-making daughter, especially after they murdered someone to keep me. But I digress. It's not the right time or place to confront them.

"Where's Al?" It should be a normal enough question for me to ask right when I get home. I'll be surprised if they expected any *I miss you*'s and *I love you*'s from me.

Mother and Father exchange worried glances before she turns back to me. "You better come inside, Cadence." I notice her eyes now—weary, with bags underneath. Father wears the same forlorn and exhausted expression.

"Is she okay? I heard that she's sick. I—"

Malore pushes me forward, reminding me that I need to move if I want to see her. Maybe that's why I keep asking questions about her. I'm scared. I don't know if I'm strong enough to face her in whatever state she's in. I pray to the gods that things aren't as bad as people have made them out to be.

"Where is she? Mother, where is she?!" I repeat impatiently when they don't reply, nearly knocking her into a pillar holding a vase behind them.

"Calm down. She's in her room," Father says.

I hold my tongue from lashing out at his insensitive first line and focus on the latter.

My feet take their time on each step to mentally prepare myself to face what I find. By the time I push her bedroom door open, I'm ready to be by her side regardless of my fear.

Her room, our little haven, looks exactly as it did when I left. And there she is, lying in bed, snuggled under the blankets, sleeping—wheezing and struggling to breathe.

An oxygen tube is inserted in both nostrils, the line wrapped behind her ears and down the front of her torso. I follow the tube to an oxygen tank at her bedside.

"Oh, Al!" I cry out, diamond tears falling, leaving a trail behind me and pooling at my feet as I sit on the edge of the bed and envelop her in my arms. "Al, I missed you so much!"

When she wakes, she seems a little shaken, but soon her hands slip from under the covers and wrap around mine. Her fingertips have a blue tinge and her hands are bony. So do her lips and the rest of her skin.

Worry spreads through my entire body, numbing me. She feels so bony and frail. Afraid I'm going to break her, I loosen my grip.

"C-Cade? Is that…you?" She rubs the sleep from her vision, but soon they become tears as the realization hits her.

"Yes, it's me. I'm back." I sniffle. I spot the fantasy book she'd been reading when I left sitting on her nightstand. "Did you…?"

She nods. "I did."

I smile, the tension releasing from my muscles. She got my note about why I left, and more importantly, why I didn't tell her before I did. "So, you don't hate me?"

"No," she says with a laugh. "You're…lucky." She goes into a coughing fit when she tries to sit up in bed, and I have to ease her back against the headboard.

She sounds so weak, so much worse than when I left her. Gods, it's been what, less than two weeks? "What's going on, Al?"

Mother and Father finally enter the bedroom, standing just past the doorway. Their gazes spark with their usual greedy glint–zeroing in on my fresh diamond tears on the carpet. But they remain far away and distant, exactly where they belong.

Mother rests a hand on Father's chest while he slips an arm around her shoulders. "She's gotten worse ever since you left. If you'd been here, you would have known. You could have helped."

My brows crash together. "Helped how? By giving you more diamonds to spend money on yourselves?"

"Watch your mouth, young lady," Father warns.

I scoff at them and turn to focus on Al. She's the only one who matters right now.

"Dr. Sammer had to delay the treatment for another week. He should be done tweaking the medications soon so that she can start again," Mother replies, no real emotion in her tone.

"So my lungs…well…they kind of suck now," Al struggles to say.

The diamonds stop pooling around her, even though I want to keep crying. My magic has its limit, too. "I'm *so* sorry, Al."

She looks like she wants to ask me more—ask me if I found the answers I was looking for. But her eyes flick to Mother and Father then back to me in frustration. Maybe she already knows the answer. If I'm still crying diamond tears, clearly I didn't find a way to get rid of my curse—gift—power—thing.

"Don't…be sorry." She lays her hand atop mine.

I feel bad asking her more questions when she's obviously having a hard time breathing, so I turn back to the people who deserve the World's Worst Parents Award. "Why isn't she at the hospital?"

"We'll bring her there if she needs it. Dr. Sammer is staying with us to monitor her in the meantime."

I squeeze Al's hand, willing my touch to transfer life back into her. "What's going on exactly?"

"Her oxygen saturation levels were dropping even with supplemental oxygen. She's in respiratory distress."

"But…you said she can start the new treatment next week, right?" My voice is calm for Al's sake but inside I'm a web of nerves, sticky and messy and unsalvageable. If it's a matter of money, I'll cry all the diamonds in the world to help her. But it can't solve everything.

Do I bring up the black market magi to Mother and Father? Ask them if there's a mage who can heal diseases? Didn't those Kinephrus guards say something about my diamonds having different magical properties?

Al talks in between gasps. "It's not like what happens...in fairy-tales. We don't...always get our happily ever after."

"But..."

Mother rushes over, fixing her hair as if her appearance matters at a time like this. "Allegra is right, dear. Stop wishing for what's only a fantasy."

I scrunch my forehead. "Al can say whatever she wants about her condition, but you don't get to say that."

Mother halts, taken aback by my bluntness.

That's right. I'm back, and I'm not taking this crap anymore.

"Can...can you leave me and Cadence alone for a bit?"

I want to jump for joy when Mother and Father concede to Al's wishes without any argument. When they exit the room and the door latches shut, I whirl to face her.

"So..." Al adjusts the oxygen tube in her nostrils and takes in a deep breath. "Now that we're...finally alone...tell me everything."

TWENTY-SEVEN

I've never felt so happy to be home. I could stay inside, within these four walls, for the rest of my life. Well, only if it meant I'd remain safe and sound with Al for the entirety of it. I hadn't realized how comforting her presence is. I've always wanted to protect her, to be there for her. But now I also know *I* need her.

We stay in her bed, but I crawl to the other side, snuggling under the covers beside her. After I ensure the coast is clear, that Mother and Father are long gone from the halls and even the second floor, I tell her everything. In a hushed tone. Because who knows who is eavesdropping to report back to my parents?

I tell her about the magi, the King's Guard, Archmage Sanora, and Raven.

She listens in silence, except for the occasional cough or gasp, but nods and squeezes my hand throughout my account of events. It's the bit of reassurance I need to confirm I did the right thing, and that she was truly with me on my journey all along.

I hadn't realized how I'd bottled everything up. The pressure lifts from my chest only slightly, because Al still has her own struggles.

"I'm sorry for the word vomit," I say, scratching the back of my head, embarrassed for dominating the conversation.

Al waves me away. "Don't apologize. You understand how *bored* I get here. A girl can only do…" She trails off as the air in her lungs runs out, then takes another breath to continue. "So much. And well, if my lungs would," she coughs, "cooperate for more than five seconds, maybe I could have…"

I squeeze her hand while she catches her breath. I don't want to cut her off, but seeing her struggle to even hold a conversation is breaking my heart.

"Done something cool while you were gone," she finishes.

"Trust me." I pull the covers over my waist. "You don't want to do the 'cool things' I did."

She offers a meager chuckle, but then she frowns, fiddling with the oxygen tube in her lap. "It was hard to pretend I didn't know where you went, but even harder to not spend every waking moment worried about you."

"Gods, Al." I hadn't thought about that. "I'm so sorry."

"Hey," she says with a smile, "don't be."

But I am. "I'm sorry I didn't get the answers we wanted."

She shrugs. "Maybe that's how it's supposed to be."

I wrinkle my nose at her response. I'm not satisfied with going back to the way things were, with returning to this life of being under Mother and Father's thumbs and accepting it as the status quo. I hope Al isn't either.

"So, what about that Raven girl?"

I want to curse my sister for bringing Raven back up. It was already hard enough telling her how she saved me from Sanora and set me free, how she hadn't betrayed me like I first thought she did. Sifting through all of those complicated emotions, I take a moment to answer so I don't stumble and trip over each syllable leaving my lips. "What about her?"

"Do you love her?"

When I picture loving Raven, my stomach squeezes and my chest tightens. It's a fire I don't want to remember. Especially how it was never fully ignited.

I burst out laughing, clutching the bedspread. "Love? Come on, Al, I'm not that easy."

A lingering kiss and a missing ache in my arms are the extent of *that*. And we can't ever be more, now that Sanora is going to execute her for stealing Tor's crown.

"Oh, um, I'm sorry…" Al must have sensed my turmoil, no doubt written plain on my face.

"No," I add. "Seriously, it wasn't love. Yet. But I think…I think we could've gotten to that point."

"I didn't mean to…"

I shake my head. "Don't worry about it." I take a deep breath and change the subject. "So, I told you what I was up to while I was gone. What about you? Did you read every book in the library?"

"You're only half right. I didn't read…every book in the library." Al leans over the edge of the bed, digging through her nightstand drawer. She pulls out a thick book, letting it fall onto her lap with a plop. "But…I found one that neither of us ever read before."

I eye the tome curiously. The pages are yellow and weathered, ready to rip with one flip of the page. The book's black cover looks gray with age, like the dust has permanently permeated into the leather binding. "What is it?"

"So, while you were gone, I did my own snooping…about what Mother and Father may have been hiding from us. I figured if you found that magi emblem, what else did we have about them?"

"I knew you were smart." I smirk.

"Was there ever any doubt?" she says with a wink. "So, from what I can tell, this…" She smooths her palm over the cover, and I catch her fingers gliding across the golden, flower-like insignia. "This is a book about the magi."

I almost leap from the bed. "What?!"

"Soon after you left, Malore revealed to me…" She takes in a shaky breath. "that he was just like you—a mage. I had him search the highest bookshelves for me…" She coughs, reminding me about her angry lung. "A few days after you left. We found the oldest ones…no one had touched in years. And, well, here this is."

"What does it say?—Wait, don't keep talking if it's too hard for you to breathe right now." I can't help but focus on her oxygen tank poking out from the bedside.

"It's okay, Cade. I'm actually feeling a lot better…now that you're here." She thumbs through the pages. "There are so many facts in here. Even I couldn't read it all before you came back. But, it does talk about…the different powers magi can have, their limits, history, how they…got their power from the gods. Everything."

I can't help but feel this book is a part of my family history. Since Tor gave me my power, in a way, it is. "Oh my gods, this is awesome! We can learn so much from this book!"

Al smiles. "Exactly. And since your birthday is in a couple of days…" She pauses to cough again, then adjusts the oxygen tube under her nose. "I wanted to be the first…to wish you a happy birthday…and give you this book as a present."

My heart swells and I reach for her hand. Not for the book, but for being herself. I wrap Al in the biggest hug I can and savor her returning embrace. It might be weaker and frailer, but it's still hers, and it's the best feeling in the world.

"Thank you." I sniffle into her shoulder.

"Hey, don't give me any diamonds. I don't want to see any tears."

"I'll try." I blink a few times, and press my fingertips into the corners of my eyes to stifle them. "Thank you, Al," I say as I take the proffered book.

"I know how much this could mean for you. I hope it helps you…find any answers you're still looking for."

With all the information in my hands, I could combust with excitement. But, in all honesty, I'm not sure I need it anymore.

I've finally reunited with my sister. We can go back to the way things were. Living with our parents, knowing that they're murderers will suck, but at least I'll have Al. That sisterly bond is one I wouldn't trade for anything. And well, isn't that the most important magic of all?

I reluctantly leave her room to stash the book under my bed where the magi emblem also resides. Now that I'm alone, I cry all the diamonds I kept inside, hoping I never have to say goodbye to Al ever again.

TWENTY-EIGHT

It's my seventeenth birthday today, but I would've forgotten if not for Al reminding me. Ever since I went on my whirlwind adventure, it hasn't been on my mind. Well, except for when Archmage Sanora revealed my birthday is the anniversary of her husband's death. But I ignore that for now so I can enjoy today.

I don't care if I don't receive any presents. In all honesty, there's nothing I want that my parents can give me. Unless they stop using me for my diamond tears, make Al feel better, and bring Raven back safe and sound. That's not asking too much, is it?

In any case, I've already got the best present ever. I roll over in bed, letting the light coming in from the split in the curtains wake me even further. My sister let me stay here last night after I had a nightmare about Archmage Sanora. Being here with her again, I'm so grateful, and I try not to let my concerns get the better of me. I guess I could ask for more, but I won't think about that right now. I inhale—oxygen easily fills my lungs, but the most important person in the world to me has been struggling to take breaths.

Al is sleeping beside me, her plush, lilac sheets bundled around her. I beam. The oxygen tube in her nostrils and looped behind her ears is hard to ignore. No one said that life was fair, but it doesn't mean it can't be.

I thought the rising sun would also be her wake-up call, but having someone burst through the door works, too.

Both double doors fly open as Dr. Sammer, Mother, and Father march in. I immediately shoot up in bed.

Al's a little slower to get going, rubbing the sleep out of her eyes before she realizes extra people are in the room. She focuses on me and yelps like her dreaming had made her forget that my return wasn't, in fact, a dream.

"Gods, you startled me," she says, and I honestly don't know who her words are directed at.

Dr. Sammer walks over with a freshly pressed white lab coat and a bag of medical supplies and helps her sit up in bed. "Sorry, Allegra, it's not every day I'm barging in here unannounced." He presses two fingers to the inside of her wrist. "I'll check your heart rate, okay?" He keeps his fingers there a long time while staring at her collarbones. "All done. I also counted your respiratory rate, which is how many breaths you take in a minute. I have to be sneaky when I do that, so you don't change your pace after the fact."

"Sneaky is right," Al says. There's more rosiness to her cheeks this morning.

Mother and Father remain watching from the doorway as the doctor pulls out a stethoscope and places it on her back. He makes her breathe deeply.

I'm pleasantly surprised that it only sent her into one small coughing fit.

Dr. Sammer loops the rubber part of his device around his neck like a scarf. "You're sounding better today."

"So…are you going to tell me why you're here at this gods-awful hour? Unless you're going to help us celebrate Cade's birthday?" She turns to me and winks.

Why is *Dr. Sammer here?*

When he doesn't answer, she continues, "Couldn't forget my girl. Happy seventeenth birthday!" She wiggles her fingers at me like I'm old now.

"I feel the arthritis setting in already," I say with a chuckle. I ignore how our parents haven't yet acknowledged my birthday. They'd say they have more important matters to tend to. "But seriously, thanks. I nearly forgot myself."

"Well, happy birthday, then, Cadence! I have a wonderful present for you!" He claps. "The new medication is ready for your sister, and so is our stem cell transplant procedure. Allegra can begin the new treatment immediately!"

Dr. Sammer better check my heart rate and respiratory rate because I'm sure they're both through the roof. "W-what? She can… start the treatment?"

"Mhm," he nods, a smile widening on his dark brown skin.

"You mean, like right now?" Al asks.

"Why'd you think I woke you up at this 'gods-awful hour'?"

Al and I scoot closer on the bed and hug each other, laughing and smiling. Diamond tears tease the edges of my eyelids. From joy. But regardless of the reason, I still have to keep them hidden.

"I'm so happy!" I say awkwardly, jumping out of bed. Dressed only in a thin shirt and shorts, I rush to the closet and say, "Oops, let me grab a robe." I do, but keep my back to the doctor.

Mother and Father are smart enough to take the hint. They know I'm about to cry and cry and cry.

Father clears his throat. "Dr. Sammer, can we discuss a few things about the procedure out in the hallway while these two get ready?"

"Sounds like a plan. Pack your things, okay? I'll be back to take you to the hospital. You'll stay for a few weeks." Dr. Sammer grins then walks to my parents, resting both hands on their shoulders before leading them out and closing the bedroom doors behind him.

With the coast is clear, I turn around with diamonds pooling in my arms. I let them fall to the floor, clinking and glistening, and rush back to Al's side. I want to jump on the bed, but she is still fragile, so I instead quickly climb back into bed beside her—making sure not to jostle her too badly.

Wanting the physical proof that she's safe, I gently hold her hands. "Thank you for the best birthday present ever."

She flips her hair over her shoulder. "Don't mention it. All in a day's work."

We burst out laughing again, and I swear I should pinch myself.

"I love you so, so much. We're going to get through this together, okay? Just you and me, like old times."

Tears trickle down her cheeks, but she doesn't wipe them away. "I love you, too, Cade." She takes a deep breath. "Which is why I can't have you by my side."

I blink. "W-what do you mean?"

"I'm going to recover from this setback. I'm going to receive the new medication and treatment I need to make my lungs not hate me. But you…you still have work to do. And I refuse to be the one who holds you back." She bows her head, picking at her nails. "You have to go back and finish what you started."

I grip the sheets and squeeze my eyes shut, afraid I'll permanently dry up my diamond tears with all my crying. "I don't want to leave you again. I should be here for—"

"For what? To sit around while I crack painfully cheesy jokes? To watch me sleep until you fall asleep? For you to still have to endure Mother and Father's presence?" I start to retort but she carries on. "All this while you'll be wracking your brain, never knowing if you could've saved Raven. You'll forever be watching behind your back for that Archmage to come for her revenge. You're not done, Cade."

I can't believe she's calling me out. "But what if—"

"Girl, there's nothing you can say to make me change my mind. I don't need your strength. I've got my own."

Her words hit me square in the chest. "Wow…I…never thought about it like that. But I never doubted your strength. I just assumed it was my job."

Al adjusts the pillow behind her back. "That's because Mother and Father told you it was. But it's not."

The thought of leaving her again breaks my heart. It's a reality I never pictured happening. But she's right. I cry the last of my diamonds for now, my skin raw and red. Surely, I'm a hot mess.

"Hey."

I focus on her.

"You better find your answers for me. You already know that I love you, but what about Raven? You have to try to save her—to love her. And stop this crazy queen's tirade—for all our sakes."

"Why do I have such a smart sister?" I say with a smirk, mulling over her words until an idea clicks in my head. "I met someone on my travels. Aura. She's a Transport Mage. Her magic allows her to teleport herself and others almost anywhere. She lives on the outskirts of Jessen. Says magi and humans live as equals there, that it's better than Kinephrus or Noravale and their leader, Bidyzen, is fair and just. Maybe we can go there after you finish your treatment?"

"Hey, you've been to so many cool places without me. No fair!" She sticks her tongue out at me.

"All you have to do to be like me is steal a horse, travel around with a mage you didn't know was a mage, befriend a bunch of pub goers, outsmart the King's Guard, outrun a sandstorm, get conned by the Queen of the Magi, get thrown in and break out of jail." I smile before I add in a chipper tone of anyone trying to sell something. "All for the low, low price of three rubies, ten copper coins, and forty diamonds!"

We burst out laughing, but Al quickly goes into a small coughing fit. She leans over to make sure there's enough oxygen in her tank before settling back on the bed. "That's crazy…" she says, "that there are entire cities where magi live. Well, even that they actually exist! And magi like Malore, and probably half our staff, were here this whole time. Right under our noses!"

"Right?! And I love that Jessen welcomes both humans and magi. Maybe we can spread our reach, one city at a time. One diamond at a time." I wink.

"Ugh, you're so corny!" she laughs, pushing me over at my arm.

Our precious time together is short-lived as one of the maids comes into the room with a wheelchair to take Al to the hospital with Dr. Sammer.

By the time she's gone, I can't remember what our goodbye was like. Blocking it out of my memory is the only way I'll be able to leave her behind like she wants. All I know is that I was so, so proud of her. She's one tough cookie. And, apparently, I need her more than she needs me.

TWENTY-NINE

As much as Al's departure was a blur, the aftermath is anything but. Mother and Father eventually return to her room to find me still in bed, now sitting on Al's side. Gods, she's not farther than a few miles away, gone for not more than thirty minutes, and I already miss her.

Mother and Father close the bedroom doors, remaining as far away from me as possible. Their impassive stares speak volumes. They probably haven't shed a single tear of joy that Al's treatment will begin, nor a skipping heartbeat from worry for her safety.

The first words to come out of Father's mouth? "If she doesn't make it through this, we're going to blame you. We'll blame you for the rest of your life, Cadence."

I didn't think I could hate my parents more than I do right now. I'm seething with anger when I should be at Al's side. Thank gods she convinced me to leave this toxic place again. Unable to hold in my rage, I scream, "Why can't you just leave me alone?!"

Mother wipes a wisp of hair off of her forehead and sighs. "Oh, don't be so dramatic."

My face twists in disgust, reflected at me in Al's vanity mirror beside my parents. "How can you say that?"

"Dr. Sammer's treatment is our last resort. She was too weak to even dance one song at the ball. It…wasn't good for our image," Mother says, biting her lip.

"You're both pigs!" I leap from the bed, hold onto the end of the bedpost, and spit out, "*You're* not good for our image. "

Father folds his arms. "Calm down. This is not the time for—"

"Calm *down*! Are you kidding me?" I swear my fingernails can dig holes in this wood.

"Just because you were gone doesn't mean you can come back and do whatever you want. We're still your parents," Father retorts.

"Lousy ones," I grumble.

Mother takes advantage of my changed position and walks closer, trying to grab some of the diamonds lost in the sheets.

"Stop!" I shriek, slapping her hand away and returning to the bed, protective over the space. "What are you doing?"

Mother rubs her wrist. "Cadence! What has come over you? I'm only collecting the diamonds we should've had last week. Maybe you can do more for Allegra, after all."

She's saying that to spite me, using it as ammunition for my clear defiance. "My diamond tears will never be enough to heal her. And I shouldn't have hidden my power from the world. Because that's what it is—not a curse, not a gift, but a *power*."

"Think what you want, but that won't change our minds. The world is a horrible place."

I scoff and say sarcastically, "Sure it is. You taught me that I needed to hide from other people who would use me, but it was so *you* could use me for yourselves."

Father shrugs. "Of course, there were added...benefits to your gift. We weren't going to deny ourselves that. Who would?"

I wanted to wait to confront them, but the one person who I need with me to get through this isn't here right now. And she gave me permission to fight for what's right. So, what do I have to lose?

"Oh, it was a gift, all right." I fume. "One you stole from the Archmage's husband." There. I said it.

My parents' eyes widen. Father's mouth opens, but nothing comes out.

"Oh, can't talk, huh? Just like the Archmage's husband. Tor can't talk anymore because you *killed* him."

"We have no idea what you're talking about," Mother finally says.

I laugh in a crazed sort of way. "I've been to Kinephrus. I've met the Archmage. I even found Tor's magi emblem under your bed. You can't hide it anymore."

Mother holds her hands out and tries to settle me like I'm a scared animal. "Cadence, please…"

"You murdered him!"

"All right, we did it," Father admits in a gruff voice. "So what? It was so you could have as much time with Allegra as possible."

"No. It was so *you* could become a baron and baroness, buy this stupid house, and hire people we don't even need and…" I start bawling again. My whole body's shaking now. "You stole my life from me…a life I never knew I was supposed to have. I never knew about the magi, the wars that happened, none of it."

"We were protecting you from those heathens." Mother lifts her head high like she's above everyone else. Gods, she sickens me. I keep the knowledge to myself that they're hiring these "heathens" to do all this work. I don't want them to know I found out, in case it can help me somehow.

"Speaking of heathens," Father says, "We know all about that Raven girl. We're not stupid. We know she didn't kidnap you."

My heart leaps at the mention of Raven, but then I narrow my eyes at them. I wasn't about to deny it. "So what?"

Mother cuts in. "Well, clearly, she's a bad influence on you. These are the exact type of people we were trying to protect you from. Thieves, vagabonds, liars, bastards. The whole lot of them are no good."

Do they even realize the words they're saying? What hypocrites! "Raven has done the most selfless thing for me that anyone has ever done. She gave me my life in exchange for hers. And I'm going to go save her."

"She's just a girl," Mother scoffs.

I stand tall. "I know. You can't stop me from going back to her."

My parents try to loom over me as they stalk closer. "What makes you believe we'd let you leave this time?" Father asks.

"Exactly. We need you here. Not for your diamonds, but for the King," Mother adds.

"W-what? What in all of Soridente are you talking about?"

Mother picks at something in her nails as if she was casually mentioning the weather. "You might remember when we sent some of the King's Guard after you? They almost intercepted you in Serency. We sent our lovely new Tracker Mage for that job."

I blink in surprise at Mother's admission to hiring magi. But does that mean King Pontifex knows, too? "Yeah, how could I forget? Raven and I kicked their asses with a bunch of cool pub folk."

Mother's eye twitches but she continues. "And then of course we've got some guards around our home now. It's all thanks to the deal we made with King Pontifex. We finally revealed to him our secret. We told him…about you."

My jaw drops. "You…you told him? But, didn't he start a war to kill and banish magi?"

"If the situation suits him to his advantage, he's open to, shall we say, making exceptions," Father says.

"Like…what?"

"Well," Mother keeps going, "We made a deal that if your Father could become his advisor, we would give you to them to marry Prince Wendell, and to provide them with diamond tears whenever they see fit. The turmoil amongst our people, as evident by those dirty nobodies from Serency, proves that another war is coming. Another war is necessary. And that requires lots of funding—hence, why King Pontifex was willing to strike a deal with us."

I haven't eaten in a while, but I still think I'm going to be sick. Just when I thought they couldn't get any worse. "I've got to be having a nightmare right now. Are you insane? I'm not your collateral!"

"There's no arguing here, Cadence. The deal is done."

"You don't *own* me!"

"Who's going to stop us?" Father marches toward me, and I back away toward the window. Jumping out of the second-floor window seems like a much better option than staying here with these lunatics, honestly.

The doors to Al's room are closed, but shuffling and bustling echo down the hallway as if people are running in a panic.

"I heard yelling. Is everything all right in here?" a voice says in worried desperation as the door opens.

Thank the gods, it's Malore—and the other hired help. There are ten of them now when there were four or five when I left...a little over a week ago.

Mother smooths back her hair and Father tugs at his shirt to get out the wrinkles. Father clears his throat. "I'm sorry for the commotion. Cadence, she's...hysterical that she didn't get to spend more time with Allegra. Dr. Sammer took her to the hospital to start her stem cell treatment."

One of the maids claps a hand over her mouth. "Oh, that's wonderful news!"

"But she'll miss the birthday dinner I have planned," the cook says, clutching his apron in disappointment.

Malore closes his eyes and his Adam's apple bobs as he swallows hard, shifting his focus between me and my parents. He knows something's up.

My lips tremble and my whole body threatens to shake. It takes everything I am to compose myself instead of confessing everything about my parents right then and there. But clearly, they're capable of murder. I have no idea what they would do if I exposed them, and I refuse to risk anyone's life here.

Malore rests a hand on my shoulder. "Are you okay?"

I shake my head. "No, I'm not." I grab Al's book off the nightstand and hold it close to my chest. Without looking at Mother and

Father, I direct the staff, pointing to the piles of shining jewels all over the floor and bedspread. "Please take these diamonds to the good people in Serency, especially Gunder at the Better Days Pub."

"Don't be ridiculous, Cadence. *We* could use the money, especially with Allegra's new treatments," Mother says like it's another average, everyday thing to plan.

I grit my teeth. "Stop manipulating me! Dr. Sammer said he has everything he needs to help Al recover. It's *my* money, and that's where I want it to go."

She actually backs off, physically retreating as well.

I push past her and Father, stalking toward the door, eager to return to my bedroom where I can lock myself away and devise my exit strategy. I'm surprised I've made it this long in the same room with them.

The staff begins gathering the gems, scooping them into their pockets and bags.

"Should we reveal it was you who sent it to them, Miss Alero?" the maid asks.

I stop in the doorway and turn halfway, maintaining a stoic expression. "Oh, there's no need. They'll know who it's from."

THIRTY

I've never rushed to my room so quickly, locked the door so tightly. I rush to pack the things I need, using the same bag I'd taken
when I left with Raven. Tradition has been broken, and death is no
longer a part of my birthday. With Al's blessing to go rescue her, I
can only hope I'm not too late.

One of the maids knocked on my door a bit ago, stating that
breakfast was ready, but I sent her away. I can't think about food at
a time like this. I don't even care if they've got the biggest birthday
cake in all of Soridente waiting for me for dessert tonight. My intestines twist at the thought.

A little while later, I hear my parents talking outside my door.
I freeze, expecting them to barge in, but then their footsteps and
voices fade away. Good. There's no way I want to see or talk to them
if I don't have to.

The book Al had been reading when I left, the one I put my letter in, is cradled in my arms. It's my stark reminder that she knew
why I left, that I didn't leave her because I wanted to, but because
we had to improve our lives, and that's why I'm leaving again. It reminds me that she loves me because she's letting me go after someone I could potentially love someday. She's proven that she can be
strong without me…and vice versa.

Still, this whole journey has been for her. Even my leaving now,
is for *her*. Because we both know I can be happy and healthy since

I discovered so much on my journey—the joy in helping others, the good parts of my magic...and Raven.

I don't know when her sentencing will happen, but time sucks and clearly isn't on my side. I have to go back to Kinephrus. No matter what the magi warned me about, no matter what Sanora says she'll do to me if I return. Al will get the treatment she needs, so there's one more important person in my life I can't lose either.

Raven wouldn't want me getting in my own head. Al wouldn't want our parents to win over us. I reminisce on what Raven said about how she lives her life—free, independent, and in control. That's exactly how I was living when I was away from home. I did the things I wanted to do, even if that meant crying diamonds for people. But it was on *my* terms. So why should I stop now? Shouldn't I embrace everything that I am and do what I want to do?

And what is that, Cadence? I ask myself.

A small smile spreads across my face.

I dash under my bed and grab the magi emblem I stole from Mother and Father, stashing it in my bag for safe keeping, along with the magi book Al gave me. Then I rush from my room and down the stairs to the butler's quarters. The door is closed so I knock. Of course, another employee answers. But I insist on speaking to Malore. The man lets me in. The room is quite nice, with all the same fixings I have in mine, the canopy beds, the chandeliers, the large dressers, the lush carpets—more unnecessary extravagance.

Malore's sitting on one of the lounge chairs, writing in what looks like a journal.

"Malore? I need your help fixing something in the library," I say, thinking quickly on my feet to find a way to pull him away from the other employees.

He offers a quizzical expression, rubbing the stubble on his chin. "Oh, well, I just started my break."

"I can help," the first man says again, having followed me.

"I want Malore," I state firmly.

He seems to get the picture with my stern expression. He stands. "Ah yes, of course, Cadence. Lead the way."

The other guy looks hurt and confused as we leave. I want to tell him he's not missing out on much, but of course, that's not true.

We walk in silence to the library, all my words waiting to bubble to the surface once we get inside. I almost gasp when we finally reach the room. The tall bookshelves, the cozy couches—I missed it so much.

Malore closes the door behind us and twists to face me, folding his arms. "Okay, is this about your birthday? I swear your parents didn't tell me about it until this morning but I've been working on a party for later and—?"

"I don't care about that. But thank you, Malore." I pace in front of the nearest bookshelf, crossing my arms to keep myself from fumbling with my hands from both excitement and fear. "I brought you here to tell you that I told Al about everything—the magi, the Archmage, what happened while I was gone. And well, because she's safe with Dr. Sammer and about to start her treatments, I have to leave…now."

"So soon?" he asks, tilting his head.

"Al showed me that she can be strong without me. She remind-ed me that we each have our own lives and we're free to live those lives, and that doesn't mean we love each other any less. And so…I have to go back to Kinephrus and face Sanora."

"It…it's for that girl, isn't it?"

I bite my lip, my cheeks warming. "Who else?"

His smile reaches his eyes. "I'm happy to help, Cadence." But then the light fades slightly. He picks up a stray book from the couch, flipping it over even though he keeps his attention on me. "You know, I never told you why I've been against Sanora this whole time. It's the same reason why I'm against the Goldins, too—their greed, thirst for revenge, selfishness, and blazon disregard for in-nocent lives. Leaders tend to develop these ugly habits. Bidyzen is someone trying to break the cycle. He started in Jessen and will work his way outward. And so, if I can help in some way, if I can stop both sides from destroying each other, I'll do whatever it takes." He looks me up and down. "Apparently, you will, too."

I flash a warm but determined smile. "You're right. This is my 'whatever it takes.' So, will you help me? There's not a moment to waste. It's time for me to go back to a love worth fighting for."

Malore helps me carve out a plan for my breakout of this gods-forsaken house—again. We don't have the luxury of a Shadow Mage to sneak me out this time. Yeah, I may not have Raven, but I have a falcon. We switch locations to the garden, where we can open windows to the outside. And with Malore and his Tracker magic, he ensures that the coast is clear so I can leave despite the newly hired guards dotting my home's perimeter.

The greenhouse shoots a little prick of sadness in my heart, reminding me of learning the names of the plants and flowers with Al, and also of when Raven first convinced me to go with her on this crazy adventure. But I stuff those thoughts away, for now, to focus on the task at hand.

Malore has to whistle for me because I never learned how—a skill Al always excelled at. Despite so many lessons, I still failed to pick it up. Not too soon after, Aura's falcon, Kazi, appears in the open window.

"Yes!" I pump my fist. "It worked!"

"So, Aura said to put a message in his little pouch, and she'll receive it? But how long will that take?"

"I'm not sure. She didn't say, but I hope not too long. I need time on my side here."

A brown-and-cream-colored, feathery blur swoops down from the window to the back of one of the benches beside us.

"Well, you're kind of cute, aren't you, Kazi?" Malore asks as if expecting an answer.

The bird cocks its head at us as if it understands what he's saying. Maybe it does.

I snicker and then get back to business. I sit on the bench and scribble out a message to Aura. The gist of the letter? *Hurry, I need you. Need to save Raven and kick Sanora's butt.* I'm almost done jotting out my note when a *fwoosh* reaches my ears. It sounds like another falcon has flown in. I spin around to see some leaves shifting.

Malore steps in front of me. Even though he doesn't have a weapon, his mage instinct to protect—if that's a thing—must be taking over.

Whether Mother or Father caught me, or another one of our hired help is going to rat me out, I stand in response, ready to run or fight or whatever I have to do.

But we both let down our guards when Aura reveals herself from behind a cluster of trees, boots clinking on the floor and her white hooded cloak swaying behind her.

"Aura! What are you doing here?" Malore asks, his shoulders easing at her presence.

My jaw drops. "Wow, I didn't even finish writing the message and you're already here! That must be some falcon."

Aura laughs and Kazi flies straight to her forearm where he rests. But her expression quickly grows dark like the growing shadows of the setting sun. "I never left Noravale. I…had a feeling you'd need me sooner rather than later."

"You're the best!" I exclaim, my tension easing slightly. We weren't home free yet. This was the start of it all, the beginning of the end. If I left now, there would be no turning back. I'd never return home, at least not with the state my parents are in. But right now, I can't see myself going about it any other way. There's no way I'd marry Wendell when I have a perfect girl for me waiting in a prison clear across the country. I just have to save her first. And there's no way I'd cry diamonds for a King who doesn't care for his people—for *all* his people—Unremarkable or not.

"I heard about your sister. I'm so happy for you both," Aura says, snapping me back to the present.

"Thank you. This…this is why I need you. My parents claimed they cared about me and Al, but that's a straight-up lie. Al's getting the care she needs so that I don't lose my best friend. I can't…I won't lose my girlfriend either."

Aura grins. "What happened to that bashful girl I met in my house last week?"

I realize how emboldened I've become and almost blush, but instead, I hold my head high. "A pretty cool girl I know taught me that." I wink.

"Well, it's about time you saved her, huh?"

I nod fervently.

Malore clears his throat, haphazardly picking at a dead leaf on a nearby plant. "I don't mean to burst your bubble, but exactly how are you going to break Raven out of prison?

I chew the inside of my cheek. "Uh…good question. I figured I'd wing it—use myself as bait or something?"

"Cadence, you said Archmage Sanora promised she'd kill you if you returned." He shudders at the thought.

"Yeah…about that…" I scratch behind my ear. "Can't you transport yourself into Raven's cell and rescue her?"

"Not with the wards her magi have built up. Come on, Cadence! We must be strategic here. I want you both coming out of this alive, okay?" Kazi flies to Aura's shoulder at a flick of her command.

"I know, I know. I feel like I'm a goner whether I go there or stay here with my parents. Sanora is out for revenge, and if I leave, Mother and Father will be, too. But I have to stay focused on Raven because I need her as much as she needs me right now." I think a moment before something clicks. "I know what I have to do."

He cracks his knuckles. "Okay, so you'll create a diversion while we bust Raven out of prison?"

"Well…not quite. I'll explain on the way."

"But I can take you there in a second," Aura reminds me.

I glance at the overcast sky, the open window once giving me all the hope in the world, and now, it's only a sliver of what I want in life. "Right. Okay, here's the plan. It's kind of messy, and it might get me killed. But if justice prevails, and good triumphs over evil, I might be able to pull it off."

THIRTY-ONE

Malore and Aura seem to think I'm only *semi*-crazy, so they decide to go along with my plan and help me. Who knew I'd have multiple magi friends when I didn't even know they existed two weeks ago?

At least I like to believe they're my friends. I've only ever had Al and Raven, so how would I know?

In the greenhouse, Malore and I approach Aura. She places her hands on our shoulders. I inhale deeply and pray to the gods that Raven's still alive.

And then…we're gone.

In the same time it takes me to exhale, I'm standing in Sanora's tower, in the grand hall where she'd previously sat on her throne. Aura and Malore are beside me for half a second before they both disappear, just as we planned.

This better work. It *has* to work.

But the moment my feet hit the blue rug, I furrow my brow. Sanora…she's…not here. I didn't expect her to sit on her throne all day. But still, her absence is unsettling. It doesn't feel right. I contemplate what she could be doing instead.

The doors to her tower creak open behind me, but my gut tells me it's not her. Not that I need to stick around to see who it is. I sprint to the nearest braided spiral column and hope I can hide in the shadows long enough to avoid detection.

Two people are talking, a man and a woman, but their voices are hushed. I strain to make out the words they're saying.

"Happening...in Esoch's tower..." I pick out in between the clicks of their boots on the porcelain floor. I lean forward, peering around the column the tiniest bit to spy where the two magi, probably guards, are headed. They walk down the hallway and past the throne room. I'm tempted to follow them.

"She deserves it...stealing Tor's crown..."

"Shadow Mage..."

I gasp and then clamp my hands over my mouth and whirl around, willing my back to become one with the column. The two guards pause in silence. My hammering heart fills my ears Who knows what powers these magi have? They could probably take me out instantaneously if they wanted.

I hold my breath. Thankfully, they continue walking, their footsteps and voices fading away. I wait a couple of seconds longer before I slink to the next column, then finally, against the wall separating the throne room from the hall. I slowly peek around the corner in time to see the heel of one of their boots disappear around the next corner. I can't lose them.

I *can't* lose Raven.

Creeping along the wall, I follow the guards' conversation, making sure to keep a good distance between me and them to avoid detection. The halls are filled with paintings no doubt of past Archmagi. I'm not even sure which picture is Tor's. Eventually, the hall leads to an outdoor walkway, thankfully a much shorter distance to Esoch's tower than any of the others.

I have to wait for the guards to traverse the whole distance to the opposite tower before I even step foot on it. With the open sky and absent walls, there will be nowhere to hide if they turn around.

When I find my chance, I rush forward, crouching slightly for fear the wind will knock me straight off this runway. That'd be my luck. The tower is stone gray, reminding me of the prison I stayed in a second too long. No windows, no decorations. I scream on the inside at its ominous vibes. I *can't* be too late.

I find an open archway and peek around the edge, gripping the stone frame. My throat catches. What looks like a hundred magi sit inside the tower, with seats rising up the walls of the tower like a stadium. I hope Aura and Malore won't have too many problems, seeing as a huge chunk of the city of Kinephrus came to this…public *event*. Gods, who would want to watch an execution? That's sick. Well, I'm not sorry to burst their bubble. Because there won't be any executing tonight.

I pull my hood over my head. It's a little beaten up and torn from my journey but still enough to cover me. I slip into the crowd, the opposite direction that the guards are walking in. Noting a spot with less foot traffic, I stand with my back to the wall behind an empty row of seats. Two rows in front of that, magi are chatting, but they're too preoccupied to notice me—or that I'm out of place.

I tune out their conversations because honestly, I don't want to know if they're saying anything bad about Raven. I'm about to slink along the side when a voice booms from the center of the tower.

"Welcome, welcome!" It's that one guard who took me to Sanora in the first place—the Psychic Mage.

I cringe instinctively, hoping he can't hear my scheming and plotting from way over here, and especially amidst the other auras around here, or whatever he reads off of people.

"Thank you all for joining us for a night of retribution and revival. Please rise and give your praise to our Queen, Her Majesty, Archmage Sanora!" He spreads his arm to the side and she walks out, looking more radiant than I remember.

Her gown looks like it's going to swallow her up, covered in intricately patterned beading, and her golden jewelry shines from the beaming lights in the tower. Her crown rivals that of King Pontifex's, fixed atop the center of her head surrounded by a cascade of beaded braids. No wonder she wasn't sitting on her throne when I arrived.

Everyone does as the Psychic Mage commands. I clap lightly to blend in, though the crowd cheers, clapping, hooting, hollering, and whistling their support. Come on, what is this? You'd think the Archmage was holding a special celebration, not the execution of an accused prisoner. The thought twists my intestines in knots. If it's my birthday today, it also means it's the anniversary of Tor's death.

Blood for blood.

Once the crowd settles down and takes their seats, Sanora sits on a golden stool, surrounded by a slew of magi guards. I can only imagine what their powers are.

"It is an honor to have my people with me tonight, to support me and pay tribute to Tor," the Archmage says. Even though there are magi way high up the tower, they are cheering as if they can still hear her. "Though Tor cannot be with us tonight, he would be pleased to know we are properly punishing those who defy us. Today, on the anniversary of Tor's death, we lay to rest the Shadow Mage who tried to steal his crown."

Now the cheers for Sanora morph into boos and hisses for Raven. I frown and cover my face more, trying to hide how upset I am.

"*And* she also escaped from my jail. But that was my mistake to underestimate her powers. I did not let it happen again when the gods decided to bring her back to me as fate intended." She claps her hands together. "All right, it is finally the moment you've all been waiting for. Let's not wait a second longer, shall we? Bring out the prisoner!"

At Sanora's command, a small door across from me opens, and the Trap Mage is there, leading Raven to the center of the room. Her cloak is gone, and her clothes look like they've been through more than one sand tornado. Her pink curls look faded and matted. My chest aches at the sight. I want to get her attention so badly, but obviously without revealing myself…yet. But anyways, Raven's staring at her feet, trudging along like nothing matters anymore. To her, nothing does.

But she won't think that way for long. She doesn't know that I came back for her.

Sanora couldn't be glaring at Raven with any *more* disdain than she is right now. "Do you admit to the crimes for which you have been sentenced tonight?"

Raven nods solemnly.

"What's that? I want to hear the words from your mouth, traitor."

"Yes," she says feebly. "I do."

Gods, she's given *up*. Oh Raven, if only you knew that I haven't.

"And you understand that the punishment for your multiple crimes is death?"

"Yes."

The Trap Mage who is binding her arms behind her back makes a face at that. He didn't end up setting me free from my cell, but he *was* intrigued by my Diamond Mage status. Maybe he can be swayed on our side if I play my cards right. Half of the damn magi city is probably in here so I need all the help I can manage.

I scan the area to find a way to sneak closer when another figure enters the room.

Sanora looks like she's on cloud nine. "Then Raven McKae, you will now face your sentence of death by poisoning.

Oh, gods. The Poison Mage.

I wish Sanora would use her Illusion magic right now so that this could be fake and just what she wants us to see. But I can't deny it. My eyes aren't playing tricks on me this time. The Archmage really is about to execute the girl I've caught feelings for—the girl who showed me what else is out there, who introduced me to a better side of myself.

If I thought the tatted-up Psychic Mage was a chunk of metal, the Poison Mage was a slice of steel. She's all limbs, wearing violet robes that cling to her tall, thin frame. Of course, she's the Poison Mage. Unassuming in her might, she can do some real damage to anyone who crosses her path.

What hurts me more than witnessing the Poison Mage stalking toward Raven is the fact that my girl isn't even putting up a fight. She's not screaming, kicking, fighting—not even crying. I guess that's her way of showing strength, by not showing any emotion. That would be one more way she's letting the Archmage win.

I don't know how the Poison Mage's magic works, and I don't want to be too late. So before anything else happens, my legs move on autopilot, rushing me down the steps, my arms pumping to keep up the pace.

"Stop! Don't do it!" I scream.

I'm sure all eyes are on me right now, but I wouldn't know. I can imagine their confused stares and Sanora's enraged glare burning a hole into me, but my attention is only on Raven. Her face brightens like the rising sun, and that throbbing in my chest when she first asked me to dance at the Summer Solstice Ball returns. Her comforting presence, the easiness of being with her, the independence and confidence she brings out of me when I'm around her. Gods, I missed her.

"Cade!" she exclaims. Her expression is one of elation, quickly replaced by fear and shock. The tear she sheds says it all.

I run to hug her, but something tugs me back as if someone pulled me by my cloak, and I fall to the floor. It must be the Trap Mage, creating some sort of barrier, preventing me from reaching her. I grunt in frustration and spring to my feet. "Rae, I...I came back for you."

Sanora laughs, acting as impassively as if I hadn't interrupted this event. "That's bold of you."

The crowd goes wild, shouting both in anger and excitement for the scene unfolding before them. I ignore them, including the Archmage, and focus on Raven. "I had to come back. You're one of the most important people in my world."

Raven's lips tremble while her eyes shut. They open, tears spilling down her cheeks. "But...what about...?"

"She's safe, getting treatment. She told me I needed to come back for you." I avoid saying her name so as not to put a target on Al's back.

"I'm so grateful…I…I wish I could meet her," she says in a soft, low voice for only me to hear.

"I promise you will." I don't know how, but I'll keep that promise. Seeing her reaction, I can feel how much she cares about my sister, just like I know she cares about me. Maybe it used to be about the money for her, but not anymore. I hope she knows I came back not because I care about her magic but because I don't. I started having feelings for her before I ever knew she was a mage. I see *her*. I'm not going to abandon her as her parents did. And me, it used to be about getting rid of my power and always focusing on others more than myself. But now, I know without a doubt, that my diamond tear ability is not a curse, it's a gift—and I fully embrace it. I embrace everything that I am—my sexuality, my independence…*me*.

I pull my shoulders back and stand tall. "Archmage Sanora, I come before you today, to ask that you forgive Raven for her crimes and set her free."

Sanora's laugh gets lost in the crowd's roar, head tipping back and beaded braids jangling. "I told you I'd kill you if you ever come back. What makes you think I'd let either of you go with your lives?"

The Poison Mage, and even the Trap Mage, take a readying stance as if they're going to attack me. I want to take a step back, but I stand my ground. As loudly as I can, I proclaim, "Because I'm the only heir you have left."

Raven's mouth drops, and equally surprised gasps escape from the magi surrounding us. The Trap Mage, who had inadvertently divulged that information to me while chatting with the other guard outside my prison cell, averts his gaze.

For once, something falters in Sanora. It feels so good to see a tiny brick crumble from her haughty tower. "I…I don't know what you're talking about."

"I'm talking about what you told me. Tor gave me my power, which makes me your adopted daughter according to the rules of the magi. I overheard that the other magi imbued with Tor's magic died in the Goldin War. Because you can't touch anyone else with magic and obviously Tor hasn't since then. That means I'm the last of your adopted children. So, are you really going to kill me?"

Sanora's eyes narrow into slits, but she shakes it off, probably realizing the rest of the magi are watching her. "I...no, you're right. I haven't given an Unremarkable any power since Tor was murdered...nor before then. It was all Tor's doing." She paces the floor, clearly trying to discover a way out of this. But there is none. "So, you're one of my adopted daughters. But that doesn't mean I shouldn't punish this heathen and thief who is not related to me."

Raven scans the crowd with disdain as they cheer in agreement.

"Then take me instead." I step forward, tipping my chin up.

"Excuse me?"

"Let Raven go, and I'll stay with you. Forever. I won't try to run. I won't make your life miserable. Just let Raven go."

"Cade, no!" Raven cries. She jolts toward me but is jerked back by the Trap Mage, conflict shading his expression.

"Hmm...interesting proposition," the Archmage says. She twirls a jeweled braid between her long-nailed fingers. "And what's in it for me?"

"Don't do it!" Raven interrupts. "Don't sacrifice yourself for me."

"I want to do this, Rae. Let me do this for you."

Something seems to come to Raven's senses, and she eases back, remaining silent. She helped create this independent girl, after all.

"Sanora, I will help build the magi kingdom in your image."

"Intriguing offer. If you stay here..."

"She's not going anywhere with you!" a shrill voice calls from the crowd.

My heart drops into my stomach as I recognize it. I spin on my heel, my pulse racing. The one person I never thought I'd see is standing at the top of the stairs, close to where I'd been spying on the scene earlier. My tongue catches in my throat in bewilderment, but somehow, I manage to sputter, "M-Mother?"

THIRTY-TWO

I never thought I would be so weirded out seeing my two worlds collide. There's Mother and Father, standing with a couple of our staff from the house. It dawns on me…they must all be magi like Malore, hired from the black market. And they must have a Transport Mage and another Tracker Mage amongst their ranks if they found me and got here so quickly.

"Cadence! You shouldn't have anything to do with these traitors," Mother says, placing fists on her hips. Back home, she looks intimating, but here she appears small surrounded by her magic-laced enemies. Magi twist in their seats to face her, glaring daggers and probably withholding curses on the tips of their tongues.

"Traitors?" Sanora has remained somewhat composed this entire time, but Mother's words send her into a rage. Her eyes go round and her jaw clenches. Her cheeks flush, not in embarrassment, but in red-hot fury. "Monticello and Esmerene…*you're* the traitors!"

Father holds a similar protective stance to Mother's. Baron or not, he also appears to have his humanity stripped down to the barest of bones. "Cadence, come here, right now. We don't care what you think of us. We're bringing you home."

Before Sanora can even retort, I chuck out a reply of my own, "I'm not going anywhere with you."

All of my parents—that sounds weird to say, but it's the truth—raise their eyebrows at my response. I trudge around the space, each step as heavy as my words. "I'm tired of people always needing things from me. This is my chance to do something for myself and get what *I* want." I whirl to Mother and Father. "I'm not getting what I want if I go home with you."

Mother dares to roll her eyes at me. "Well, too bad. You belong to us and soon, you'll belong to Prince Wendell and the King."

"Belong?! I'm not some piece of property you can sell or some object you can trade away. I don't *belong* to anyone!"

Raven's getting riled up now, too. Even though she can't move, she can still speak with that autonomy of hers. "She can do what she wants! Stop controlling her!"

"Oh, so you're the little heathen who's screwing with our daughter's mind," Mother spits out, taking a step down the stairs. She ignores the surrounding magi ready to pounce on her. "I hope you're not actually screwing her."

"Mother!" This situation is already completely mortifying but she knows how to take it to the next level.

"Hey!" Sanora's voice cuts through our argument. "Don't you dare talk like I'm not here." Her visage holds so much intensity lightning could've ignited them. "There's no way you're going to take Cadence. She's just offered herself up to me in exchange for this…" She cuts a glance to Raven. "What did you call her—little heathen? In any case, I'm going to accept her proposition."

"No! You can't go in my place!" Raven cries, but I'm determined.

I have to do this to save her from the Poison Mage…and death.

I don't understand why the magi in the stands are watching the scene below them as if none of this is happening. From what I can make out, their expressions look as if they're watching a play or a musical out on the town. I ignore them for now and turn to all my focus onto my parents.

I don't know what powers the magi have that Mother and Father brought with them—the ones they bought off the black market, ugh, probably with my money. But whatever they are, they must not be strong enough, because the Archmage's guards have surrounded them, fully encircling them like prey. I back up slowly until I'm at Sanora's side. "Please, let me do this," I say to no one and everyone at the same time.

She nods to the Trap Mage, and in that moment of silent understanding, Raven's arms break free from their binds. She immediately runs toward me, and this time, no one stops us. We're tangled in each other's arms, and I nuzzle my head into her shoulder. Despite what she's gone through, she still smells like, well, like Raven. Like ivory and pine. Her arms fit around me perfectly, and mine have settled around her like a glove like we were made for each other. When we pull back from our hug, she brushes my cheek and cups my jaw, then pulls me in for the most painfully sweet kiss.

I almost curse the Trap Mage for letting her go, and Sanora for letting us finally reunite. It's so bittersweet, this taste of love and happiness and a future I want to live for, that will all be snatched away from me in a moment.

When we break away, I'm hot-faced, and Raven's cheeks are as pink as her curls. I find her beauty almost too much to bear.

I want to stay in her arms until the end of time, but the Trap Mage taps me on the back. I swivel.

"You are the last of my heirs, the last magic-touched Unremarkable from Tor. It's been sixteen long years, but now you are finally home." Sanora opens her arms to me.

"I will miss you forever," I whisper to Raven, and surprisingly, I find I can shed no tears. I guess I've accepted this cruel twist of fate. I turn back and approach Sanora, painfully aware of each footfall closer to her and further from Raven. The sight of Sanora and knowing my back is to the girl I was falling for…it kills me.

I stop halfway to Sanora but she tuts at me and spreads her arms even wider. "All the way, daughter."

I'm about to puke, the bile ready to release. I slowly walk the rest of the way to Sanora and let her envelop me in her arms. Mine slowly rise to wrap around her as well. It's so awkward and…unnatural. I can't remember the last time I hugged Mother—my *real* mother. I can't imagine it would feel any different than it does now, hugging a stranger who wants to take away everything and everyone I love.

Her hold loosens, but no sooner than it does, she spins me around and locks me against her with one arm, a cold slice of metal against my throat.

I'm dizzy with confusion. Raven's screaming, my parents are yelling. But when I scan the crowd, again they act as if nothing is happening. I realize what Sanora is doing. This is how she's remained the magi's beloved queen. She's probably masking this from them right now, maybe even reflecting a scene of me attacking her so that when she kills me, it will look like self-defense to them. They would be none the wiser. How can they live under such a tyrant's rule?

But why is she showing it to Raven and my parents? And then Sanora's words come back to me. *Sweet revenge.*

I try to break from her grasp, to claw at her skin, but the Trap Mage must have me pinned in place. The biting edge of the knife pierces my throat ever so slightly, threatening to end all of this.

To end me.

"Stop! What are you doing?!" Father screams.

"Let her go!" Mother yells.

Raven's voice joins the commotion. "Please, Archmage! Don't do this!"

Sanora's laugh is maniacal. I'm sure every mage from the highest point in the tower to the bottom would be able to hear it. "Oh, how the tables have turned. Look who's in the position of power now? *Me.* As it always should have been."

"We need our daughter!" Mother screams again. I've never seen her so angry, but I know she's fighting for my diamond tears, not for *me.*

"Oh, it's funny how you want your daughter. Do you know who I wanted? Tor. And you killed him. You went back on your deal and murdered him in cold blood. Why should I show you mercy now? Shouldn't this be equal retribution?"

"He deserved to die!" Mother snarls, lunging forward like a crazed woman.

The guards immediately zero in on her. Sanora didn't use her Illusion Magic on them. They hold her back by her arms as she kicks and screams. I'm surprised she isn't foaming from her mouth.

I flick my focus to Raven, and the concern in her eyes could start a fire. She notices me and her expression changes to an odd look, then she winks. I tilt my head in confusion, but before I know it, she's gone. *What the….?*

Malore appears in the center of the room, several tens of feet away from me. When he spots me being held hostage, he yells, "Sanora! You don't want to do that! Unless you want your people to die tonight as well."

I can't see Sanora's face, but she's probably narrowing her eyes and raging on the inside. "And why not?"

And then Aura appears beside Malore, but she's not alone. I can't count the number of people that pop up beside them. If I hadn't been able to cry before, somehow I can now. Tons of magi and humans are among their ranks. But I don't recognize a single face.

"The citizens of Jessen are ready to help our cause, ready to fight against you," Aura announces.

My parent's magi abandon them and also join us at the bottom of the stairs.

Sanora scoffs. "A bunch of half-witted, dead-beat magi? I'm shaking under my crown! And Unremarkables? You think you can beat a room full of magi with Unre—"

And then she screams. The cool blade slips from her grasp and clatters to the floor. I'm immediately released from her hold and fall to the ground myself. I sputter and run my fingers along my throat where a thin slice of skin sliced open, and only a bit of blood coating my fingertips.

I press myself onto all fours, then spin to find a giant shadow over Sanora's face, blinding her in darkness. In an instant, the crowd regains their composure and witnesses the true scene unfolding before them. Sanora's illusion over them has fallen. But now they don't know what has happened, only that we're attacking their Archmage.

They ready their weapons, arms raised with colorful swirls of magic. And it's as if everyone hears *Go* at the same time.

The fight is on.

THIRTY-THREE

Some of the magi's magic takes an actual physical form. Swirls of gas and sparks of light fill the air. I've only scratched the surface of the extent of the magi's powers. I thought I would be excited, but with everything occurring around me, all I am is terrified.

One of my parents' magi appears to be gathering the wind into a mass of magic before stretching it into a long object like an arrow. Then she fires them off one by one as if she had a bow, piercing the Archmage's magi in the stands.

Those who are higher up make their way down to the fight using various means. Soaring through the air, creating slides to whip their way below, transporting like Aura does in the blink of an eye, or sprinting at an incredible pace.

My eyes round at the enemy magi's retaliation. One thrusts his hands out, and sound waves crash into the opposition. My hands clamp over my ears to stifle the aural disturbance, a cacophony of screams and explosions. A man from Jessen is about to punch a Kinephrus mage, but the mage stops him mid-swing with the snap of her fingers. He moves in slow motion as she side-steps his fist before landing a blow to his back. Time resumes to its normal speed in his world.

The variety and control of their magic are impressive. I want to stand here and study the different powers, well, if they weren't trying to *kill* me.

I dash to the lowest row in the stands, praying to the gods I remain invisible to the Archmage and the citizens' attention while I devise a plan.

But what can I do to help? My diamonds can't help me fight back against these magi. A strong call catches my ear and I whirl to the sound. Another human from Jessen is going to town, beating on a mage whose power must be invisible, like Sanora's illusion magic. One of his comrades is legit wrestling with another mage like they're alone in a bare-fisted match.

Here these people are, clearly devoid of magic, out here kicking ass. Why can't I do the same? Why can't I be enough? Use what I have, do what I can. I take a deep breath and locate the nearest free object—a small podium off to the side. I lift it with both hands and launch it at a group of Sanora's magi ganging up on one of my parent's magi. It crashes into one of them, who stumbles into another mage. My breathing is ragged and I wipe my mouth with my forearm. "*We're* not the enemy here, you know?!"

They turn to me now, malice in their eyes. I guess they found a new target. They stalk toward me and my hand shoots to the bag slung across my chest. I fish around and clasp the hilt of the dagger Raven had started to train me on before the sandstorm. I whip my hand out, pulling it from its sheath, and stab the nearest magi in the shoulder. It may not be graceful but it worked.

The mage snarls in pain, grabbing her shoulder and doubling over. I survey my surroundings, readying for the next attack with my dagger's blade a glinting warning. But this physical threat is foreign to my grasp. I don't want to hurt anyone, even if they are considered my enemy. I only want peace.

A blur to my right catches my attention. It's those two brothers, the Prowlers from Raven's crew who I met in jail. Aura and Malore must have busted them out of their prison cells. Better yet, the thieves must have forgiven Raven for her past errors, because they rush to fight Sanora's magi and aid in our crusade.

The scene is pure chaos, and when I search for Raven, I can't find her. Damn it, where did she go? Did she use her shadow magic to escape? I do another cursory scan for my parents this time, but again their presence eludes me. This fear isn't fair. It's bordering on paralyzing and I wonder if I can make another move. Is Sanora using her magic to hide what's actually happening, to show me what she wants to show me? I don't know exactly how powerful she is. How many people can she trick with her Illusion Magic, and how long can she hold onto it? Maybe with these attacks, she's in a sort of weakened state. I can only hope.

"You might want to watch this, Cadence!"

I spin to find Sanora in the stands, hands clawing the air. Her attention is off me, and I follow the direction of her sneer...toward my parents!

"No!" I exclaim, stumbling around the fighting magi and humans. But I'm too far away to do anything. Somehow, I'm watching myself directly across from Father, holding a dagger. But then the scene seems to glitch, and Mother is where I was, but now I've become Father, still holding the weapon.

My eyes widen as I realize what she's doing. She's making them think I'm going to kill them. If they fight me in self-defense, they're going to kill each other instead. I can't believe Sanora has a power *that* strong.

My parents have done awful things to me, but I hope they wouldn't attack me, that they wouldn't kill me. But they killed Tor to protect their chance at wealth, not to protect me. The thought rattles me to my marrow.

I scream, but nothing reaches my ears as the calls, clangs, and crashes of the fighting masses swallow up my voice.

It happens in slow motion. Mother tells Father to stop, and Father tells Mother to stop. But the fake versions of myself won't lower my weapon.

"No!" I cry out.

Mother stabs Father, and Father strikes Mother. They both double over on each other, slipping to the ground. Blood gushes from their wounds, revealing they were truly human, not the monsters they made themselves out to be my whole life. I'm scared. And how do I know what's real? is the Archmage showing me an illusion, too, to devastate and distract me?

Arms wrap around me, nearly giving me a heart attack, but it's Raven. She must have heard my scream.

Mother and Father weren't about to win any parenting awards, but they didn't deserve to kill each other…for Sanora to murder them—even if it was in retribution. I don't have time to process any relief, any feelings of freedom if my parents are truly dead.

I try to fight my way out of Raven's grasp, fury burning through me at the sight of Sanora's wise-ass smile. I don't want her to think she has any power over me, especially when it comes to my parents. Al and Raven? Completely different story.

"A life for a life. Now we're even, Cadence," Sanora says. Her tone is flat.

I guess I should be happy she's not maniacally gleeful about just killing them—even if she made them physically do it to each other.

"But that's not how it works. You're a murderer, and now everyone you rule over knows it."

Her face changes as she scans the crowd. The other magi are fighting, but a few must have seen what Sanora did, for they have looks of shock and disgust. She must have been so focused on conjuring up this illusion that she forgot to hide it from her people.

"Your parents killed my husband…before we could have any children of our own," she says, stammering a bit. "Don't turn this on me, you ungrateful wretch!"

A blue mist swirls in the air as a mage uses their power on another mage.

Through the haze, the Poison Mage steps into view.

My stomach churns. No…

Sanora adjusts the crown on her head. "Now, there's still the matter of making that little thief pay for what she did. Trying to taint Tor's grave by stealing his most prized possession. Let Raven be an example to magi and Unremarkables alike. If you cross me, you won't get me a third time."

"Leave us alone!" I cry out, clinging to Raven now, no longer wanting to claw my way out to attack Sanora, but instead to stay in the place where I've felt safe, the place where I belong.

But Raven pushes me away. "I need to take care of this, Cade."

"Rae...don't! You'll die!"

Raven takes a wide stance and cracks her knuckles. "Show me what you got, mage." She turns into a shadow, her body becoming an ephemeral vapor, black as the night, and likely Sanora's soul. She swirls around the Poison Mage, who lunges for her and tries to grab every which way, but Raven zips from her grasp every time.

I stand there, shaking, clutching my torso. I can't take this. I can't lose Raven.

The tall, lanky mage reaches again for Raven, and before I know it, she's somehow grabbed onto her. She pulls her down, forcing Raven to change out of her shadow form. The mage locks a hand around her ankle and drags her to the ground.

"Raven!" I hope she hears me among the clang of swords and swoosh of spells.

The Poison Mage mumbles an incantation and closes her eyes. When she opens them, they're straight up purple when before they were brown.

The color drains from Raven's face, likely mirroring my own.

And then Raven's paleness turns purple, like she's turning sick like she's being...poisoned.

"Stop! Stop it now!" I pound my fists on the Poison Mage's back, to no avail. She's a solid statue, immovable, unstoppable.

"I won't stop. This is fair retribution," Sanora howls.

"This is fair retribution!" a voice calls from the top of the tower.

I don't recognize the voice, but apparently, some of the magi do—on both sides of the fight. I find Malore and Aura in the crowd and sigh in relief, but my muscles tense at the look in their eyes.

Shock...and awe...and confusion.

A man storms in from the tower's peak, and at first I think he must be a Transport Mage or something, but then I realize there's another mage with him who's moving his hands in an odd motion as if controlling them toward the floor.

"Who's that?" I ask no one in particular.

"Bidyzen!" Sanora sneers, though her expression changes and she takes a step backward.

The man is younger, around Malore's age, but has dark skin and long black hair, along with a trim mustache and goatee. His clothes are light and flowy. They kind of remind me of Aura's attire.

He and the mage land in the center of the room, and the Poison Mage steps away from Raven and out of their line of sight. If I heard Sanora right, this must truly be Bidyzen from Jessen! But I'm not about to let Raven die just so I can find out. I rush to her side, shaking her shoulders when I noticed her unmoving form. I zip my hands back, for her skin is ice cold.

"No...no...you can't...you can't be..." I won't admit it. I can't admit it. Diamonds scrape my eyes and cloud my vision as I bend forward to check her pulse, placing two fingers at her upper neck. I feel nothing. I immediately attempt to resuscitate her, placing the heel of my palms on Raven's sternum and starting compressions.

Her chest lifts and falls from the ebb and flow of my pressure, but not of their own accord. After I press my mouth to hers to give her air, I return to compressions. But she's still not breathing.

"Raven!" I sob, diamonds spilling onto her and down to the stone floor, my eyelids raw and sore from their slices.

"It ends now!" the man says.

"Bidyzen!" Aura exclaims, hopefulness replacing her previous distraught state.

The mage raises his arms above his head, moving them in a circular motion. It's as if he's creating a vacuum. The room glitches like there's a ripple in time.

Magi and humans alike gasp in awe. He's made the whole room stop and watch him.

The guards around Sanora disappear in the blink of an eye as if she'd used her illusion magic to put them there.

Sanora snarls. "This isn't over, Bidyzen!"

The Trap Mage stands beside her now, along with the Poison Mage and one of the Transport Mages I recognize from one of the towers. He touches their shoulders and in an instant, Sanora and her magi are gone. To where, I don't know, but I hope it's far, far away from here.

The other magi in the stands flee the scene, either running away or leaving with Transport Magi. The humans and magi Aura brought to help us from Jessen are cheering around me, but many bodies are lying on the floor that aren't getting up– the casualties of Sanora's rage. I can't help but feel like it's my fault. If I hadn't come here trying to rescue Raven, these other innocent lives wouldn't have been lost.

But they're gone...just like Raven.

I can't turn around. I can't look at her still form.

I cry out in anguish.

She's gone.

Forever.

THIRTY-FOUR

The tears keep falling and I can't help it. I don't *want* to help it. My diamonds pile up on the floor, but I wouldn't have it any other way. If I wasn't crying for Raven, it would mean I didn't care about her. The pain is a sign that she was important to me.

I'm still processing the image of my parents killing each other. Well, when Sanora made them kill each other. But did they have a choice? Who knows how the Archmage's powers actually work? In any case, they're dead and gone, too. My stomach lurches in disgust that I almost upchuck on this concrete floor. But on the flip side, elation fights to bubble inside me and the knowledge that they can never use me or Al ever again. A weight lifts off my shoulders like an anchor rising to let a ship set sail. Their actions today haven't overpowered the relief I feel for finally being free.

I flinch when a hand lands on my heaving back.

"It's okay, you're safe now." It's that calm yet commanding voice I heard earlier.

Bidyzen.

I sniffle and sit back on my heels, quickly and roughly wiping at my swollen cheeks.

He walks around to face me, stooping to meet me at my level. His eyes are yellowish-orange like a cat's. I find strength and comfort in them, though the stinging in my chest still overwhelms me. "Turn around," he says.

My lip trembles. "No…I'm not ready to see her…"

"Please, just turn around," he repeats.

I shake my head, pressing my thumbs to the corner of my eyes to staunch the tears. "I can't…"

But I find more hands on my back now. Malore and Aura come into view. "It's okay, Cadence," Malore says.

I breathe in deeply and exhale. Remaining on my hands and knees, I turn inch by inch. And I'm glad I'm on the ground already, because if not, surely my knees would have buckled. Because standing there, in all her beauty and glory…is Raven.

"Is this…is this an illusion?" I manage out.

Raven smiles warmly. "Oh, that Poison Mage was no match for my shadow magic. But apparently, Sanora didn't want you to think so. She must have created an *illusion* of the Poison Mage killing me. But I'm as real and alive as can be."

"She grabbed you…and filled you with poison. I tried to save you."

"I saw what you did, and it broke my heart, Cadence. The mage never touched me. I'm safe. You're safe."

I push myself to my feet and run to Raven, and she meets me halfway. I wrap my arms around her neck as she pulls me in from my waist. She's warm, comforting, and safe, and…and *alive*.

"We did it, Cade. We made it out of this together," Raven says softly. Her lips find mine and my heart might explode from pure joy. And now, I'm crying diamond tears of happiness. It takes everything in me to let go of her, but I'm not ready to leave the present moment, because right now, it feels like we're the only ones in the room.

When Raven parts from me, she wipes away her own, real tears. "I want to thank you for everything you've done for me. You could have left me here. You could have never come back. But you did. It made me realize that I don't have to be defined by my past." She brushes my cheek with the back of her hand. "It's never too late to start a new family. And well, money is nothing if you don't have love or trust."

I sniffle and nod. "So true. And…if you don't have control over your life, you're not really living. And so…I choose you. I choose this life for myself."

"You better, because I choose you, too."

Someone clears their throat, and I swivel to find both familiar and strange faces staring back at us. I lace my fingers with Raven's, not ready to let her go. My spirits lift when I spot both magi and humans alike huddled around us. And it appears as if Raven's thief friends made it out safe and sound.

Aura steps over to Bidyzen. "Well, I'd never guess this is how you would meet the leader of Jessen," she says.

Well, that introduction jolts me. "Oh, my gods, the ruler of Jessen! That's right!" I wipe my palms on my pants, now sweaty from being all nerves.

He bows to me, even though I should be doing that to him. "It's a pleasure to meet you."

"So…can someone tell me what happened here? How did you get Sanora to stop?"

Bidyzen flashes a devious grin and folds his arms. "Like you, I also possess a rare magic. I'm what they call a Cancel Mage."

"Whoa…" Okay, I definitely wasn't expecting that.

"That's some major *whoa*!" Raven exclaims. "I…I thought Cancel Magi were a myth."

"Nope," Bidyzen says. "I'm as real as can be. So, you see, I can cancel out any mage's power. You're mid transport to Kinephrus? Nope, now you're in the middle of Lake Urso. Creating an illusion? Forget about it. Can't do it."

"And crying diamonds?" I ask expectantly.

He smiles. "You can cry regular tears like everyone else."

"Wow…that's…I never thought I'd see the day. Kind of scared to have you try it on me…" I rub my chin.

"Don't worry." Bidyzen laughs. "I don't have to use my power on you if you don't want me to. It only lasts a short while, anyway. You know, rules of the magi and all. The gods weren't going to give us complete power, so we each have our limitations."

I chew the inside of my cheek. "What's my limitation? I've never been able to stop crying diamonds. And it's not like I churn up any bad ones."

"Well, you do cry different colored diamonds, don't you?"

My eyebrows rise like mountains. "What did you say?"

"Diamond magi cry different colored diamonds that have different properties, such as healing, poison, and the like."

Whoa, wait a minute. Did he say different *properties*? "I've only cried regular diamonds—nothing special about them."

Bidyzen shifts his feet against the cement. "Your 'regular' diamonds are powerful enough. However, you can train yourself to produce colored diamonds with different magical properties—at least, the Diamond Magi in the past have, so I'm sure you can, too."

The ground sways beneath me and I catch myself on Raven's shoulder. Here I am, thinking I'm good for nothing. But no, my diamonds are powerful. And now I can become even more so. My mind whirls at the possibilities.

Bidyzen turns to address the masses, the few confused magi residents of Kinephrus, the citizens of Jessen, and more. "Sanora slandered my name since we split many moons ago. I tried to ally with her, but when I found out her true colors, she tried to have me killed. I escaped and joined the Everyfolk, a group of humans and magi alike who live in Jessen."

"We are a good many people, who cast no judgment and consider us all equals." He looks to Aura and she nods. He weaves in between the crowd as he continues, "When Omaru, the leader of the Everyfolk, passed away earlier this year, the citizens elected me as their leader. And so, I ask of you, please join us on our crusade, our journey to bring peace throughout all of Soridente."

"How are you going to do that?!" one of the Kinephrus mages shouts from the stands.

"Yeah, how do we know you're not another tyrant?" another mage asks, stepping closer from within the center circle.

Bidyzen nods knowingly before addressing them. "I understand your concerns. Our citizens are free to come and go as they please, but they choose to stay because of the kind of world we've created upon our island. They will vouch for everything I have stated here tonight. I want to stop not only Archmage Sanora but King Pontifex as well. Otherwise, they will both be each other's and our undoing. Their tyranny must be put to an end. And I will do that with my power…and anyone who would like to help me, because I can't do it alone."

The questioning magi talk amongst themselves, whispering and gazing up at Bidyzen, Aura, and even me, every so often. Eventually, they come out of their huddle with their shoulders back and heads held high.

"We'll join you, Bidyzen…" the first mage announces.

"Darc. Bidyzen Darc."

"We'll join you, Bidyzen Darc."

The Cancel Mage bows in thanks then turns to me and Raven. I twirl to my left and right, surveying who's around us. He can't possibly want me to come with him, could he? "And you…"

I point at myself, and he nods. "Cadence Alero…"

"And Raven McKae!" Raven flips her hair and winks.

Bidyzen smirks. "Cadence and Raven, will you also be joining our cause, joining the Everyfolk?"

My lips part in hesitation. I hadn't had time to think about that. "My sister, she's not a mage but, she's back home in Noravale receiving a stem cell transplant and new medication to help with her worsening symptoms. She has a neuromuscular disease."

Bidyzen approaches, resting a palm on my shoulder. "I would love for her to come, too. We need someone strong like her."

My lips turn up in a half-smile. Starting a new chapter scares the demons out of me, but Bidyzen allays them quite nicely. "Thank you. She'll be eager to set foot outside of Noravale for good. And I want peace in the land as much as you do. What can I do to help?"

"As if you don't know?" Raven squeezes my hand. "You're the heir to the Magi Throne, girl."

"*And* you're a Diamond Mage," Bidyzen states. "You have more in you that hasn't been discovered yet. We can help you tap into your potential in Jessen."

Everyone's stares bore into mine, but they aren't gazes of hate or anger. They're of expectation and hope.

Jessen's leader holds his hand out for me. "So, what will it be?"

Raven is about to shed tears of her own. She emanates complete trust in me. "I'll go wherever you go, okay?"

Her words melt my heart. They give me the last bit of clarity I need to step forward and shake Bidyzen's hand. "We're in."

"Perfect. We can leave whenever you're ready," he says.

I'm sure the hope and anticipation in his eyes matches my own, but my mind nudges me to remember the world I left behind. "I can't wait to see all that Jessen has to offer, but there's somewhere I need to stop at first—and more importantly—there's someone I need to see."

THIRTY-FIVE

I've already experienced enough pain—from my diamond tears, when I thought I lost Raven, and when I thought I'd never see Al again—when I thought she wouldn't get the treatment she needed to fight the good fight. But today, the only pain I feel is from mourning the loss of what should have been. I should have been raised by happy, loving parents. I should have had parents who cared for me more than money or status. But that was never the case. And so today, all of this becomes real. There is no Archmage's illusion, no nightmare to wake up from, no fiction story I close the book on, no story about someone across the street I can make up.

It's *real*.

Mother and Father are gone.

The funeral procession happens in slow motion, making it even harder to watch. I almost didn't go, but Al urged us to, even though she hated what our parents did to me in the name of helping her. She said we both needed closure. I guess we do. But it doesn't mean it's easy. Al told me forgiving them isn't something we need to do to heal from their abuse. It's a relief knowing we can move on. But for now, they still haunt me, silent but present like a shadow.

Raven's shadow covers Al and me against the afternoon light, as we sit on a covered balcony overlooking the streets of Noravale.

Al already looks brighter, displaying more fervor than I've seen in months. She no longer needs oxygen, but she's been sticking to her wheelchair more lately to conserve energy, which is also increasing every day. I can't tell you how grateful I am that Dr. Sammer's treatments are working. It's not a cure, but it helps with her pain and weakness immensely.

Trumpets play a somber tune, and black horses pull a golden carriage with our parents' caskets in the back. It, too, is black and gold. I roll my eyes, surprised it's not covered from top to bottom in my diamonds.

The citizens of Noravale are standing on the sidewalk, many dressed in black, weeping and mourning the loss of esteemed and distinguished nobility. Their performative grief makes me sick.

Beside me, also shielded by Raven's shadow magic, are Bidyzen and Aura. Aura brought us here in time for something I needed to see but never want to experience ever again. Bidyzen's hand rests gently on my shoulder. I needed him here, too, to conceal me from the outside world. Sure, Raven's hiding me in her shadows, but Bidyzen is hiding me from something else. Without him, my tears would give me away.

And so today is the first time I've ever cried real tears. They're wet and cool against my skin, and instead of rolling down my lap and clinking to the floor like gems, they soak my clothes. It's a reminder of my humanity.

They're not happy tears, but they're not sad ones either. Al's cheeks are also damp, and her small sniffles reach my ears. I imagine she feels the same as me, disappointed in the past our parents made but grateful we can move into a brighter future of our own creation—together.

Raven and Al give me hope that everything can improve—that despite the shadows, there is always sunshine. Raven's arm is wrapped around my waist, a comfort in these uncertain times.

I exhale and focus on the scene below. They've ended the procession right outside the royal castle. Standing there is King Pontifex, Queen Consort Natali, and last and most certainly least, is

Prince Wendell. The memories of Captain Rioza and the King's Guard trying to capture me and Raven, the king and queen consort conspiring with Mother and Father to wed me off against my will, the behind-the-scenes lying and swindling and abuse of the magi, are further tainted by their presence.

Aura transports us closer to the scene so we can hear what's going on. Lines of people are gathering outside the castle now. We settle in the confines of another covered balcony that's free for us to use. The house it belongs to is on the market, and therefore empty.

"Thank you for gathering here today, to remember two lives lost too soon," King Pontifex says, his voice reaching the crowd.

I narrow my eyes. What more does he have to say?

He wraps his arm around Natali's shoulder, who, in turn, has an arm around Wendell. They've dressed appropriately in black, but their fingers and necks still shine with gold. "It is with a heavy heart that I officially acknowledge the deaths of Lord Monticello and Lady Esmerene Alero."

People gasp, others cry out, and still, others are silent, probably in disbelief. The announcement of my parents' deaths, the finality of it, sends a burning to my chest. Despite their cruelties, they were still my parents, but they will never hold space in my heart. Al and Raven will take all of it up for the rest of my life.

The King clears his throat, jolting me back to the present moment. "We confirmed this after their house staff recovered their bodies. The Aleros were killed trying to rescue their daughter, Cadence, from Kinephrus."

The crowd boos and hisses.

"Archmage Sanora must be stopped at all costs. We believe she has captured Cadence along with her older sister, Allegra. More likely than not, she has brainwashed Cadence to join her ranks, her army against humans like you and me. She is a mage, after all."

My jaw could hit the floor. What. The. Heck?! He just gave me away to everyone. Everything my parents did to keep me a secret, to selfishly hide me away from the world, all comes undone at this moment. I'm fuming.

Al wheels herself closer to me and squeezes my hand, easing my frustrations a little as I return my attention to the scene.

Wendell's expression flickers, like he's surprised but trying to hide it. I'm surprised he didn't know about it, what with the King eager to marry him off to me and all. I feel sorry for the prince, having a father like that. Guess we have that in common.

Pontifex continues, "We don't speak of the magi anymore since the war, but the truth of the matter is that they still exist. The queen is still out there, working behind the scenes to bring us down. Before the Aleros' untimely deaths, they entrusted their daughters to us. We cannot allow the magi to take one more life. And so, if anyone has news on Cadence and Allegra Alero, please report it to me or a guard immediately. And if you encounter them, please bring them back to us…safely, of course."

I rush to the balcony's edge, gripping the cement with white knuckles. Raven's fingers grip my upper arms to hold me back, even though I wouldn't actually do anything.

"That is all. Stay strong, Noravale. And I will see you at the Autumnal Equinox Festival in a few months!" The family turns to leave, and the procession continues.

"Of course, he'd find another excuse to flaunt his power and wealth." I wait until the crowd clears out before Raven pulls me, her back sliding down the wall as she takes me with her. "Why can't he leave me alone? Haven't I been through enough?"

Raven hugs me tighter. Aura and Bidyzen send me a look of genuine sympathy.

"I'm so sorry, Cadence," he says. "If it's any consolation, the king is out for me too, but he tells people they're allowed to bring back only my head."

I bite my lip. "If Pontifex knew I'm on your side, he would've changed that part of his speech about me."

"Ditto," Al says, folding her arms yet still managing to shiver.

"We'll all be safe in Jessen for now. We're like an island, plus the magi here are hard at work ensuring only the right people enter. It'll take a lot for Pontifex and his army to reach us. We're hoping to right their wrongs before they do."

My stomach churns from my emotions. "Can we get out of here?"

Raven stands and then helps me to my feet. "Are you sure you're ready to go?"

"I'll be able to continue my treatments in Jessen, right?" Al asks.

Bidyzen nods, warmth and comfort flowing from his very, well, aura. "Yes, you will. You'll be in the best of hands there."

She bangs a fist on her armrest. "Then, hells yeah, I'm in!"

"Cadence?" Raven asks.

I peek out from the slats of the balcony railing. Noravale is as foreign to me as Jessen is now. Al and I don't belong here anymore. The only way we'll ever come back is to stop Pontifex. "I'm ready."

Aura bows her head slightly. "Then, to Jessen we go." She gathers us closer to her, and in a second, we've arrived on the outskirts of Jessen.

Waves crash behind us, and it could be an ocean. Looking forward, I'm grateful the city is not the desert oasis on the other side of the water where Aura lives. Instead, it's a lush grassy plain with flowers the colors of the rainbow. Beyond that are the city streets, and they hold so much promise.

Whinnying resounds and I whip my head to the side to find King and Clove galloping toward us. Raven jumps in place and I giggle, petting their noses and flanks when they reach us.

"Okay, I'm officially pumped that you still have horses. I always envied the other families!" Al says as Clove walks up to her for some extra special nuzzling.

"I thought you'd appreciate some familiar faces here," Aura says with a smile. "There are a lot of people you already know settling into their new home, like Malore!"

"Oh, good, I like him!"

I raise an eyebrow at Al's enthusiasm and tuck the image of her blushing cheeks in the back of my mind to inquire about later. For now, my heart is full and my eyes are probably shining like my diamond tears.

"Well then, what are we waiting for?!" Raven exclaims.

"Let me introduce you to the Everyfolk," Bidyzen says, and he starts walking toward the city.

A part of me is scared to move forward, physically and mentally. We're going up against King Pontifex and Archmage Sanora, along with everyone who's been led along the wrong path. It scares me because I don't know where this road to Jessen will lead me.

I never wanted anyone to get hurt, especially for me, or because of me. But I understand this fight isn't about me. It's about the greater good for all Soridente citizens, for peace between magi and humans. It hasn't happened yet, and it seems so far away, but maybe it will come.

No, it's not something that might come. It can't just arrive. It's not a passive thing, this struggle for peace. It must be created, worked on, and fought for.

I take a deep breath then grab Raven's hand as we follow after Al and lead the horses, stepping forward toward a better future, one that must be fought for, tooth and nail. It will cost blood, sweat, and diamond tears.

And, well, I guess that means I have some work to do.

ALLEGRA

HARDCOVER EXCLUSIVE SCENE

Cadence is going to be in such big trouble today.

  I'm going to talk about this book until her ears fall off. She's going to wish she never got me hooked on this series.

  I had woken to the birds chirping outside my window, reminding me that even they have more freedom than I do. But I didn't dwell on that fact for long, instead focusing on the faint lavender scent from the candle I'd burned last night as I read *Flames of Destiny* before my eyes became itchy-tired. The bed and I became one just *three* chapters from the end.

  I propped some lilac satin pillows behind my back and sat up against the headboard, snatching the book off the table where it had sat all night. Thank the gods I'm never hungry first thing in the morning. Cade wakes up like a ravenous beast and rushes to the kitchen to stalk her prey—usually fresh-baked bread with peanut butter and a bowl of mixed fruit. Me? I take my time waking up. Becoming human, I like to say. Today, that means finishing the first book of Furia and Elden's story. I pray to the gods it's not a cliffhanger. Granted, there are five books in the series. I could finish them all in a week. But it's the principle of the matter. Readers like me demand justice!

Instead of food, I devour each page, reading at an unnatural pace. Elden had just been saved by the dragon he'd been hunting the whole book, but Furia was still leading the attack on the creature, not knowing its true nature.

My toes wiggle under the blankets as I turn to the last page. A folded-up piece of paper slips onto the bed. I ignore it, focusing on how Elden escapes on the dragon's back and Furia thinks he's betrayed their clan. *Not fair!* How could the author do that to us?

Cade will have to grab the second book from the library stat because I don't want to waste another moment not knowing what happens next! I start to read the back matter of the book before my eyes flit to the paper that fell out. I pick it up, wondering if it's a makeshift bookmark Cade forgot to take out. But, after carefully unfolding the paper, I quickly realize this isn't a bookmark at all.

It's a letter.

A letter from Cade…to me.

Dear Al,

I hope you are reading this not too upset at that ending. You'll be able to read the next book whenever you like. I've already stashed that in your nightstand drawer for easy access. What I really came here to say is that we've got stories of our own with endings I hope we won't be upset about. The reason why is because I'm going to try to do everything in my power to change the endings Mother and Father have doomed us to have.

Everything they told us about my "gift" is a lie. The new friend I told you I made—the girl at the masquerade—she said I was cursed with my diamond tear ability and that maybe it can be reversed. She was sent by the Magi Queen to bring me to their city to find answers. Oh, and she explained that I'm a mage, too. I found evidence in our parent's room confirming that they have a connection to the magi. I know it sounds crazy, but it's more than fantasy.

So, I'm taking a chance and leaving with Raven tonight. Trust me, I don't want to leave you right now, not ever. But if there's a way I can reverse my curse, or find another way to help you get the treatment you need, it's worth it for me—for us. I think you would agree.

Al, you're the most important person in all of Soridente to me. I love you more than words can describe. Know that I will try to come back to you as soon as I can. Hopefully, I'll return with the answers we need.

Cade

P.S. Don't get into too much trouble while I'm gone. I can't promise I'll do the same ;)

I must have read the letter three times again before I realized how slack-jawed I am. Cade's gift is a curse? And she's a mage? What. The. Hells? What else don't we know about ourselves? About the outside world?

In any case, that sneaky little Cade actually did it. She busted out of here! And I'd bet my golden wheelchair I'm the first to know. My heart beats wildly as I clutch the letter to my chest, grateful for the tears I'm allowed to cry—tears of joy for Cade's bravery in trying to save us. I just wish I could do something to help. I reach to my nightstand and pull open the top drawer to find a crap ton of diamonds as well as *Inferno of Fate* inside, just like Cade promised in the letter. I have a feeling she's going to keep some other promises that are in there, too.

I stash her letter in-between the pages of the sequel and close the drawer again, my heart still pounding.

"Allegra! Allegra are you in there?" Mother calls from outside my bedroom door. Perfect timing.

"Yeah, come in!"

I expected Mother to burst inside with her usual haughty gusto, but she's joined by Father and a few of the staff who tail behind her as if she's Queen Natali herself.

"Allegra, is Cadence in here?" Mother asks, rushing to my bedpost. Her hair and dress are a bit haphazard, definitely not like the normal prim and proper appearance she tries to uphold no matter the time of day.

"No? I've been here by myself all morning," I say.

"Well then where is she?!" She snaps as if I'm my sister's keeper. Her tone is sharp, but there's a bit of a waver to it. She's worried. I smirk internally. Good. Let her *perfect* little system they've had going crumble.

I grip my bed sheets so hard I'm afraid I'll rip them, raging on the inside at their selfish concern. I swallow the coarse words I'd like to say to them until the anger settles like a stone in my belly.

They're only worried about Cade because it means their source of diamonds is missing.

I feign ignorance. "How am I supposed to know? Did you check the library?"

"I don't *believe* this," Father murmurs to himself. He paces before the staff, looking equally as disheveled.

One of the men among them locks eyes with me, an inquisitive glint catching me by surprise. He's one of the newest hires brought on to make "our"—my *parents'*—lives easier. His dark hair is slightly styled and flipped over his forehead, highlighting his stark green eyes. Usually, Mother and Father hire boring old coots or middle-aged stiffs to do the grunt work at home. But this guy can't be past his early twenties and is the freshest of the batch.

"Why are you all bent out of shape? Cade's probably chilling in the greenhouse, or causing mischief in the laundry room." They don't know that I know, do they? They can't find out as long as I keep my cool and play along.

"We looked there!" Father huffs out. "She…she's been missing all morning."

"She's got to be here somewhere." My stare drills a hole into the shaggy rug floor. Cade and I are the queens of keeping secrets and I'm not about to let my expression give any of hers away.

"She's usually the first in the kitchen but *poof!* Nowhere in sight," one of the maids adds. "I even checked her room to see if she wanted me to bring her something in bed."

"I last saw her in your bedroom late afternoon, actually," the young butler I noticed earlier states.

Mother's eyebrows rise like jagged hills. "Our room?"

"Her mask had gotten mixed up with your things. She left promptly, I think back to her room."

Father scoffs and folds his arms. "Well, she was there for dinner last night, too, Malore. Nothing remarkable happened after that. So, where is she *now*?"

So, his name's Malore.

At first, I assumed Father's inquiry to be rhetorical, but he expected his daughters' whereabouts to be easily accounted for. After all, Cade and I are trapped inside and there are only so many rooms. Surely, they haven't already searched them all?

Malore adjusts the black and silver sash across his white button-down shirt. "I think it best we search the greenhouse again. I thought I'd heard voices in there last night but when I scoured the area, it was empty."

His gaze zeroes in on me and I stiffen.

What if he knows I'm lying? He looks sharper than anyone else under Mother and Father's employ. I remain silent and his focus moves back to my parents.

I'm in the clear, at least for now.

"All right then. Round up the mag—" Mother stop herself. "I mean, round up the rest of the staff. We need all hands on deck."

Father balls his hands into fists. "No one is to rest until we search every inch of this place. We *will* find Cadence."

I smile as Mother and Father rush from my room, their frantic and erratic movements amusing as they usher the present staff out. They're louder than the Summer Solstice Ball.

With them gone, I finally swing my legs out of bed and transfer to my wheelchair. There's a ton more interesting things about to happen in this house than reading about Furia and Elden right now, and I'm not about to miss a second of it.

ACKNOWLEDGMENTS

There have been so many people who have stood by my side throughout my writing journey and believed that I would become a published author someday, especially on the days I thought I never would.

There is such a special bond between sisters, but there is a whole other level between twins (especially if those twins happen to both be writers). Heather, I truly wouldn't be where I am today without you. I remember we used to draw our book covers and write stories from as young as six years old. When we got to high school, we found fanfiction.net and began writing *Kingdom Hearts* fan-fiction. We'd dangle our USBs in front of each other to signify when we'd finished a chapter, and enthusiastically read what we wrote—glaring at each other when it ended on a cliffhanger or was too short and we wanted more.

And then, we began to write our own stories, devouring each new chapter with that same excitement. When the days were tough and the words didn't flow, or self-doubt crept in, you were the one who kept me writing because I knew there was at least one person out there in the world who wanted to read my work. It's why I never gave up. We had stories to be told and characters we cared about it. Our books are more than just words on a page to us—they're a part of our hearts. I can't thank you enough for being my cheerleader, my inspiration, my accountability buddy, my alpha reader, and my biggest fan. I love you to Pluto and back.

To Chris—with all of your support for me and my writer life, I know without a doubt that you love me. The times I stowed away on my computer to write or edit, my never-ending to-do list and 'relaxing' weekends, and the years I participated in NaNoWriMo and left everything to the wayside while I tried to write 50k words in a month, you took it all in stride and never guilted me for the time and energy it took because you knew it was leading me to my dreams coming true. You'd cheer me on with each draft finished or agent request and stay quiet when we shared an office and I'd be editing a YouTube video or doing live writing sprints. Your support never ceases to amaze me. I already loved you before, but all this makes me love you so much more.

To Savannah Goins, my first online writing friend. When we followed each other on Instagram back in 2016, I was trying to build my author platform because that's what writers recommended we do. I had no idea when I clicked that button that we'd become beta readers, critique partners, Mastermind group buddies, and, most importantly, real life friends. You were my first friend who was a published author and I loved bragging to my coworkers when I'd leave for the weekend that I was 'visiting my author friend.' I'm still so inspired by your hustle and drive to succeed as a full-time writer—self-publishing a trilogy and writing the best books (with animals in them)!

To Antonia Ryder, my first critique partner who I met on the NaNoWriMo forums in 2016. Your constructive feedback has indefinitely made my writing stronger. You first showed me how to line edit Ranokori Realm and it blew my mind that I had to go word by word and line by line through my entire manuscript. Ha ha. Thank you for all the tough love!

I'm so grateful to my Mastermind group of Savannah Goins, Alicia Grumley, and Brittany Wang. When I came to you all with concept for *A Diamond Bright and Broken*, you suggested the brilliant idea that Cadence's parents guilt-trip her into paying for Allegra's treatment as a way of 'keeping Rapunzel locked in the tower.' You not only gave me invaluable feedback to help me grow along my writer journey, you were so supportive during my roughest mental health days. Even when I wasn't accomplishing any of the goals I set for myself each week, you all were non-judgmental, reminding me I'm allowed to "blob" if I need to. You were listening ears on Marco Polo when I showed my face and said words, sent tons of prayers, and Alicia sent much needed Alicia-isms.

Lenn is my ride-or-die writer chica! As I was brainstorming my novel, your suggestion of a female Flynn Rider shaped it into the best story it could be. You helped me survive the query trenches for more than one manuscript. When I felt the sting of rejections, I thought about how much I loved your writing and how you never gave up, always working on another story. That helped fuel me to keep going, too. Your story ideas and perseverance are an inspiration to me and I can't wait for the day we get to meet in person!

Thank you Vanessa Marie for being my disability sensitivity reader to ensure I properly wrote Allegra's arc and disability representation.

To the AuthorTubers and those whose online writing advice helped me learn and grow: Kim Chance (thank you for your editing services too!), Bethany Atazadeh, Jenna Moreci, Jessi Elliott, Abbie and KA Emmons.

Thank you for your support and friendship Ryan Medina, Teresa Beasley, Autumn Ashleigh, and Kristin Ardis. Renee Dugan—your writing is such an inspiration to me. Thank you for making me a better writer by just being you!

To my publisher, Zara Hoffman and Inimitable Books. None of this would be possible without your excitement for and dedication to my book. I'm so grateful and honored to be chosen so that I can share my book with the world.

Thank you, Keylin Rivers, for my gorgeous book cover. And thank you, Grayson, Wilde for the amazing world map. You guys are the best!

For you who are holding my book—thank you for supporting me and reading my work. I hope I can share many more words with you for years to come.

For those of you interested in writing your own stories—do it. But know that like every book's story, every writer's story is different. Some people go the self-publishing route. Some people take the traditional publishing route. Some get a literary agent, while others don't. It took eight years from when I started writing again and realized I wanted to be published until I actually was. I'd written three manuscripts, started one, and queried three of them before finally getting a book deal.

This journey isn't easy, but it's sure worth it.

ABOUT THE AUTHOR

Holly Davis is a kidlit author who started her writing journey as a child, often drawing the book cover and only writing a couple of chapters. In high school, she wrote fanfiction for the video game, *Kingdom Hearts*, before eventually wanting to write stories of worlds and characters all her own!

Now Holly gives writing advice and interacts with the online community via her YouTube channel. She's also a Page Turner Young Writer Awards judge and the host of the Diversity is Lit Book Club, which promotes BIPOC authors (buy Diversity is Lit merch).

You can find her in the Chicago suburbs helping people in the hospital as a physical therapist, enjoying the company of her two babies who have fur, and binging Netflix shows.

Map of Soridente

Kinephrus

Lake Urso

L

J